TIGERS BURNING

TIGERS BURNING

A Duffy House Mystery

Crabbe Evers

William Morrow and Company, Inc.
New York

Library of Congress Cataloging-in-Publication Data

Evers, Crabbe.
    Tigers burning : a Duffy House mystery / by Crabbe Evers.
        p.   cm.
    ISBN 0-688-11469-5
    1. House, Duffy (Fictitious character)—Fiction.
    2. Sportswriters—Michigan—Detroit—Fiction.   3. Detroit (Mich.)—
Fiction.   I. Title.
PS3552.R33T5   1994
813'.54—dc20
                                                            93-43125
                                                            CIP

Printed in the United States of America

First Edition

1 2 3 4 5 6 7 8 9 10

BOOK DESIGN BY LISA STOKES

To Mark Fidrych, the sublime Tiger, and his summer of '76—
"Come on, ball, stay low. Stay low, ball."

Acknowledgments

The authors wish to thank the Detroit Tigers Baseball Club and spokesman Greg Shea for their kind cooperation. We are also indebted to Monica Vitlar for her hospitality, pith, and an unforgettable midsummer night's ride down Michigan Avenue in her convertible.

Tiger! Tiger! burning bright
In the forests of the night,
What immortal hand or eye
Could frame thy fearful symmetry?
    —WILLIAM BLAKE, "The Tiger"

TIGERS BURNING

Chapter

1

"DE-TROIT NOW, THEY HAD THE WOLVES, THE DE-TROIT WOLVES,"
Biz said. "And the Stars, 'cept they weren't around long 'cuz the
money run out."

I had snuck up on Henry "Biz" Wagemaker's sentry post in the
lobby of the overpriced Outer Drive sardine can that passes for
my residence. Wagemaker, formerly of the Chicago American
Giants of the Negro American League, is a cotton-haired dodger
who ran with Satchel Paige and called Jackie Robinson "rook."
He serves as my joint's bow-tied doorman, traffic cop, and social
historian. He and a panoramic fifteenth-story view of the Sheffield
Avenue entrance to Wrigley Field had sold me on the place.

"Wasn't no *De*-troit colored team ever got goin' good, Mr.
House," Biz went on. "Not like the American Giants here. Good
job town like *De*-troit. Lotta colored up there. Cool Papa played
for the Wolves, I think he did. And Pete Hill. Pete was up there.
He was with me on the American Giants too. Lotta people don't
know that."

You could prime Biz's pump with an eye dropper. Get him going
on the minutiae of the Negro leagues, which have been gone forty
years but which exist like crystal in Biz's mind. Biz was an outfielder. Little guy, even littler now, likened himself to Jimmie

Crutchfield, the mite from Moberly who played for those good Pittsburgh Crawford teams. If you lingered too long, Biz would go into all that too, then recite some poetry of David Malarcher, his fine Louisiana-born American Giant manager. He had a port-folio, Biz did.

"Why you goin' to *De*-troit, Mr. House?" he said as my cab pulled up in front.

"See an old ballpark and talk to a fellow who lost his job," I said.

"Don't have to leave town for that," he said.

It had been early A.M. when the call came in. The light was low, a table lamp with a green glass shade, but enough to illuminate the prose. I was rereading Bill Veeck's horseracing book, a memoir he fragrantly titled *Thirty Tons a Day*. A very good recording of Mahler's Symphony Number Two was Sturm und Drang-ing on the stereo. It was music a tone heavy perhaps for Veeck, a man who once stocked his Seeburg phonograph with ten different cuts of Bunny Berigan's "I Can't Get Started with You" when he was courting his second bride.

I was sipping a serviceable brandy, and the windows were shim-mying with late October gusts. It was the kind of chill wind that makes most people pull up the comforter and dream winter dreams. My lids, however, were light. Sleep at my age is an after-thought, especially when the reading is rich. Wrote Veeck: "I always had a lively interest—precocious, my daddy thought—in chicanery, the uses and abuses of power, the flashing arc of the knife into the underbelly, and the dull thump of a body in the alley." And after that line, I didn't put the book down until the phone rang.

"Duffy," the voice said, "I'm out."

Only three words, but offered with timbre and precision. It took but a moment to know they came from Jimmy Casey, a man who had made a career out of chatter. I muted the record player.

"They canned me—I'm through," Casey said. "It'll break to-morrow morning. Thirty-five years, and I'm out the door like a pitcher with a dead arm."

"Shit, Jimmy," I said. Not too eloquent, but from the heart.

A silence draped the line. I could hear Casey's breathing, then a swallow of something probably harder than I was nursing. It was one A.M. my time, which made it two in Detroit, where Casey was calling from. I could see the spot in my mind: the wet bar in his Dearborn basement, a room festooned with mahogany plaques and black-and-white photos and quaint mementos from his three and a half decades as the voice of the Detroit Tigers. And Jimmy himself, a little guy with pipes, the Tigers' radio and TV play-by-play guy, a tenor-voiced natural, who was as much a part of the Detroit franchise as the famous Gothic *D* on the uniform. Was.

"I'd take the shitcan if I deserved it," Casey said, his words slowed some by the alcohol. "If I blew calls . . . or couldn't tell a curve from a slider. . . ."

I could feel the chafe. Casey was my peer, sixty-five years old, and he'd never lost a job in his life. In broadcasting, a business where they measure you by the moisture your presence puts in a viewer's palm, that's saying something. He'd perched himself in the WJR booth and peppered Tiger baseball out to Kalamazoo, Petoskey, and all points within earshot of the Great Lakes like a fog-cutting clarion.

"Worse, if the fans were just sick of listenin' to me," he went on. "But they love me. Got the numbers to show it. Goddammit, I'm as good as I ever was, Duffy. *Better* than I ever was."

The light over my shoulder flickered, and I could hear the refrigerator kick on. All was still except for the anguished throb in a friend's chest.

"The bastards settle with you?" I offered.

"I don't wanna settle," he said. "I don't want a package. I don't want a sweetheart annuity and a fairway condo in Sarasota. That's what *they* want."

He was bitter and plaintive all in the same beaker, like Canadian whiskey and 7-Up, his last-call libation.

"You gotta help me, Duffy," he said.

"How do you mean, Jimmy, how in hell—?"

"Listen, Duffy," he said, "this is me, not the booze talking. They canned me because of what I *know*, not because I'm washed up. The ballpark, Duffy. I now what they're doing. I know whose pockets they've stuffed and the phony engineering study—"

"Hold it. Slow down, Jimmy," I said, even though I knew what he was talking about. The current Tiger owner wanted to abandon Tiger Stadium. It was a familiar flap in yet another town. Except that Jimmy sounded like an assassination nut. Conspiracies. Grassy knolls, all that celluloid intrigue. But he beat me to it.

"Think it's horseshit, don't you?" he said. "Drunk talk. Stuff that goes thin in the light of day. . . ."

My silence agreed.

"I'm sober as a judge, Duffy. Pissed off, sure. If I had a bat in my hands, I'd measure somebody," he said. "But I'm not wrong, dammit. What's wrong is over there in the front office. They took me out because I called them on it. Called them frauds and thieves. And they nicked me."

"You wouldn't be the first, Jimmy," I said.

He snorted something unintelligible at that.

"And you didn't ring me at two A.M. for sympathy."

"That's right, Duf," he said. He leaned into the phone like a play-by-play announcer calling a ninth-inning rally. "You got an audience, Duffy. People who count still read you. That piece you did when Jack Remsen was killed in L.A. ran in every paper in the land—"

"Jack was *murdered,* for godsakes, Jimmy! The story wrote itself."

"No, it didn't. You know it didn't," he said. "You wrote it. *You* got inside Jack like nobody else. You made us ache for him. That story, Duffy, it counted."

I suddenly felt very tired. Sportswriters are not in the business of deliverance. We don't save souls. I can't remember when we even saved someone's job.

"Your guys will rally around you, Jimmy. Joe Falls, the TV guys—"

"Sure, they will," he cut in. "They'll raise hell here. All over Michigan. Even into Canada. Tempest in a teapot. But you, Duffy, you can reach out."

That was code. Casey knew I'd worked for the office at 350 Park Avenue. The commissioner of baseball. I'd investigated murder and treachery in the national pastime—in both leagues. Never say the game is old-fashioned.

"Do this one for me, Duffy. I'm on the carpet. Don't wait until they kill me."

"Come on, Jimmy."

"They threatened me, Duffy."

It was my turn for a swallow. Jimmy Casey was either a wracked, desperate man, or he was piping me like a pro.

"Do it for me and for that old ballyard on Michigan and Trumbull, if that's what it'll take," he said. "I haven't asked you a favor in a long time. Come out here. See it for yourself. At least give me that."

He did not have to say anything more. I told him to get some sleep and I'd call him over his eggs. But he knew he had me. I taste blood in my throat when I hear of old friends being kicked around. Or old pros, for that matter. Jimmy Casey was an original, so authentic and rare that he would not stand a chance of getting hired for the same job today. He was that good. And now, having been cut loose, he was tossing in a cruel Detroit wind. At least I could be there to help stem the gale.

The next morning I had a satchel packed and a reservation made on the morning train to Detroit. Biz Wagemaker waved over a cab with that good right arm of his.

My Amtrak crept out of Union Station, made the bend around Lake Michigan and the tip of Indiana, then pushed east across the autumn-colored flatlands of lower Michigan. It was a six-hour trip if the lead car didn't hit anything en route. I could have flown. I could have driven. The train, however, even in the context of Jimmy Casey's dire straits, was my speed.

It was midweek, and the coach cars were lightly populated. I spread out with a pack of newspapers and my copy of Casey's memoirs. A few years back he'd put them together in a low-priced volume called *Casey at the Mike* and peddled it like red-hots at banquets, grand openings, and baseball-card conventions. The copy he sent me was inscribed "To Duffy, my good, good friend and fellow traveler." This trip, I feared, might test that friendship. As I opened it to the first chapter, the spine cracked.

But I was glad to be headed into the fray. I needed a scrape. The season was over. A Canadian franchise had beaten an American squad in a World Series conducted in domed stadiums. Not a blade of grass or a cloud came into play. Grown men spit on carpet. It was baseball, played at the same distances with wooden bats and mud-rubbed balls, but it was painful for this old purist to watch.

Nevertheless, the Series' conclusion left me with the off-season, the hot stove, that frost-lined, stationary time when the system is likely to grow listless and die. I've long believed that box scores keep the chambers pumping. A good pennant race can sustain the terminally ill, keep them hanging on until it's clinched. But when the umpires take off and the bases are pulled up, well, things go morbid in a hurry.

Jimmy Casey's firing—and I had to rely on his version of the details—stirred the pot. That and the fact that he was tying his demise to his public affection for Tiger Stadium, a wonderful old ballpark at death's door. In the decade before the twenty-first century, only three originals remained: Wrigley Field, Fenway Park, and Tiger Stadium. I've watched a lifetime of baseball in each one of them. I would not go so far as to say they are temples. Or maybe I would.

Of the three, the Detroit park, a post-ridden double decker with massive light towers and an outfield roof, is least appreciated and most vulnerable. Built of concrete and steel in 1912, its modern owners have lately yearned to tear it down—for all of the usual, fiscally responsible but repugnant reasons. Like Casey, I always liked the place, its character, how it gave grit and texture to the Tigers in their linen-white uniforms. I'm a sucker for old ballparks, zealous in my hatred of the wrecking ball.

Casey wrote passionately about the place. "This ragged, charming den of lower decks, upper decks, posts, poles, and overhangs," he said, turning a phrase better than your average raconteur. "A park to lose yourself in as a child, and savor as an adult." He could not conceive of its demise. Of course, he is of a generation that does not comprehend private suites or seven-million-dollar salaries.

Lost in his memoir, with the jostle of the train a kind of background music, my eyes played easily over those sentiments, and even more easily over the horsehide stories and radio-booth anecdotes Casey fed the reader like hot chestnuts. I knew most of the characters and crumbums he wrote about; I even saw myself every so often. Casey was kind to me, gave me good lines I didn't remember uttering. His were soft, I-can't-believe-they're-paying-me-to-do-this strokes, and, given his current status, were bitter-sweet to read.

After a couple of hours of reading and riding, a tuna sandwich on wheat bread and some ice cream, I dozed off like a pensioner who'd been up most of the night before. The clack of the wheels and the swaying of the train's huge carriage put me under. I was always a customer of vibrating beds back in the days when they came with the motel room and hummed to life with a quarter. Alone or not alone, I loved them.

I don't know how long I slept. I don't know if I was jostled awake by a lurch of the train or the kick of a clumsy passenger. I do not know if I was still unconscious and dreaming, only that I suddenly was aware of people all around me huddled at the train's windows. They were young and old, black and Asian families with babies, students with backpacks, a soldier, a bird-thin, rouged lady with a green wig, and they were all staring open-mouthed into the now darkened terrain as the train groaned on. I sat up in the seat, or maybe I was already sitting up, and felt grit in my throat.

I turned with the others and saw a sky aglow with an orange collar, a filmy, other-worldly emanation. I blinked and began wiping the window with my forearm when a dank, acrid gust of air filled the car. One breath of it was enough. It was fire, a massive, organized blaze somewhere near the tracks. Then the train moved around a bend and into a level open area, and suddenly the distance was a bed of flames.

"The Hawk," someone said. I turned to the perspiring face of a redcap, a black man with glistening skin and a look of total dismay. "The damn Hawk," he intoned as he stared into the fury.

In Chicago, the Hawk is the icy, unforgiving wind off the lake. In Detroit, however, the Hawk is the night of the devil, a single terrible evening in late October when the city burns. I'd read of it, seen newsreels of the city lit on fire. Anything flammable is ignited. Abandoned automobiles, some with junkies inside, bubble with flames and toxic smoke. Tenements, abandoned or occupied by terrified familes, are torched. Wooden porches are stuffed with gasoline-soaked rags and go up like dry brush. Sheets of flame slither up clapboard. Tar-paper roofs explode with black smoke and white-hot gases, then collapse into roaring, angry infernos.

Unless I was dreaming it all, this was a night of the Hawk like no other. Everywhere I looked, on both sides of the train as it groaned on into Detroit, there were outlines of flames and billowing smoke. I blinked and swallowed and clutched my chest. I heard muted explosions and shrill sirens. People gasped and children cried. The smell was undeniable. The train seemed to slow, and my gut ached at the notion of being stranded in an aluminum tube while flames nipped at the ties, but then the wheels quickened again.

Suddenly a massive, magnificent structure came into view. And it was familiar to me. It was Detroit's old Union Station, a grand central depot for decades of train travel into the city but which I knew had been abandoned for years. I had come and gone with visiting baseball teams through its ornate doors. At fifteen stories, it was a proud, imperial building full of windows and cornices, the brick-and-stone craftsmanship of a century ago. And now it was aflame.

Though our train followed a track that took it hundreds of yards from the old station, we had a startling view of it. Pennants of fire shot out from windows on every floor as if the entire building had been ignited at once. The sight was breathtaking and awful, and neither I nor my fellow passengers on this train ride through hell could take our eyes off it.

The flames reflected in our eyes. We were speechless witnesses— maybe victims—of the Hawk. The train kept on like a slow, metal mole, moving relentlessly by its past, the besieged, incinerated old station, and edged deeper into the present, the inferno that was Detroit.

Chapter
2

Jimmy Casey hugged me, he did. Gave me one of those extended, lost-relative embraces that told me plenty about his condition.

"This is a *friend*," he said into my neck as his paw slapped my back.

The embrace was accompanied by fumes of Old Spice and Stroh's. He'd been waiting for me at the entrance of the Dearborn Inn, the colonial, white-pillared hotel in Henry Ford's suburb. It was nearly ten o'clock; it had taken hours for me to get from the downtown train station back out to Dearborn. The fires had turned Detroit on end. There was not a cab or a limousine to be found. It took a double sawbuck to get the station manager to get one for me.

The cab arrived with its dome light dark. The driver was a chunky black guy with white hair and a dashboard full of tiny plastic saints. He motioned me over. "Gon' cost you," he said. I'd have mortgaged the condo. Once I was inside his jitney, he hurtled into the street. "The fires," I said. "What in *hell* is happening?"

"Hell," he said. "Madness. I pray to God for deliverance."

We ran into police everywhere. Apparently in an effort to keep the Hawk out of downtown, they were blocking just about every main thoroughfare. The cabbie spat curses, rattling his saints. He finally got on the Lodge Freeway and was waved off before he could cut over to the Fisher Freeway. It went like that forever, with the cabbie getting more and more exasperated. His anger, my money. Somehow he caught an open ramp onto the Edsel Ford Freeway heading west toward Dearborn. He drove like a man running from a fire. In the skies beyond the concrete walls of the freeway we could see the glow, the cinders, the smoke. The taxi fairly flew. When it landed, it cost me.

"Why didn't you get off here in Dearborn?" Casey said.

"Wish I had—I must have snored through Dearborn," I said. "The fires, Jimmy. I've never seen anything like it."

"It's a nightmare. Worse this year than ever. Firemen get shot at. It's like the Third World, Duffy."

"Union Station, Jimmy. Good Lord. And no firemen, at least none—"

"They let the shells burn," he said. "Firemen, the poor bastards, they try to keep what's still good from going up. It's unbelievable, and I've seen it now for years."

He leaned down to hoist my satchel. He was a slight man, and I could see he was exhausted.

"Makes *my* situation trivial, doesn't it?" he said.

I wiped a smudged hand over my face. I smelled of smoke— even out here everything smelled of smoke—but I followed Casey inside the hotel.

"What happened today?" I asked.

He handed me the *Free Press/News,* the amalgam of what had been two competing Detroit newspapers. The story of his firing and his doleful mug were at the top of the front page. He'd probably spent the day in front of television cameras. He braced himself against the counter.

"I've talked all day. Feel like I've just called an extra inning doubleheader," he said as I checked in. "And I'm supposed to go live on the eleven o'clock news."

We moved into the lobby, but did not move far. Casey was spotted immediately. People stopped him, gathered around him, reached out to pat his shoulder, and to get in a word of sympathy and encouragement. On better days Casey would have reveled in the attention, in the confetti and the kudos. He was a short, utility-infielder kind of a guy with thin hands and quick feet. Tonight, however, he seemed overwhelmed by it all, his smile weary, his eyes sunken behind the bifocals.

As we were about to break free, an elderly lady in a chartreuse jogging suit and makeup to match hustled over and hugged Casey as if he were a member of the Publishers' Clearing House giveaway team. She clung to him. A cloud of Jungle Gardenia blew over us. She withdrew with tears flowing, then kissed him heavily on the cheek. "I'm Stella from Livonia, and I've loved you all my life," she said.

He held her hands and thanked her and used all his might to pull away. He turned to me with a smear of lipstick on his cheek.

"The Stellas love me, they really do," he said.

I saw that his eyes had clouded.

"God, I want my job back," he moaned.

I let him have that for a beat, then motioned toward the bar.

"Got time to grab a drink?" I said.

"I want a bed, Duffy. I'm whipped. Been on the air all day, and I'm still not through," Casey said. "Now these fires. That's the story now. Bigger than me."

"Go home then, Jimmy," I said. "Recharge. I can take care of myself. New game tomorrow."

"Okay," he sighed. "But we go at it first thing. I asked you here and I want you to get into it. It's more than just my job, Duffy, like I told you."

"I don't follow you, Jimmy. All your fans . . . Stella from Livonia—"

"I know all that. How it looks—poor, pitiful me," he said. "I apologize for being in my cups last night. But I'm only part of the story here. It's the worst situation you can imagine."

With that, another pair of fans approached.

"Tomorrow morning, Jimmy," I said.

"Eight sharp. There's a person you have to meet," he said, and once again waded into his public.

I found my room and heard my stomach growl. My paunch does not need encouragement, but I was hungry. I backtracked to the inn's restaurant, a place called the Early American Room. It was closing up, linens were being stripped from the tables, but I managed to convince the maître d' to prevail upon the chef for some eggs and fried potatoes. They arrived gloriously—three yellow eyes over easy—a few minutes later, complemented by a pot of coffee. I sat in the rear of the dining room and ate like a man who'd just fled a fire.

I also devoured the day's Detroit *News* and its stories of Casey's dismissal. I knew many of the details of baseball in Detroit, but this account brought me up to date. The Tigers were owned by Joe Yeager, also known as "Little" Joe Yeager, or just "Little Joe." Yeager was actually tall, a good six-three, who got his name, as I heard the story, not out of irony but because his father was known as "Big Joe." That fact, of course, did not keep the well-endowed sporting press from lewdly suggesting other sources of the "little" part of his moniker. I did not contribute my own, to be sure, as those kinds of barbs tend to come back and bite. One day's virility, I've been told, is the next week's prostate problem.

Nevertheless, Yeager was a man made abundantly wealthy by the worldwide proliferation of Little Joe's Chicken and Pasta shacks. He'd purchased the Tigers a few years earlier—a "childhood dream" fulfilled, he'd said—and infused the franchise with chicken-shack money. When millions spent for free-agent arms and bats did not result in championships and playoff payoffs, Yeager, like many of his fellow modern-day owners, grew disenchanted with his dream acquisition. The Tigers became just another business, and a losing one at that. Professional baseball teams, contrary to the beliefs of many dreamers, are seldom lucrative.

To turn things around, Yeager had brought in a tough new vice president and general manager whose mission was to shake up the tired, stodgy Tigers franchise. That is not uncommon; all owners do the same thing now and again. But when I read of Yeager's choice, even my bushy brows were raised. The new GM was Walter E. "Sport" McAllister. Sport was, of all things, a former college basketball coach in Michigan. A legendary one, to be sure, a screamer and a referee baiter whose teams had brought a Final Four slot or two back to the peninsula, but a basketball coach nevertheless. McAllister was an odd choice—hell, he was a *loony* choice in my book—and Yeager admitted as much, but the Tigers owner made it anyway.

That McAllister fit in at Tiger Stadium about as well as a basketball lodges in a catcher's mitt did not seem to bother Yeager. In no time, McAllister's personality duked it out with the sports media. The former coach was a blowhard, and he blew a good lot about how the Tigers were a dusty mess and he was going to wield a big broom. According to the *News,* it was Sport McAllister who had publicly fired Jimmy Casey.

What I did not know was how vigorously Casey had gone after them for wanting to abandon Tiger Stadium, "our ballpark," as he called it. The newspaper had a detailed chronology.

"There's nothing wrong with our ballpark, and everybody knows it," Casey had said early in the season. He told his listeners to write in and say what they thought, and he got buried in mail. He read choice letters on the air. Instead of interviewing old ballplayers and relief pitchers on his postgame show, he shared the mike with engineers, historians, and stadium-preservation rabble-rousers. It got so hot, the *News* said, that Joe Yeager himself threatened to muzzle Casey if he did not stop the crusade. Jimmy ignored him. He joined a group called S.O.S., which stood for "Save Our Stadium." Casey said it should be S.O.B., for Save Our Ballpark and because "that's what my boss calls me."

I took pause in reading all this. The eggs and potatoes had been superb. The coffee had warmed and settled me. I'm of Casey's generation, semiretired now after four decades of plying the bat-and-ball beat for the Chicago *Daily News.* I wrote a column called "On The House" in which I hashed and rehashed spats and con-tretemps like this one here in Detroit. Nowadays, when the commissioner of baseball is not paying me to look into big-league mayhem, I am supposed to be pasting together my memoirs. It is a ponderous, suck-my-thumb exercise. Roast us some chestnuts, Duffy, about Joltin' Joe and Campanella, Feller and Hal New-houser, and Kaline when he was a kid.

Jimmy Casey, on the other hand, was punching rather than pasting. At a time in his life when he could go along and get along, when he could read the script and retire with garlands, Casey had raised his fist. Where most people our age look inside and find mold, Casey was summoning guts and gristle. And plenty of people around here, according to what I had just read, backed him mightily.

Now Casey never struck anybody out, never scored a run or knocked one in. He neither won the Tigers a championship nor did he blow any for them. For all of his patter, Casey, to my knowledge, never did a thing for the Detroit Tigers as far as the box score was concerned. But when he took his stand in favor of

the ballpark and got canned, you would have thought he was Ty
Cobb or Denny McLain in their salad days, Hank Greenberg in
'38, Gibson or Fielder on a tear, for the earth beneath Detroit
shook.

That and a city on fire were what I had gotten myself into this
Halloween Eve, Devil's Night. I folded the paper and left the
lounge. My room did not beckon with any ardor, so with my
hands in my pants pockets, I headed toward the rear gardens. The
night was just warm enough to be comfortable in a sport coat.
Though I smelled smoke in the air, this place seemed far removed
from the inferno only miles away.

The Dearborn Inn was a proud, stately old place once used to
accommodating visiting tycoons and muckety-mucks of Ford
Motor Company. Lately, it had been made posh again by a big
hotel chain. They kept Henry Ford's portrait over the fireplace,
and appointed the lobby with mahogany writing tables, overstuffed davenports, fine rugs, and piped-in Mozart over the stereo.
It was a cut on the elegant side for me, but I've always appreciated
fine old hotels and this was one of them. The rear grounds which
I now trod were rich with grass, fall flowers, and a gazebo at the
center. Ringing the lawn were replicas of five colonial homes that
also served as guest rooms. There was Edgar Allan Poe's place,
Barbara Fritchie's, Walt Whitman's, that kind of thing. They were
so clean and authentic-looking that I expected somebody from
Disney World to jump out and announce that the monorail was
about to arrive.

The garden's lights were styled like gas lamps, the kind of thing
they were phasing out in my youth; now replicas of them were
all the rage. I seemed to be alone. The sound of my brogans on
the pathway was the loudest thing going. The Poe house was dark,
which may or may not have been a good sign, and I reminded
myself to reread *The Murders in the Rue Morgue*. My stroll was
nice, a little lonely, but, given the chaos in Detroit, this pampered
little patch of Dearborn green was idyllic.

As I turned and walked into the copper-roofed gazebo, I sensed
someone behind me. The someone was a woman; the knock of
her heels gave her away, something she didn't seem to mind. She
was tall, trim, in her thirties perhaps, wearing a pale business suit
and light-colored hose and possessing the carriage of a professional
woman on her way to sue somebody's ass off. Instead of a brief-

case, however, she clutched a large purse. I figured her for one of a group of cosmetic salespeople the maître d' had told me were rife at the Inn. Then she headed my way.

"Hi," she said, sitting on the bench across from me and crossing her legs. She ran a long-nailed hand through her hair, which was thin and a little too blond. It was as sincere a greeting as they come, however, and I smiled at her like an uncle. She was nice to look at, some Dietrich mixed with Dickinson—Angie, not Emily—so I looked. As I did, I saw a little bit of a rough edge, a crust, or maybe it was just fatigue.

"Avon calling?" I said.

"Come again?" she said. She had a great voice, deep and a bit flat, the type capable of a growl.

"Seems like the place is full of cosmetic agents," I said.

"Not me," she said. "I'm just a girl looking for a date. I was stood up, thank you."

"His loss," I said.

"And mine," she said on an exhale. She had heavy lids on dark, lined eyes that were fastened on me like magnets on a refrigerator door. "But the night doesn't have to be a total tank, does it?"

It was my turn to come again. Just then something beeped inside her purse, and she rummaged after it. "Fuck," she hissed once she found it and read it. I winced. I am still amazed at the casual profanity of the day, particularly from the mouths of women. This one's little beeper exercise told me that I was not dealing with an Avon lady.

She looked my way again, smiled, and cocked her head ever so slightly. It is an endearing quirk in young women and terriers.

"Staying here?" she asked.

I nodded.

"Interested in a little room service?"

I smiled. She was glib, to the point, and when a breeze stirred, instead of smoke, I smelled a scent of musk that would seal most deals.

"A tussle with my slippers and pajamas before bed is all I can handle nowadays," I said.

"I could tuck you in. I give good tuck," she said.

I shook my head and released a toneless whistle.

"Don't act surprised," she said, getting up and smoothing out her skirt.

"But I am," I said. "Always will be. I still have my illusions about witty, pretty ladies."

"This is Detroit," she said. "Illusions went out with the Corvair."

With that she lifted her eyebrows and strode back toward the Inn. As she went, her beeper sounded again.

Chapter

3

"So one night—get this, Duffy—instead of chatting up a half-assed pitching coach on my postgame show, I put on this lady who heads the group to save the park—"

"S.O.S.," I said. We were in Casey's Cadillac heading down Michigan Avenue toward Detroit.

"That's right. Her name is Kit Gleason. Now this is a sharp lady, Duffy. You'll see. A looker. Grosse Pointe money. And she can talk. Sharp tongue. She gets on the air and tears Yeager a brand new asshole. Calls him a fraud and a blowhard—every name in the book! She stopped just short of saying Little Joe's chicken'll give you angina, the pasta is cold, and Yeager molests children. My director is screamin' in my earpiece, he's so shook up.

"Best show I ever did. Lit up the phones. So good it cost me my job. My spies in the front office said Yeager blew a cork. The missus says to me when I get home, 'Jimmy, you forget who you work for?' Did I forget? Sure, the radio station signs my check, but it's no secret that if management wants a guy out of the booth, he's gone. I know that, and I knew it then. But it didn't stop me, Duffy."

He was rested and hale now. His voice had that early innings chirp. He had a radio talk show to guest on, and he was driving

me to meet the lady about whom he'd just spoken. It was midmorning and traffic on Michigan Avenue was light. The street is
one of several broad thoroughfares that leads into Detroit, the city
that invented traffic.

Nowadays, however, there is not a longer, more painful drive
in urban America. Once over the border, out of Dearborn's suburban landscape of country clubs and affluence, I was slapped in
the face by the faded, bankrupt, commercial corridor that began
at Detroit's city limits. It was a quick, depressing change. There
is nothing subtle about a city going to pot, about the pitted face
of neglect, of broken concrete and storefronts faced with plywood.
Many of them were newly burned.

"Look at that," I said pointing at the smoldering rubble of what
had been a corner building. "Those fires, Jimmy. Is it business as
usual after that?"

"Papers said they stopped counting at two hundred fires," he
said. "Business as usual? Detroit hasn't had that for years. City
jumps from one crisis to the next."

We drove on.

"Sorry," I said. "Where were you?"

"That show. Kit Gleason. I said that's what did me in," Casey
resumed. "But, Duffy, I don't regret a minute of it. It was like a
vision for me. What would you call it—"

"Epiphany. Try that."

"An epiphany, that's it," he said. "Suddenly it hits me that going
to bat for Tiger Stadium is the best thing I can do before I call it
quits. Best thing. Once started, I couldn't quit.

"Yeager, McAllister—they'll do anything," he went on.
"They'll eat their young to get a new ballpark. I was the first
course."

"This woman—"

"Kit Gleason."

"Kit Gleason," I said. "Tell me more."

"As I said, vintage Grosse Pointe. Husband's a plastic surgeon.
So she's got class," Casey said. "Somehow she got involved with
the save-the-ballpark group and boy, did she ever. Stepped in and
turned it into a real protest outfit. She organized it. Put out a
newsletter. Held fundraisers, auctions. Next thing you know,
there's a couple thousand members.

"And she's everywhere. In the paper, on talk shows, the news.
And oh, boy, is she good. Nice to look at, and she knows her

beans. She put out white papers on how the stadium could be saved, and she even got a bunch of architects to come up with a plan to renovate the place. Got 'em to do it for nothing. She ran the plan all over town to where the newspapers and TV stations endorsed it. I mean, she's a force, Duffy, a banger.''

"And she got to you, right, Jimmy?"

"That she did. I'll admit to that," he said. "She said, 'Jimmy, they don't own Tiger Stadium. We do. We're caretakers. We use it, have a lifetime of baseball memories in it, then pass it on in better condition to our kids.' Hell, Duffy, I've said that a thousand times myself, but this is the first time I actually did something about it."

We crossed streets named Lonyo and Livernois, glided past a big General Motors complex at Commercial. The sights got no better or worse as we went. Casey fought over a lane with a groaning garbage truck that dripped effluvia from its hopper. Plenty of trucks, tankers and semis, loaded and wheezing and headed for somewhere, rumbled past us.

At Grand, the area began to look familiar, and I realized we were closing in on Tiger Stadium. Yet before my eyes set upon the ballyard, I was suddenly taken with an open park area to my right.

"Pull up, Jimmy!" I said.

Casey threw me a look and moved to the side of the avenue.

"Turn in here—this park area," I said.

He did so, and there it was again: Union Station. Casey slowed, and I gawked at the building just as I had the night before. It was a burnt-out case, its windows now charred holes, the brick facade scorched. And it was still smoking.

"My God. I saw it burn last night, Jimmy," I said as I peered up at the ruin.

"It's a damn shame," Casey said.

"That was our depot. Our main stop," I said. "The old team trains. . . .''

"How well I know, Duffy," he said. "Everybody who came to town—from Rita Hayworth to Hank Greenberg—came through there. Now look at it. It's a goddamn shame."

He sped up, pulling around the cul-de-sac and past the makeshift cyclone fencing erected around the station area.

"But it won't happen over there," he said, braking at Michigan.

Across the boulevard was Tiger Stadium. Its silent white walls and daunting light towers stood before us like a fortress.

"That's what this is all about," he added. "Me. Yeager and McAllister. Kit Gleason. Right there's our fight."

We did not linger, and only a few minutes later we were in downtown Detroit. In the light of day, as opposed to my frantic exit last night, the central city was as I remembered it. At Fort and Shelby, Casey pulled into a parking lot in the shadow of the venerable Penobscot Building. The lot was crowded. People with business faces were coming and going. It was a good sign.

"My interview is here too," Casey said as we walked in. "In the meantime I want you to get chapter and verse from Kit. She knows you're coming. I'll join you when I'm done, maybe an hour or so."

I found my way to a seventh-story office. The door was clear glass, locked, and dressed with more propaganda than I had seen since my last I.W.W. convention. *S.O.S.* in gold and black letters was painted on the glass. SAVE OUR STADIUM below that, and then a full-color aerial photo of Tiger Stadium. Festooned all around were bumper stickers and cartoons, headlines and photographs, buttons and patches that had something to do with the grassroots effort to save the ballpark. The face of Tiger owner Joe Yeager had a diagonal red line across it. That was mild compared to remarks about what he could do with his chicken—PLUCK YOU, JOE—and pasta—YOU TOUCHA TIGER STADIUM, I SMASHA YO' FACE.

I stood taking it all in, feeling like a parent who'd just gotten his first glance at his kid's college dormitory door, when the door-lock buzzed me entrance.

Standing inside was a gray, pin-striped suit containing a gray-eyed woman with steel-gray hair.

"I am a sucker for this place, this curio, this Wrigley Field," she said. "There is no more beautiful sight," she added. "I read your book, Duffy House," she finished, lifted an eyebrow, gave me a thumb up, and shook my hand.

"We need that kind of poetry around here," she said. "Wrap Tiger Stadium with a coat of metaphor, how 'bout it? You Chicago guys could do that. Starting way back with Lardner. You know, my dad used to take the train to Chicago every week and come home with the *Daily News* and your column inside. Best writer in the Pie Belt, he called you."

I swallowed. The butter was slathered on my kisser and dripping on my collar.

"I read every word," she went on. "Your White Sox got Billy Pierce from us, you know. And Walt Dropo. 'Course, we stole Cash from you—"

"And Chet Lemon and Willie Hernandez," I cut in. It was apparent with Kit Gleason that you had to.

I ran an eye around the office. It was a good-size room with more stadium baloney on the walls, stacks of flyers and banners on the floor, two copy machines, a long table with a dozen phones, and boxes of what looked like S.O.S. newsletters, T-shirts, bumper stickers, and postcards. On Gleason's desk, which was cluttered but orderly, a lit cigarette with a crimson gash of lipstick on the filter was propped in an ashtray. This was Agitprop Central. Its proprietor, however, looked more like a Ford Motor Company executive than a holdover from the local SDA chapter.

She caught my eye pausing at a poster of Sparky Anderson and his 1984 world championship Tigers.

"Bless those boys," she said, her thoughts drifting into an earlier October.

Just then an inner office door opened and another woman appeared. Tall, about forty, with a solid head of blond hair like that favored by today's First and Second Ladies, she wore a sleek dress full of flowers, a lot of jewelry, and a countenance as lovely as Catherine Deneuve's. She stood there with her hand on one hip like women do when they're beautiful and cocksure. She was one of those women you couldn't take your eyes off after a first glance, so I didn't.

"You're talking baseball with one of the best, Mr. House," she said, and stepped forward with an outstretched hand. "Georgia here was named for Ty Cobb, you know. I'm Katherine Gleason. Welcome to S.O.S., where the little people have a voice."

I stared at her, and at the lady next to me, then back at her again. Standing there, like a rabbit between a steel trap and a velvet one, I felt like a mope caught in a rundown.

"Georgia Stallings," my pin-striped admirer explained, "in case you were confused."

She lifted her cigarette to her mouth and dragged on it like Denny McLain did in his organ-playing days.

"Georgia's the nuts and bolts of this place," Katherine Gleason said as the phone rang. Georgia reached for it and shot me an I'll-talk-to-you-later nod. Gleason waved me into the rear office.

"She knows Tiger baseball forward and backward," she went

on as she headed for a soft leather sofa and sat down. "Edits our newsletter. We call it *Bleacher Views*. People call her with trivia questions . . . the newspapers even call her. Named her two cats Trammell and Whitaker."

I sat down on the other end of the sofa. It was a great piece of furniture.

"Jimmy Casey can't say enough about you, Mr. House," she said. "And he's the best thing that ever happened to this organization."

"He says you got him canned," I said.

She laughed. "Jimmy Casey got Jimmy Casey fired. But we did add insult. Jimmy wanted to be used, and we used him. I'm a crass woman, Mr. House, and I use all the media punch I can get."

With a scrape of silk she got up, went over to a fancy coffee machine, and fussed with a cup of something that included a spritz of steam and cinnamon.

"Coffee? Cappuccino?" she said. I declined.

I looked the place over. It wasn't what I expected. Instead of the fluorescent lights of the outer office, a pair of brass lamps lit this room, and the low light gave it an executive feel: fine wood and draperies; nicely framed prints and photographs with my hostess in them; a hint of perfume in the air; and soft jazz emanating from an étagère in the corner. This was not a take-me-out-to-the-ball-park cubicle, and Katherine Gleason was no bare-bones organizer operating on a pass of the hat.

"If we operated out of a storefront, nobody'd take us seriously," she said, reading my thoughts. "Gadflies don't stop anything. We're lobbyists, and we have to look the part."

"Subscriptions to *Bleacher Views* don't pay for this," I said.

"That's where I come in," she said. "You can't look like a loser nowadays. That's the whole problem around here. 'Oh, Detroit, Murder City,' or 'Detroit, where lemons are made.' This city's the pisspot of America, Duffy. Until—and I said *until*—you get to the Tigers."

She was sitting partially turned toward me, homing in.

"There's still a sheen on the Tigers. Our Gothic *D* is a classic. You've read Roger Angell. There're Tiger fans all over. Tom Selleck—he's a *degenerate* Tiger fan. Tiger Stadium's part of that, everybody knows it, but it's old, and they're making it part of the loser image of Detroit. And nobody wants to stick with a

loser. So that's why you see all this. We have an operating budget
here. It takes *money* to fight money. I know Joe Yeager's crowd.
I know the buttons to push."

She sipped her drink, which was frothy, and came away with
white foam on her upper lip. I had once helped remove a similar
mustache. Slowly. The bearer had been gorgeous. I was twenty-
two at the time, and it was wonderful.

"When Yeager fired Jimmy Casey—and we all knew that was
coming—he blundered big time," she went on. "What public
support we didn't have until then we have now. So it's time to
strike. Go in for the kill. That's where you come in, Mr. House."

I wished I had taken that offer of a drink.

"You'll have to explain," I said.

"Let me backtrack," she said.

"You may think it's a familiar story. Run-down stadium in a
bad part of town. No private suites, no revenue makers. Worse,
Tiger Stadium isn't an icon like Wrigley Field and Fenway Park,
so it doesn't have museum appeal. I'll admit, Tiger Stadium is an
old maid with bad teeth and brittle bones. But she's still a lady.
She makes money. The Tigers always have. She has a future. And
a *lease,* I should add."

I made a face. Stadium leases are hot-dog wrappers.

"The stadium's owned by the city," Gleason went on. "Its lease
with the Tigers binds them there until the year 2008. 'Course the
mayor would eat the lease in a minute if Joe Yeager builds downtown. Detroit doesn't have a lot of building going on. But Yeager
wants out. Anywhere—suburbs, city, riverfront, Florida. And he
could build a new stadium tomorrow if he used his own money.
He won't do that—"

"So the city builds it. . . ." I said.

"The city's broke."

"County or state money," I countered.

"Nothing out there either," she said, "Unless . . ."

By now her drink was gone, the cup and saucer put aside. She
rubbed her well-manicured hands together and her bracelets jan-
gled. She was a striking, intense woman. I'm not dead yet, and
her beauty, the skin, the thin wisps of hair on her temples, dis-
tracted me.

". . . unless Yeager seeds the landscape. And that's what he's
doing. McAllister, really, this kind of thing is Sport McAllister's
kind of action. He did everything with grease when he built his

basketball programs, and he hasn't changed. We think we can show a pattern of payoffs. To state officials, developers, assessors, anybody who needs to be bought. And they have McAllister written all over them."

She leaned nearer as she said it.

"And that's where I come in," I said.

"Yes," she said. "You can bring in the commissioner."

"I can?"

"You can. You've got his ear. You've done a lot for him recently."

She smiled when she said it. I had the feeling I was being rushed and romanced all in a single move.

"Chambliss is a strong commissioner," she went on. "Unlike a lot of his predecessors. He could convince the other owners that Yeager is bad for baseball."

My mind spun at the notion. I'm no lawyer, but I know litigation when I hear it.

"Whoa! There's a lot on your plate," I said.

She smiled again. Perfect teeth. The tip of her tongue playing fast and loose.

"This is all or nothing for us, Mr. House," she said. "A full-course meal."

I got up and walked across the room to a wallful of photographs. Most of them featured Ms. Gleason. There she was with a middle-aged Al Kaline and a jowly Mickey Lolich. With Sparky Anderson. With Jimmy Casey.

"My clout may not be as heavy as you think," I said. My back was to her.

"You underestimate yourself," she said.

I continued to scan the photos.

"This is a big thing in your life, isn't it?" I said.

"It *is* my life, Mr. House," she replied. "It replaced the tennis club, the riding stable, the charities, garden clubs, and luncheons. It got me out of Grosse Pointe Park."

I pondered that.

"Grosse Pointe," I said. "Most people want in, and you want out. How's that happen?"

"That's a long and different story," she said.

"But a good one, I bet," I said.

She inhaled at that, stood up, and straightened her dress. She was not biting. I'm a nosy sonofagun.

Just then I spotted a photo of Gleason and Al Shaw, the current
Tiger cleanup hitter. I liked Shaw, who had arms the size of beef
shanks and who wore a baseball uniform as well as Julius Caesar
wore armor. In this shot Shaw was wearing an old-fashioned Tiger
uniform, one I'd not seen before, and a white hat with a black
visor. The uniform, I figured, was a Cobb-era jersey. Instead of
the Detroit *D* over the heart, it featured the orange head of a fang-
bearing tiger. It was a remarkable shirt, the tiger's toothy puss as
arresting as Kit Gleason's smile. The photo was personally inscribed by Shaw.

Suddenly I realized she was standing at my side.

"Al," she said, noting my fixation. "He's in this too."

I lifted my eyebrows. Shaw was a franchise player.

"The Tigers haven't signed him for next year," she went on.
"He's going to insist that part of his new deal is a guarantee that
the club stays in Tiger Stadium. Claim it's vital to his knees, his
numbers, et cetera. Wait 'til Yeager hears that."

I shook my head.

"Shaw's a ballplayer," I said. "Money suits him, not sentiment."

"You'll see," she said.

"You are going for broke, aren't you?" I said.

"Nothing less. Can you help us?"

It was my turn to inhale. I had to watch myself and any com-
mitment that I made. I don't speak for the commissioner of baseball, but Kit Gleason was right: He'd listen if I asked him to.

"I like old ballparks and I like people who like them," I said.
"I cut my teeth in most of them. Hats full of memories. These
days, as far as I'm concerned, anyone who saves one is a saint."

She smiled, that same toothy flash she had offered in the photos
on the wall.

"But I cannot guarantee anything," I added. "I can't save Tiger
Stadium. Maybe nobody can—"

"But you'll suit up with us?" she said.

I nodded. She gently squeezed my arm. It was a gesture that
would have been dismissed by stronger men. With me it went to
the bone.

We were interrupted by a rap on the door. It was Georgia Stallings with Jimmy Casey in tow.

"Don't let me interrupt," said Casey as he walked in.

"I think you should," I said. "Ms. Gleason here has sold me the
farm."

Casey laughed loudly at that. He came over and gave Kit Gleason a hug. He was doing a lot of hugging lately, and I was not sure I blamed him.

"I like this man," Gleason said, nodding at me.

"Watch out, Duffy," Casey said, still with an arm around Kit. "You saw what happened to me."

The phones were ringing in the other room. More S.O.S. memberships, no doubt. Georgia Stallings went to accommodate them.

Kit Gleason went over to her desk.

"Let's talk," she said to both of us.

Chapter
4

OVER A LONG LUNCH AND MUCH OF THE AFTERNOON, I LET CASEY and Kit Gleason show me their stuff. It was voluminous. Some of it was factual and damning; some of it, hearsay and innuendo, as the attorneys would say, and just as damning. There was no denying the homework that Gleason and her S.O.S. people had done on this thing. And the passion. They were dead earnest in their intent to show that the operatives of the Detroit franchise were going above the law in their attempt to scrap the stadium.

By late afternoon we were all tired. My head was blipping like a scoreboard run amok. I needed time and distance to get a handle on things. I told Gleason and Casey that, and they understood. I was not certain, I added, exactly what or how much of this I was going to put to the commissioner. Or when.

I told Casey I had made plans to see an old Detroit friend for dinner, and this was as good a night as any to do it. I needed some time away from Jimmy and his zeal. He dropped me off at the Lindell A.C. Tap on Michigan and Clinton. It was a legendary Detroit watering hole just a half mile from the stadium. Billy Martin used to compose lyric poetry there. Alex Karras read

Proust at the bar. Or something like that. I walked in and was happy to see its interior once again.

I had lied. I did not have an old Detroit friend to meet. I sat alone in a booth. I ordered drinks. I ate a fried steak. I read the newspaper and glanced at a few of the documents that Gleason had let me take along. The hours passed. I don't know what time it was, or how long I had been sitting there, when suddenly a midget with a fireball voice ran in and started shouting.

"The stadium's on fire! Tiger stadium! Burnin' like hell!" the little guy howled. It was Halloween, and this had to be a trick. The midget had to be Eddie Gaedel come back to life.

But the Lindell patrons leaped from their seats and ran out the door. The bartender surfed the TV channels for news. I grabbed my reading matter and rolled it together like a newspaper, then followed the horde. On the sidewalk, I gawked to the west in the direction of the stadium. Police cars and fire trucks roared by. I was jostled by patrons hustling to their cars.

A cab pulled up and four of us went for it. In jitney style we all got in—two fellows my age and a woman wearing blue jeans and a Tigers jacket—and the hack sped off for the stadium. He drove with one arm on the wheel; the other, I noticed, was missing. Streetlights and stop signs meant nothing to him. He nearly rear-ended a hook-and-ladder truck, and almost rubbed out a Vietnamese can picker. He nearly gave me a stroke. But in minutes we were within a block of the stadium.

And it was burning. The sky, which only a night earlier had appeared as though it could ingest no more cinders and soot, was swirling with smoke.

I made my way up Michigan Avenue, past the police roadblocks to where I was standing on a curb near Cochrane Street. The walls of the stadium, and the core of the park in the area behind home plate, shook with white-hot explosions. Orange fire and pitch-black smoke billowed above the roofline. It was an urban volcano, a fury of gases and echoing blasts.

I was struck dumb at the sight of it. Big fires, the genuine infernos, stoke up with a roar, with explosions and heat that singe your eyebrows and knock you backward. The horror of them is that they can be so awfully gorgeous. Flames hop with orange tips and glow red and blue at the core. White, nervous smoke hovers like good fingers on a piano, or the thick stuff billows like storm clouds. Smoke that will kill you on the inhale. Fire and smoke, it's just a hell of a thing.

Then it hit me as I gawked, my eyes watering, at these flames that stabbed the starless Michigan night: This inferno was consuming not an empty warehouse or a row of tenements. This fire was far more cruel. It was eating the guts out of an eighty-year-old ballpark. This was Tiger Stadium.

By now there were firemen everywhere—on the street and running into open stadium gates, perched on cherry pickers two stories up. They were throwing torrents of water into the old walled structure, but the fire raged, obviously feeding on innards that were not iron and concrete. Black smoke pumped into the sky as if it were coming from a blast furnace.

I could hear and feel the rumble and roar as I stood there. Like a thousand empty oil drums thumping on the pavement, like thunder in my gut. The smoke, so toxic I could taste it, settled in a gritty haze that hovered at shoulder level. Sirens yelped and whined all around as more alarms sounded and squads of police hurtled to the scene. Fire trucks with their bullying engines were stacked up along Cochrane Street, named for Black Mike, and skirted the hind side of the stadium only yards from where I was standing. Thick hoses crisscrossed the sidewalk like giant, leaky anacondas.

Suddenly I was jostled out of my trance and saw that I was now among a mob, a gathering crowd of hundreds, maybe thousands of people who had heard the ballpark was burning and felt they had to be there. Except for a few jerks who aped for the TV cameras, the gallery was as smitten as I was. There are not many intelligent words to say beyond those that you blurt out at first glimpse. Reality sinks in, and the face draws taut. This was Tiger Stadium burning—Briggs Stadium, named for old Spike, before that; Navin Field, if you go further back; and Bennett Park, named for the guy who invented the catcher's chest protector (and was too embarrassed to let his teammates see him wearing it), at the very beginning. This was home to the ball clubs of the boys in linen white and that Gothic D on the navy-blue hat. Tyrus Cobb. The G-men: Goslin, Gehringer, and Greenberg. Al Kaline. Trammell and Whitaker and the Bless You, Boys. Tigers, Tigers, burning bright. And they were all burning in this fire.

As the heat and flames warped and melted and blackened Detroit's tired, toothless maiden, as fire wracked this cool autumn night, those memories burned within me, as they did in the others, Tigers fans, gathered around me. You could see it in our faces. Silent, stunned, moist-eyed people of every age and color, we stood there like widows and orphans.

After a time, I was pushed back by police trying to control things, so I moved east toward Trumbull. The street and sidewalks were now jammed with people, like the crowds on Opening Day, which are always good in Detroit—except this was not Opening Day. I searched the faces on the off chance that I might spot Kit Gleason. I knew she'd be here somewhere.

Just then a helicopter flew over us, its burping motor cutting through the bellow of the fire trucks' idling engines. As it hovered above the park, I could see the Little Joe's Chicken and Pasta logo on its fuselage. So did the crowd, which put up a noisy boo and holler at what it figured was the Tiger owner riding inside. I'd never seen a helicopter booed before, and I hoped for Joe Yeager's sake that nobody was packing an antiaircraft gun. In Detroit, you never know.

The ruckus stopped only after the chopper disappeared behind the stadium's walls, a dangerous maneuver, I thought, given that the fire and smoke were still thick and swirling. Yeager, no doubt, wanted a view from center field. From what Gleason and Jimmy Casey had told me, it was probably as close as he'd ever been to the cheap seats.

I turned to get far from the maddened crowd and saw Jimmy. He was standing on top of a television news truck parked in the intersection of Michigan and Trumbull. Camera lights were in his eyes, a microphone was in his face, and even from a distance I could see he was carrying on as if Bill Freehan had just caught Tim McCarver's foul fly to end the Series of '68. Casey was back in the saddle, even as cinders rained.

As the crowd and mayhem grew so thick I could hardly move, I decided to get home. Smoke was still rising from the stadium, but the explosions had stopped. The air stunk.

Returning to the Dearborn Inn was no easy sell. Cabbies wanted to stay and watch, fares be damned. I bid up the pot, and finally found myself a ride from a fellow who could have been a twin of Gates Brown.

"They takin' this Halloween shit too far," he said, and drove the rest of the way in silence.

Back at the Inn, I activated the television and was right back at the fire, complete with Casey's play-by-play. Live television covers breaking chaos better than any other medium, and without the smell. One station had hired a chopper for an infield fly's view, and it showed the stadium burning in several areas. The press box three levels up behind the home plate—the ink-stained wretches of the baseball beat saw things *ninety-five* feet up in the air while covering the Tigers—was an inferno. It had burned before, Jimmy Casey reminded, back in the off-season of 1974. Which prompted Tiger General Manager Jim Campbell to crack, "What a shame that it happened in the winter when the writers weren't around."

In all, the home-plate axis of the park had burned. The press box and adjoining broadcasting booths were gone. Flames had turned the tar-paper roof above them into lava. From the helicopter it looked as if nothing was left of the stands behind home but a huge, scorched crater. It was a sight. For me, someone who had spent so many hours in that very area, it was a depressing, almost sickening scene.

I watched on into the night, now after midnight, expecting Casey to share the mike with Kit Gleason at any time, and once again to hear her distressed tones. But he never did.

When the phone rang, I half expected it to be Kit.

"Why aren't you down there, Unk?" exclaimed my niece Petrinella.

"They don't need my help, Petey. Bucket brigades went out with Ty Cobb."

"It looks bad," she said.

"Looks worse close up," I said.

"So you *were* there."

"On Cochrane Street. I could hear the sizzle."

"Is it curtains? The excuse to tear it down?" she asked. A fan who read out-of-town datelines, Petey knew the dubious status of Tiger Stadium.

"No excuses needed, from what I've learned. But this can't help, Pete."

There was a pause.

"I've never even been there," she said.

"Too bad. The old girl was worth a visit. . . ."

Petey asked about me and my plans. I filled her in on Casey and Kit Gleason and the affairs of the stadium before the fire.

"Tell me this," she said. "Was it set?"

"God knows," I answered.

"Is *he* a Tiger fan?" she asked.

"I would think so," I replied.

I took a shower before I went to bed in order to wash away the smell of fire. My day's wardrobe was beyond help. I was exhausted on several fronts, but I still did not sleep worth a damn. I dreamed, I think, a silly dream of running the bases in my underwear. In my dreams I am always being chased, and I am never wearing a damn thing. I awoke in the dead of morning with a full bladder, bled it, and returned to a bed that offered no sleep at all. Lying in a hotel room staring at the ceiling is a curse of youth and nerves. Without much of either, I usually sleep when I put my mind to it. That night I lay there like a dull fugitive until I heard someone pad down the hallway and lay something at my door.

I got up to discover a fresh Detroit *Free Press*. Tiger Stadium in full-color flames spilled over the crease. Turning on a lamp at the room's cherry-wood reading table, I spread out the full-size newspaper. Though the fire had occurred only hours earlier, the *Free Press* covered every angle of it. Reporters and photographers got inside the smoldering stadium and detailed the damage to the third-deck press box, the radio and TV booths, and the dining area behind them. They were a total loss. The corporate boxes were gone. Before firemen arrived, flaming debris had dropped into the lower levels and ignited. The home and visiting clubhouses, the lounges and weight rooms, sports service facilities, and stadium operations offices were badly damaged by fire and water. As I had seen on television, fire even reached right-field's Campbell Box, named for the longtime general manager. The narrow, enclosed box, which held only a dozen or so and was often cited as having the best seats in the house, was gutted.

Only the Tiger business offices, the two floors of corporate, public relations, ticket, and operations offices located in far–right field were spared. A snarling *Free Press* columnist called that an oversight.

I read all about it. In my mind I retraced a lot of my own memories of the ruined areas many times. I'd jabbered with George Kell, and pried bromides from Virgil Trucks. I'd watched as Kirk Gibson bellowed in a shower of champagne. I could go on and on.

Just as I was putting the paper aside, as the light of day rinsed the window, I glanced at a short paragraph which said that firemen had reported the discovery of a body. It was presumed to be that of a security guard, or the arsonist himself, which is always a hopeful thought. Nobody was sure, or if they were, they were not saying. The body was badly charred.

Then the phone rang.

"You're up. Knew you would be. I been up all night. I smell like a goddamn kielbasa."

It was Jimmy Casey.

"I just read the *Free Press*."

"Old news already. They found somebody in it, you know," he said. He was breathing heavily, his system highballing.

"Did you get in?"

"An hour ago. It's a mess, Duf. Looks like a bomb hit it. Roof behind home is gone. Everything between first and third is cinders. Pillars are warped like pretzels."

"You should go to bed, Jimmy. Something like this could kill you."

"Forget it. I came home to take a shower and change my shirt. Goin' back down at seven for the morning news. You wanna come along?"

"Include me in. How about Kit?" I asked.

"I'm tryin'. Been callin' her all night. No trace," he said. "Georgia doesn't know where she is. Her hubby hasn't seen her—which is no surprise, apparently. Nobody knows where the hell she is."

A half hour later, Casey's Cadillac swung into the Inn's semicircular drive like a B-52.

"Get in! Get in!" he shouted through the open passenger window.

He had a portable phone wedged in his neck and he was yakking into it as I slid onto the leather. He was flushed, bug-eyed, looking like a man who'd been up all night looking for a lost kid.

"The body's a woman! The one they found!" he said, talking

awkwardly over the receiver under his jaw. He squealed the Caddie out onto Oakwood Boulevard. "I got a guy at the station plugged into the cops. Says they're positive it's a female."

"So what?" I said.

Casey pulled the phone away from his face and held it in midair. He fixed me with a look reserved for cadavers.

"Kit," he said. "I think it's *Kit*."

Chapter 5

CASEY PUSHED THE CADILLAC DOWN MICHIGAN AVENUE, AND GOD
help anything in the way. One hand on the wheel, the other on
the phone, his tongue wagging at me and whoever was on the
line, his foot a sash weight on the accelerator.

"How do you know it's Kit?" I asked.

"Believe me, I know," he said, hanging up.

"What's that supposed to mean, Jimmy?"

He pulled up at a stoplight and thumped the heel of his hand
against the wheel.

"Because she had my keys," he said.

"Wait a minute," I said.

"She had my keys," he repeated. "To the press box, the clubhouse. Some of the gates. . . ."

"How'd she get inside in the first place? Past security?"

"First, with me. When the season was still on. I took her around
and she got to know the boys at the gate. They liked her."

"But this is the off-season. . . ."

"Off-season's easier. They wink her by. You know Kit. You
saw what she's like."

I still wasn't buying it.

"Come on, Jimmy. What does she want with a dark ballyard?"

"She was putting together some kind of journal. A book, you know, about the stadium and the whole fight. She'd wander around the place at midnight writing things down. One night I sat in the old press box with her. Way up on the rim of the third deck. Pitch black. Colder 'n hell. Bats flying around the field—bats with wings, that is—and she's telling me how lucky we are to be there. That kind of thing. I let her have my keys so she could get into the upper-level boxes and the catwalk gates. Anywhere she pleased. That's what she wanted. I figured, what the hell, I wouldn't be needing them anymore."

"And you know she was there last night?"

"I know Kit . . . put it that way," he said, staring ahead. His mug was taut with concern—and guilt.

We could see the smoky haze before we saw the stadium itself. The adjoining streets were a parking lot of vehicles with flashing lights. Without Jimmy Casey, I could not have come within four blocks of the place. With him, I found myself in the infield with a gaggle of reporters and shoulder-held cameras. Casey was once again being interviewed. While he talked, his patter a stream of Tiger lore and lament, I looked around the smoldering, bare ruined choir. It was London during the blitz. It was Dresden. It was Detroit.

There was not much I could do but gawk, and then it started to rain, a cold, clammy drizzle that matted what hair I have on my head. I stood there in the rain, my hands plunged in the pockets of my trench coat, looking at the blackened carcass of a ballpark, and I realized dismally that I had defined myself through baseball, through games and teams and places like this. At that moment it seemed a trivial, childish pursuit, even more hollow in the dank vapors of the rubble in front of me. Had a part of me been cauterized with these flames?

And Kit Gleason. Beneath her pluck and sharp mind, her beauty and class, was she simply a lost girl groping for some form, some sentiment, and finding it in her crusade to save a pile of bricks used by wealthy transients to play their pampered games? Had it defined her too? And consumed her? I overheard reporters saying her name, adding questions, speculations. Had she been part of the heap? Brazed like the girders?

The wind shifted, the rain increased, and I was buffeted by a gust of dirty, fetid air, the stench of burnt asphalt and melted resins. I suddenly felt the urge to get Casey out of here and de-

termine once and for all if Kit was dead or alive. The rain drove
everyone in the infield toward shelter in the outfield stands. The
broadcast crews, of which there were a half dozen, stayed live.
Well-coiffed, well-intoned talkers mined every cliché to fill un-
prompted airtime. I hoped Casey could pry himself free.

Finally I saw him shuck his headset and come my way.

"Let's go. Nobody here knows anything," he said.

We wound our way past the strips of yellow plastic and knots
of fire officials and cops standing in the expanse of the lower
grandstand in right field, the area closest to the undamaged Tiger
offices. Just then Casey motioned at a cluster of men in sport coats
sipping coffee from Styrofoam cups.

"Erve!" he said.

One of the sport coats looked up and came over to us.

"Duffy House, Lieutenant Erve Beck," Casey said. "Erve's a
homicide detective."

He was a thick guy with a chafed neck, about fifty.

"Can you tell us anything?" Casey asked.

"Wagon took remains away at maybe six o'clock or so," Beck
said. "Boys said it wasn't much. No I.D., far as I know."

"But female? You still saying that?" Casey asked.

"Never did," Beck said. "We got a security guy said your friend
was here. Went in about nine or so. But he don't know if she came
out or not. A real winner, this pooch."

"Hold it, Erve. So you don't know who it is?" Casey said, his
voice rising.

"What we know, Jimmy," Beck began, "and this is off the record, okay, is who was workin' park security. Two male subjects,
one Caucasian, one African American. We interviewed both of
them. They identified Katherine Gleason, female, Caucasian, ap-
proximately forty, as entering the premises at nine-thirty-eight
P.M. Last time I knew, she hadn't turned up at her place of residence
in Grosse Pointe Park. That's where it is."

Casey ran his hands over his face. They were wet and blue from
the cold rain.

"How soon before you get a positive identification?" I asked.

"Can't say. Check at Beaubien. I'm on my way there now.
Wanna come along?"

We followed him.

"This joint's history, Jimmy," Beck said, tossing his cup into
the seats. "Just as well, if you ask me."

Casey threw a snarl at him.

"I'm tired and talked out, Erve," the old raconteur said. "My second home of forty years has just burned before my eyes, and a fine woman maybe went down with it. So, Erve, with all due respect to your badge and your point of view, don't you tell me what's history and what's not history as far as this fine ballpark is concerned."

"Apologies," Beck muttered.

"Necessary," Casey said.

In an unmarked police car that smelled like a shoe and rattled like a plumber's truck, we drove down Michigan into downtown until we got to Beaubien. Detroit is full of streets named after Frenchmen who stayed long enough to build a fort, kill some Indians, and move to the suburbs. Police Headquarters at 1300 Beaubien is just south of Gratiot at Clinton Street. It is a tired old municipal building that has seen too many bad guys and felt too many steam radiators, but it overlooks Greektown and downtown Detroit like a stern reminder.

Detective Beck led us to the fifth floor and into a large, fluorescent-lit squad room, the usual detective den complete with a wall of hundreds of black-and-white photographs of men and a few women so ugly and mean as to make Kirk Gibson look wholesome. They were mug shots of mechanics, street killers, the baddest ones in a bad city. The cops working out of this room pursued felony-related homicides, those passionless murders that garnished drug deals and robberies—or arson—like afterthoughts.

I was so taken with the wall of bloodletters that I nearly missed the couple passing us by on their way out.

"Jimmy," came the voice, "and Duffy House again."

It was that of Miss Stallings, secretary to S.O.S. and Kit Gleason, the movable baseball encyclopedia whose first name I madly scraped for as I clasped her outstretched hand.

"Georgia," Jimmy Casey said, rescuing my memory lapse. "Tell me—"

She shook her head, speechless, with a look that said everything. She was heavily made-up but not enough to hide the blear. At her side was a tall, tanned, extraordinarily good-looking man with a silver scalp that said he was at least fifty-five but paid age no mind. Even at this time in the morning, he was a Cutty Sark type of guy, razor cut and manicured, no doubt with perfect teeth if he

was in the mood to flash them. He was in no mood. He looked
like someone who had just lost everything.

"Dr. Nance . . ." Casey said.

The doctor nodded without breaking his look. I tried to figure
out who he was, why, and what he was doing here, when he
wavered a bit, sort of lost his balance. It was the only fissure in a
veneer as smooth as a cummerbund.

Then, like a dunce losing at ticktacktoe, I got it: This was Mr.
Kit Gleason.

Before I could say anything, he left us in the wake of his after-
shave, the kind that waters your eyes when you read slick men's
magazines. Georgia Stallings's heels hurriedly clacked down the
hall with him. I looked over at Jimmy Casey.

"Kit's husband," Jimmy said. "Dr. *Cooper* Nance—"

"Cosmetic surgeon. Face-lifts, nose jobs. Best in town," came
a voice that sounded like that of a Vienna choirboy.

The two of us turned to Beck, who was standing next to a
mound of a black fellow in a windbreaker who sat in a wooden
swivel chair. *Straddling* may be a better word, for he must have
gone four hundred pounds. His body covered the chair like a load
of topsoil. His was the falsetto voice.

"Dr. Cooper W. Nance. Husband of the deceased," he said.
"Got her I.D. from a wedding band. There wasn't nothin' much
else to get."

Casey looked at me and groaned, his shoulders slumping. The
two of us wilted with the confirmation of the news we had dreaded
hearing. I leaned on a wooden table for support, then slid into a
chair that put me at the same level as the hefty tenor.

In the man's hands was a notepad that he held out in front of
him like a conductor holds a baton, because his arms were incap-
able of tucking beside him. His shirt was open and his rippled
neck was big enough to lay a carpet runner on. He was the fattest
guy I'd ever seen.

"The doctor said he had a matchin' gold band," he went on
with a short falsetto gasp. "He wasn't wearin' it. Said it has the
same initials inside." He gasped again. "K.A.G. and C.W.N. The W
stands for William. Okay?" Gasp. "Piece of work, that cat. Had
to call him up to ask where his ol' lady was at." Gasp. "She didn't
come in last night. Nothin' unnatural 'bout that, he says."

"Make sense, will ya?" Casey said to him.

The fat guy broke a smile.

"What say, Jimmy," he said, slowing down and offering a hand the size of an eggplant. "Wynton Mercer."

Lieutenant of Homicide Wynton Mercer, I learned. No more than thirty-five years old but looking older, he had pomaded hair, light-brown skin that constantly perspired, liquid eyes, and clothes straining to contain him. With all that in his disfavor, I figured he got to his level with brains. Upon my introduction, he offered me a mitt that felt like a soft cantaloupe.

"What we got," he began, "is a fire lit in two places. Security says so. Boom! Boom! And the place is goin'." He gasped. His delivery was that of a man on a respirator, and sooner or later, I figured, he'd be on one. "Firemen say that's right, so that's a lock for the arson unit." Gasp. "They went in couple hours ago lookin' for where it started, maybe get some flash points, you dig?" Gasp. "They got a sniffer gadget can pick up gasoline fumes even in all that mess. Your firebug likes gasoline." Gasp. "Maybe charcoal lighter or grain alcohol, shit like that. Then the boys find a body pretty burnt up. White female, maybe mid-thirties." Gasp. "Find it up high in the radio-TV booth. That's no night watchman-type, so they call us to say maybe we got a homicide."

"Kit was murdered," Casey said.

"Somebody dies in an arson, that's a homicide. Yes it is," Mercer said. "Intentional or otherwise."

"You mean," I said, "you don't know if Miss Gleason was murdered, or if she died in a fire that was deliberately set?"

Mercer nodded. "That's what I mean. Either way, it's my puppy. 'Course, we gotta find out how she expired."

"And security said they let Kit in?" Casey asked.

"They didn't say it right off. We like to pried that out of 'em," Mercer said. "They said, 'Oh yeah, we let her in. She likes to come to the ballpark, roam around, do some dreamy shit. Just about any time of the day or night.'" Gasp. "Had her own *keys,* they say, which would get her in those booths up there. That makes no sense to me. She's not even with the club. . . ."

"But they didn't see her go out before the fire started?" I asked. "What's that all about?"

"Well, they *thought* they did," Mercer said. His tenor pipes reminded me of some actor, and I couldn't put my finger on which one. It was irritating.

"Come on, Wynton," said Casey.

"Thing is, she didn't go in alone. She went in with a ballplayer,"

Mercer went on. He swiveled in the chair he was anchored to as he spoke, his face shiny, plainly enjoying this.

"Who—?" Casey snapped.

"Nine-thirty. Ain't that sweet? Two of 'em drove in, parked the car, went inside," Mercer said. "Maybe an hour later, they drove out. Least the guard man thought it was the two of them." Gasp. "Ballplayer's car has that damn smoked glass. Nighttime you can't see shit inside." Gasp. "On the way out he lowers the window is all. Guard sees him. Figured she's inside too. Figured wrong."

"Who was it, dammit!" Casey said.

"We locate the lady's spouse on Windmill Pointe Drive in Grosse Pointe Park. Ain't happy to hear from old Wynton Mercer at six o'clock in the A.M." Gasp. "I say you better get your Grosse Pointe Park ass down here and tell us how your wife gets dead on Halloween in Tiger Stadium." He gasped twice. "He came in with that female Caucasian you saw. She's the lady's secretary, and she knows a lot." Gasp. "How the lady can go in the ballpark when it's the off-season. How the lady had a dinner date with the ball-player. Nails it down for us."

He stopped with that and swiveled hard in his chair, causing it to shriek. I thought Jimmy Casey was going to bite the cop's head off, he was so livid.

"Al Shaw," Lieutenant of Homicide Mercer said, a rivulet of sweat running down the ziggurat that was his neck. "Lady had dinner with Al Shaw. Showed up to the ballpark with Al Shaw. Last seen with Al Shaw."

"Oh no," sighed Jimmy Casey, wilting even more than he had wilted before. His world was unraveling like a sandlot baseball.

We stayed on for a quarter hour on account of Mercer kept on with his halting, gasping delivery, and he knew that my name had been on Kit Gleason's agenda for the last day of her life. I could tell him nothing. She had not invited me to the ballpark. She had not told me of her dinner plans with Al Shaw, the Tiger slugger. All that noninformation made me small potatoes on Lt. Mercer's considerable plate.

"You go catch your Chicago plane, Mr. House," he said to me. "This is a down-and-dirty Detroit thing."

"Commissioner of baseball may be interested," I said, deciding I did not much like Lt. Mercer and that he did not like me at all. "If he is, I stay."

"Hell yes!" Mercer said. "Burn down the ballpark and where

the white folks from Bloomfield Hills and Birmingham gonna get their baseball?"

He wasn't done.

"Expensive Grosse Pointe lady burned up in it! *Doctor's* wife. This is a big one for us, my friend! No damn Devil's Night bums gettin' their ass barbecued in some crack house. No way. This is a big-league incident! The commissioner of baseball! We're proud!" Mercer said, adding a few pods of spittle to his gasp, his smile gone.

On the drive back I tried to pry something out of Jimmy Casey. Al Shaw and Kit. What did he know? What *was* there to know? But he was wrung out, almost in shock. If Jimmy knew anything, he was not in the mood to expand on it. There is nothing more silent than a play-by-play guy who won't talk. No totals. No wrap-up. No nothing. He even drove slowly.

"I may not survive this, Duffy," he said after he'd pulled to a stop in front of the Dearborn Inn. He looked like hell, and I believed him.

Back in my room, I called home and found that my answering machine had messages stacked up. Several were from the commissioner's office in New York. That meant Marjorie, Commissioner Granville "Grand" Chambliss's private secretary, general manager, director of operations, and the glue that held him and his office together.

I called her first.

"Reporting in," I said.

"Finally, babe," Marjorie said. "You should answer your machine. Where are you?"

"Detroit. And I'm a busy boy," I said. "Things are bad here."

"Detroit—I should have known. Count on you, Duffy House, to be close to the flame, so to speak," she said. "The boss is en route as we speak. Grand wants to see the damage firsthand. Lands at Detroit Metro at noon."

"Don't say you want me to pick him up."

"No. Joe Yeager's people are meeting him and he goes right to the ballpark. You meet him there. One o'clock. Your meter is running again."

"Ee-yah," I muttered.

"What's that?" she said.

"Something Hughie Jennings used to yelp," I replied. "Ol' timer who led the Tigers to a couple of pennants."

"He still around?"

"Not for a long while. Where's Grand staying?"

"He's not. Has to get back here tonight. But he wanted to get out there and see it."

"He'll get an eyeful. And an earful, for that matter. Place was lit. Arson. And someone was found in the rubble. That makes it arson-murder."

"Not again," Majorie said.

"My exact words. It's a bad, dirty ball game."

"And the end of Tiger Stadium?" she asked.

"I don't know. The fire took out most everything between first and third. It's a sight."

"Got you. I should really visit one day. See the Bengals."

"You may be too late."

"Hmmm," Marjorie sighed. "One this afternoon. Got it?"

"You're an ace, Marjorie, a marvel of planning and execution when the chips are down."

"Nothing less, babe," she said.

Chapter

6

Then I actually took a nap. A leaden, dreamless catnap with no images of fire or Kit Gleason or overweight homicide detectives. The shut-eye was needed if I was to be in scintillating form for Grand Chambliss, baseball's high hoo-haw and my boss. He landed in Michigan at about the same time that I, rested and spunky, boarded a cab. We'd meet at the sopping, scorched debris of Tiger Stadium.

I was waiting at the entrance to the stadium's front offices when his Lincoln Continental limousine drove up. The long carriage fit him like high heels on a duck, for Chambliss was a stubby mess of a guy, past sixty years of age but ageless, with unpressed pants and an open collar.

"Duffy!" he exclaimed as his heel hit the pavement.

"You got him!" I replied.

"Look like you just got out of bed."

"How 'bout you, Grand? Sleeping well lately?" I asked.

"Like a toothless dog in a field of bones," he said.

He wrung my hand and clopped me on the back. It was good to see Grand even though he looked drawn and irritated. He also looked like he'd been dressed by a pawnbroker, but I expected that. A pair of brown slacks had lost all crease. His camel-hair jacket was one big rumple. His tie was loose and stained. The combination brought a smile to my face. Chambliss was a welcome sight: an old, weathered chum you could rely on.

"How are you really feelin'?" I asked as we entered the lobby.

He snorted.

"Blood sugar's under control. Prostate's quiet. Cholesterol is out of sight. Don't sleep much. But I survive. The job keeps me alive. I love trouble."

He was a brilliant liar.

"Fact is, Duffy," he went on, "every time I turn around I'm puttin' out some brushfire. Game is coming apart at the seams, Congress throwing antitrust at us, television backing out, attendance is down, and I'm running around trying to figure out what player's coked up, which one gambled on his kid's soccer match, and now one of the best old parks in the circuit goes up in flames like a bankrupt liquor store. Brushfires, Duffy. I'm putting out brushfires."

"No brushfire here," I said. "This was a big one. And the fire may be the least of it."

"Huh?" he said, throwing me a look.

"We got a homicide, Grand," I said after we checked in with the guard. "Arson-homicide. This fire was set, and a woman died in it."

"A woman? Security?" he asked.

"Far from it," I said. "She wasn't with the club. And a player may be involved."

"Jesus," he said under his breath. "You make my job a migraine, Duffy, and where in hell is the chicken man?"

Chambliss did not like waiting for owners, even though, as Commissioner of Major League Baseball, he works for them. To his credit, Chambliss spent much of his time trying to buck them. The good ones always do. Fay Vincent bucked too hard, and they showed him the gate. Chambliss, an ex-soybean trader, millionaire, and amateur politician, had been brought in to put the bazaar in order. He was a merchant, who, it was thought, could deal with the merchants who ran baseball. Still, it seemed to be an impossible task, even for a guy with Chambliss's dough and moxie. His undiluted love of baseball, a game he saw to be in a swamp of trouble, kept him on.

It helped that Chambliss was a smart guy with informed opinions on everything from yoga to concert pianists. He could drink beer like Bill Veeck, philosophize like Sparky Anderson, and sit in a room with two dozen owners and cut a deal. He was made for the commissioner's job, and I worried that he was now ruing it.

Just then a functionary appeared, and only a few moments later Chambliss and I were being escorted across the damp outfield grass by Little Joe Yeager, owner of the Tigers, and Sport McAllister, his general manager and the hatchet on Jimmy Casey. Yeager, who was about fifty and whose height made him anything but little, was impeccable in a gray business suit over a white shirt and hand-painted tie, black wingtips. He had the look not of an ogre, as I had fashioned in my mind from Kit Gleason's descriptions, but of a stern accountant. McAllister, on the other hand, was a pug of a guy, maybe five-ten and two hundred twenty pounds, with a tight gray brush cut. He wore a blue nylon windbreaker over an orange Tigers shirt, dark slacks, and a slick pair of black leather gym shoes.

To their credit, Yeager and McAllister had left their flunkies behind. It was just the four of us. The press had also gone home. Apart from a handful of firemen still on the scene, the park seemed quite empty. Unmanned hoses still pissed on portions of the burnt rubble.

"Looks like a missile hit it," Chambliss said.

We had stopped as a group at second base. He was right. The home-plate pocket of the park looked like it had taken a direct hit.

"The clubhouses, the training and weight rooms, the video room, umpire's room, the lounges—all lost," said Joe Yeager. He spoke evenly, like a claims adjuster. "We had service and stadium operations offices in there, and they were gutted or so water-damaged as to be total losses."

"Where'd it start?" asked Chambliss.

"Press box straight up there," Yeager said, pointing above home plate. "And the Campbell box," he added, turning to the area beyond first base.

"Two spots at once," I said. "Textbook arson, according to the police."

"That's not official," said Sport McAllister, cutting in as if I were an umpire and he was setting me straight. "Nobody's come out and said that."

"They will," I said. "Kit Gleason was found in the press-box area. If the fire was started up there, it's an arson-homicide, plain and simple."

"She was up there on her own—" McAllister blurted, only to be silenced with a raised hand from Yeager.

"A body was found, Mr. Commissioner," Yeager said. "We don't know the details. We're cooperating with the police. We're as much in the dark about what happened as anybody."

He glanced my way as he spoke, and I glowered at him. A *body*, for cying out loud. Kit Gleason was now a "body." I wondered how he classified Al Shaw, for Joe Yeager surely knew of Shaw's involvement. I waited for him to say more. He didn't. So I didn't.

Sport McAllister, meanwhile, was biting the hell out of the inside of his cheek. Fidgeting like a basketball coach, he was a guy who had found success in air-conditioned arenas and had declared Tiger Stadium a "rust bucket." I knew all this from Jimmy Casey and Kit Gleason, who had nothing but spit for the guy; and now he was standing at my shoulder.

"This is a real tragedy here, you know that?" Chambliss said. "I look at this place and I see Cobb and those good teams of Goslin and Gehringer . . . Denny McLain, Sparky's teams—you can just go on forever."

The commissioner bent down and swiped his fingers through the wet turf. Major-league grass.

"We're all in shock, Mr. Commissioner," Yeager said. "I'd rather lose my own home than see the park like this."

I winced at that. Chambliss said nothing.

"It was always my dream to own Tiger Stadium—"

"Spare us, Joe," Chambliss said. "This place is a trailer park as far as you're concerned. Don't get misty-eyed with me."

Chambliss turned his back and looked off into the stands. God love him.

"I resent that, Mr. Commissioner," Yeager retorted. "I've always loved this stadium. I've invested millions in it that I'll never get back. What I've said about how its condition impacts the health of the franchise has nothing to do with the respect I have for the stadium and its history."

"Try sellin' season tickets with history," said McAllister.

It was Yeager's turn to wince. But his loose cannon was already lit.

"History is crap, if you ask me," McAllister went on. "Guy forks over fifteen hundred bucks a year, he wants a class joint, not Ty Cobb walkin' out of a cornfield."

"Hey, Sport, baseball and history go hand in hand," I said. "It's different from basketball. And it was Shoeless Joe Jackson who came out of the cornfield."

"Whatever," McAllister replied, "Basketball's puttin' fannies in the seats. The NBA's wipin' our ass."

Chambliss raised his hand as if to cut off the debate. He walked onto the infield dirt. We followed.

"What are you going to do, Joe?" Chambliss said. "Give me a clue."

"Until our people give us some estimates, we don't know," Yeager said. "It may take weeks to assess the infrastructure damage. Gonna cost us a bundle just to clean it up so they can do that. So we don't know."

"Contingency plans?"

"Putting them together now."

"Where could you play if construction went past Opening Day?" Chambliss said.

"We haven't even looked into that yet," Yeager said.

I rolled my eyes. Somewhere Kit Gleason's soul did a turn.

"Keep my office appraised," Chambliss said. "Every minute."

At that moment a piece of debris fell from the upper deck onto the floor of the dugout. Had a manager been standing there, he'd have been beaned.

"What a mess!" McAllister growled.

Chambliss turned to the three of us. "I don't have to tell you the whole thing stinks, Joe," he said. "Arson, for chrissakes. A homicide. Tell me, Joe, can it get any worse?"

"We go with facts, not appearances, Mr. Commissioner," Yeager said coldly. He put his hands on his hips and leveled a look at Chambliss that he had probably used to good advantage in boardrooms. "We couldn't be in a worse situation, public relations—wise. We know that, but we want fair treatment. A full investigation. Until that happens, don't nail anything on us. I won't be called a criminal."

"Not my style," Chambliss said. "The league will be part of the probe, though. Duffy here. He's old and grumpy, but he's pretty good at this sort of thing. Give him whatever he asks for."

"We'd be nuts to torch this place, Commissioner," McAllister said.

"Enough, Sport," Yeager said. He turned to me and offered a business card he'd extracted from his suitcoat pocket. "My direct number, Duffy. Use it."

We looked around a little more, walking into the concourse behind first base as far as we could before the debris allowed us to go no farther. A rumbling front-loader had come into the infield and began scooping wreckage off the field and into a pile in the lower box-seat area. We could hardly hear each other over the engine and the front-loader's reverse-gear beeper. It spewed diesel fumes into the air. The dank smell of melted plastic and scorched rubble hit us in waves.

Back in the front lobby, Yeager invited us to stay on for a bite. My mouth tasted like burnt cork, something only bourbon could wash away. Chambliss said thanks, but no thanks, he had to be getting back to Gotham. McAllister, who looked like he could eat a tennis ball if it were properly salted, did not appear distraught over our exit. We shook hands all around.

We did opt to accept Yeager's offer of the use of his limousine, however, a black Lincoln with the license plate LIL JOE 2. So much for anonymity. Its driver wore dark glasses, said not a word, and looked like Billy Rogell.

"Remember Rogell?" I said, sliding into the backseat.

" 'Course," Chambliss said, nodding almost imperceptibly at the chauffeur. Chambliss turned to me.

"Marv Owen, Billy Rogell, Gehringer, and Greenberg," he said. "I'd take that infield *any* day."

He looked off. Chambliss was back in Detroit, back almost sixty years.

"I wanted to get away from those two and that park," Chambliss said, his voice low. Chauffeurs, he knew, have great ears. "It's worse than I thought. Wretched."

"Hurts Joe Yeager worse than if his own joint had burned," I said.

"But which one—the house here or in Florida or his place in Saint-Tropez?" said Chambliss.

He made a face.

"Say, how's your niece, and why hasn't she gotten back to me about the engagement ring I sent her?" he said.

I laughed. Chambliss was crazy about Petey. He'd tolerate a lot of pox from me in order to keep in touch with her.

"She's supposed to start law school second semester," I said. "Supposed to. Unless she blows it working for the commissioner of baseball again."

The Lincoln eased us soundlessly into downtown, taking the same route as Officer Beck had taken this morning, right past 1300 Beaubien, until we got to Monroe Street in Greektown. It was good to see the neon, to smell the olive oil and the ouzo. Leave it to the Greeks to put something into this battered city.

Marilyn's on Monroe was a little bar full of the kind of M.M. memorabilia you'd expect. Here's a woman who not only sang a hell of a "Happy Birthday" to Jack Kennedy but captivated DiMaggio and Arthur Miller, three heavy hitters in three different playgrounds. She had a tip of my hat.

It was not yet noon, so we had the place pretty much to ourselves with the exception of a table of burly Greek debaters drinking beers and brandy and exhaling great clouds of cigarette smoke. Overhead fans dispersed the fumes. There was dark oak everywhere—tables, benches, chairs, and a spectacular pillared frame around an enormous mirror.

We sat at a table beneath a poster of Marilyn posing in a brassiere with pointed, rocket cups that could poke your eyes out. It took no leap of imagination to see where Madonna, a Michigan kid, got her look.

A guy with a gray-haired ponytail brought us the Canadian beers we'd called for, then stepped back and did a double take.

"Well, Mr. Commissioner," he said. "This *is* a pleasure. Welcome to Marilyn's."

Chambliss accepted the welcome and introduced me.

"It's a goddamn disgrace, Tiger Stadium," the ponytail went on without further ado. "And it was torched, believe it."

He loomed over us, a guy in his fifties, with a rugged face that was softening with age, and a glint in his eye; he was rangy, still able to wear jeans and boots, and that damn hair down his back.

"I'm Al Bensmiller. Own this place with the missus. Detroit PD for thirty years. Last ten worked security at the Stadium. Know the park like my own closet. Let me get your orders first."

We took him up on that, putting in for big sandwiches with a lot of meat in them. This was Detroit, after all.

"Two questions before that guy comes back," Chambliss said.

"Who's the player mixed up in this, and what's the story on the woman who was found?"

"Al Shaw—" I said.

"Aggh!"

"They got him inside the stadium with her. Don't know what they were doing or why. An hour later or so, he left. Security thought she was with him. She wasn't. That's all I know so far."

"Who is she?"

I filled him in on Kit Gleason. Every detail and a lot of personal impressions and unabashed superlatives. The more I said, the more I ached for her, for her fate, her last minutes on earth and how dreadful they must have been. In my mind, as fresh as the light of day, I saw her face, heard her voice, felt her touch on my arm. Her loss, the damnable snuff of a vital human, hit me as I spoke. I paused and tried to deal with the knot in my throat.

"A damn shame, and I'm sorry," Chambliss said. "She puts a whole different rinse on this thing."

At that moment Al Bensmiller brought out our grub, threw in plenty of pickles, and sat down with us whether we wanted him to or not.

"I locked up the ballpark for ten years," he began. "Great shift. Entrances and egresses—" It had been a long time since I'd heard the word *egress*. Bensmiller was cued. "I don't see anybody getting in there to light it. Stadium's a fortress, guys. Closed-circuit TV, computer monitoring, twenty-four-hour guard duty, only but one entry in off-hours. No fuckin' Halloween pyro lit it."

We chewed on the sandwiches and on what Bensmiller had just told us.

"But it *was* lit," Chambliss said through his corned beef.

"From the inside, my friend," Bensmiller said. He leaned in. "What about the broad? TV just said it's the woman from the Save Our Stadium committee. And my people tell me she wasn't alone, Commissioner. They're putting Al Shaw in there. Al Shaw. That's golden, so help me. He and this chick had somethin' in the air. Ho-ly shit."

We shrugged and kept chewing, not contradicting or adding a word.

"Arson's one thing," he said. "Arson-murder's another. Actually, it's pretty easy to spot. Coroner'll do it for you. It complicates things, is what it does."

The sandwiches were great, the pickles better. The beer as cold as Opening Day. In Montreal.

"So where're your instincts, Al?" I asked. "Ten words or less."

"Lotta people start fires to conceal homicides. That's about ten words. Here's ten more. Lotta people start fires to get out of buildings they don't want to own no more. That's more than ten more. And insurance causes a lotta people to start fires."

For a guy with a ponytail, he was no bullshit.

"This is Detroit, guys. Think the worst," he said. "Like I said, the ballpark was torched."

With that, he let it be. He stuck around and talked some baseball. He asked the commissioner to sign a menu. I got his card and his home number. Nowadays, I cannot know too many ex-cops. Then he let us be.

Chambliss wiped his hands and tried to tidy up the crumbs of a kaiser roll.

"You're on again, Duffy. You know that," he said. "And Petrinella, of course. Only this time stay hard on the ball-club end of it. You're going to want to solve the lady's murder, I could tell it in your voice. Don't. Put it on hold. Stay on Yeager, I mean it. If he's involved in this, his ass'll be out of baseball so fast he'll think he fell in one of his deep-fat fryers."

I exhaled, resigned once again to the chase.

"And Al Shaw, goddammit," he went on. "Let's hope we don't have another Hall-of-Famer with his dick in a wringer. But him too—I want you to find out what you can. As far as the deceased is concerned, I repeat, Duffy, let the cops worry about that. You let her rest."

"Not sure I can do that last one, Grand," I said. "Kit Gleason was a hell of a woman. A hell of a Tiger fan."

Chapter 7

"BOOK ME A SUITE, UNK," PETEY SAID. "I JUST TALKED TO MAR-jorie. She told me to let the expense account rip."

After leaving Chambliss, I'd returned to the Inn and phoned Chicago and my niece and aide-de-camp, Petrinella Biggers. I needed a valise of clothes and my Volvo. Petey had anticipated such, but not before she had gotten to the commissioner's office and slipped herself onto the payroll. Actually, that was quite easy. She was invaluable to me, and Commissioner Chambliss knew it.

"What about those fat tips you'll miss?" I said. In the months before she was to begin law school, Petey was working tables at an overpriced hash house and making a fortune. To hear her tell it, she was milking home more in a night than I had made in a week as a beat writer.

"Treachery in the ballpark, Unk. The unspeakable, and my true calling," she said. "Not to mention that I negotiated a better daily fee."

"Cripes," I said, remembering that I had let Chambliss go without doing the same.

"I'll get that roadster gassed and I'll see you tomorrow noon," Petey said, her fingers drumming the telephone.

"Observe speed limits," I said. "Stay in the right-hand lane. Bring long underwear."

"Right," she smirked, "and don't eat fried meats 'cuz they angry up the blood," she added, which was a great but irrelevant Satchel Paige line. I laughed and couldn't wait to see her freckled face.

In the meantime, I negotiated—at least, I inquired and they dictated—a weekly rate with the Dearborn Inn for her and me. Then I dug in. I'm an old reporter, so I sleuth the same way I used to ply my beat. In my younger and more abominable days, I went after a story like a large-mouth bass strikes bait. I opened my big puss and swallowed the hook, then struggled and fought and ran with it, fully knowing that I was the aggressor *and* the one mortally bagged.

The story, the piece, was the goal. Forget all the honorable stuff you hear about the game or truth or the exalted craft of reporting. Any writer worth his byline will tell you that it is the writing— and only the writing—that counts. Real writers stay with the bait, quest after it like chefs pursue the perfect soufflé, oboists the perfect reed. The other guys go into television.

If only detection—this maddening bloodhound craft that I am thrust into as an amateur by the commissioner of baseball—were as straightforward. It is not. It is not as methodical as running down a story, certainly not as linear, seldom as predictable. And it never, never comes to you.

By now the afternoon *News* had arrived in the lobby, and I spread one out on the bed. The paper was bold and black on the fire's aftermath. Kit Gleason, with her lovely, tragic smile, was all over the front page. So was Joe Yeager, who had no smile at all. And Al Shaw, whose mug shot was borrowed from the sports department.

The coroner was not saying yet whether Kit had died from the effects of the fire of if she had been murdered beforehand. The revelation of her assignation with Al Shaw rated the biggest head-line, even though the text was slim. What meager details the press had came from unidentified sources. Detectives were not saying anything for the record. And Shaw himself had not surfaced for the press. I was certain, however, that Wynton Mercer had gasped with him.

I sat and compiled notes while switching the TV channels. There are four network stations in Detroit—and, with the *Free Press/*

News amalgam, one major paper. A sign of the times. The video newsies were uncanny in the sameness of their coverage. "Imitation is the sincerest form of television," said the wag Fred Allen.

In these early hours, I had no desire to join the reporters' scrum, but I had to make some contacts. I called Del Howard, my G-man back in Chicago. Howard is a longtime FBI agent, still on the bricks, a guy who refers to J. Edgar Hoover as "Mister Hoover," or at least he did before all those stories came out about Hoover's penchant for wearing frocks.

"The Bureau has an arson unit, but we don't automatically go in," Howard said. He was busy and could not linger, but he gave me a Detroit agent.

"Good man. Member of the Mayo Smith Society," Howard said.

I chortled. Mayo Smith was a brief, somewhat beige Tiger manager who blew the pennant on the last day of the 1967 season and then won it all with that great team of 1968. Today his name and memory binds middle-aged Tiger zealots into one of those daffy, trivia-soaked, sentiment-oozing confederations. God love them.

"When the smoke clears, Duffy, get to him," Howard closed.

With my list started, I kept dialing. I dug out his card and called Al Bensmiller, the Greektown sandwich guy. He had been a Detroit cop, and I needed Detroit cops.

"Who should I know in the Detroit Police Department?" I asked. He knew what I meant.

"Wynton Mercer," Bensmiller said.

"Rats," I said, and explained my lack of glee.

"That's Wynton. He don't let you in the club very easy," Bensmiller said. "But he's the man. He may not look like it. Last I heard, the doctor told him he'll be dead in five years if he don't shed the bulk. But Wynton knows everything. Forgets nothing. Smartest guy in the DPD, hands down."

"How do I get him to love me?" I asked.

"I can help. Wynton and I go back," Bensmiller said. "Let me know when you want in. Wynton likes my corned beef. Likes my ham too. And he's especially partial to my roast beef, my turkey, my pork chop sandwich . . ."

I couldn't help but laugh.

"Get Cecil Fielder in there with him," I said. "Show Cecil his future."

"Don't knock the franchise," Bensmiller said.

Then, on the offhand possibility that Georgia Stallings would answer the phone, I rang the S.O.S. office. I got a recording. I expected as much. Georgia had also given me her own number and I noticed it was a single digit different from the first. I rang it, again got a recording, but this time there was room for a message. I left mine.

For the next hour I kept the television on and pored over the newspapers. I clipped articles, underlined names, added to my notebook. Then the phone rang.

"This is Georgia Stallings, Mr. House," she said. "I only have a minute. I'm helping Dr. Nance with . . . with . . . all this." Her voice was shaky.

"I'm staying on as the commissioner's point man," I said.

"Tell me he thinks Joe Yeager smells in this," she said.

"You're told."

"I'll help all I can as soon as I can," she said. "We built a file a yard thick on Yeager."

"Has the autopsy—"

"I'm sorry. I have to go," she said, and rang off.

It is a five-hour, 275-mile trip by car from Chicago to Dearborn, and Petey made it in four. The Michigan state troopers never touched her, which is amazing. My Volvo, a scarlet coupe with more than a few miles on it and plenty of character in it, was foaming like a racehorse when Petey pulled in.

"Huz-*zah!*" she exclaimed when she spied me in the lobby. "What say, Uncle Duffy! Boring damn trip. Break out the milk-shakes, bartender, I'm *here.*"

She had the red hair pulled back, the dark glasses perched on top, and those House-family good looks that drive honest men to commit felonies. She wore a loose, pea-soup-green top that looked like a surgeon's scrub shirt, and a pair of jeans with a French label on the fly. At twenty-four, as lean and toned as a red fox, Petey was simply a swell-looking young woman. When she dropped her grips to give me a wet kiss and a hug, every clerk and bellhop in the place got envious.

"I'm your relief corps," she said. "Hiller, Hernandez, and Henneman all rolled into one."

"I need a starter, Petey," I sighed. "I need a Hal Newhouser."

"Prince Hal," she said.

Petey was a baseball scholar, historian, trivia maven, and fan.

Though Newhouser's career ended long before she was born, she probably knew his stats better than I did. It was a pleasure to see her. Petey energized everybody close to her, particularly her uncle, with a direct current of pith and personality, piss and vinegar, and a sense of humor a little too raunchy for me. She was real bright, maybe a little overeducated, what with a degree from Oberlin, and a list-maker who had her young life managed in columns and color codes. Right now I needed her spunk and her organization to jump-start my Detroit nosings.

Once registered and ensconced, she joined me over beer and peanuts at The Snug, the Inn's tiny watering hole hidden behind the Golden Eagle lounge. I had poked my head in earlier and lingered. The bartender, whose name was Monica and who had raven hair and the loveliest Italian eyes this side of Sophia Loren, had welcomed me with a quick delivery and a wink. I'm a sucker for winkers, and I had suggested to her that if she were not encumbered she might like to share my IRA with me. I've always been frisky on the road. It was an incorrect, crude, and altogether offensive remark, and Monica had appreciated it.

She was working once again, and after slapping two coasters, two napkins, and a bowl of nuts before Petey and me, she winked. She also gave Petey a once-over that bordered on a frisk.

"Whew," Petey said when Monica turned away. "She's a cutey, and she's workin' on you."

"The young lovelies come on to me like horses to oats," I said. "I'm safe, I'm old, and I tip like a sheikh."

"She's not so young, but enjoy it, Unk," Petey said. "I think it's time you fell in love again."

"Never fell out of it," I said.

"Then it's time you got your proverbial ashes hauled."

"Whoa! Listen to you talk."

She laughed, drank too fast, and stifled a belch.

"How about you, Petrinella? You haven't been in love for a while that I know of," I said.

"Not true. I fall in love daily," she said. "On street corners and in Laundromats. Then I fall right back out again. My luck is bum and choices are worse. I date guys who have pagers so their mothers can call them. I date guys who have the number of their probation officer on their speed dialers. I date guys who still go trick-or-treating."

"You've been working on that answer."

"True. Just for you, Uncle Duffy," she said, and leaned over and gave my cheek a beery kiss.

I loved this girl, this woman. I never had children. I never had a daughter sit on my lap and fall asleep. I never played with pigtails or wiped away tears caused by a wounded heart. Petey, my sister's girl, was the closest to the real thing. Many times in these years that she has lived in Chicago and spritzed my existence, I've felt what fathers must feel when they see the glorious product that is a daughter.

"Unk, get back in the game," Petey said, jogging my reverie.

We talked some, catching up, Petey telling me what was in my mail and the good word from Biz Wagemaker. Then I brought her up to the hour on the stadium fire, ending with a personal profile of Kit Gleason, full of dismay and a little anger.

"You liked this lady," Petey said.

"Couldn't help it. I expected a moth. A fraud maybe. A mon-eyed, bored woman who'd latched on to a cause. Like a Hollywood actor swooning over this year's fashionable disease."

"Was she a threat to anybody?"

"At first I didn't think so. Those Save-Our-Ballpark organizations seldom are," I said. "Now I'm not so sure."

"So tell me this, Uncle Duffy," Petey said. "Was she murdered? Does anybody know yet?"

"Not officially. At least they haven't said yet."

"Let's find that out first."

"Commissioner wants us to stay on the Tigers and on Al Shaw," I said. "Not murder."

Petey sniffed. "Yeah, right."

She finished her beer and turned to me. The brain was clicking and whirring.

"First thing, we're sure we have an arson. You confirmed that," she said. "Tough crime, Unk. I've been reading about it. Arson detectives sometimes work years on solving them. Second thing, we gotta see if this was a homicide. The coroner should know pretty quick. If it's a murder, that makes it personal. We're good at the personal. Then we get to Al Shaw. Famous ballplayer. Sec-ond-to-the-last person to see her alive. Pick his brain, if he's got one. That'll be easy for you, Unk. Like old times."

"Is that right?" I said. "But I used to ask questions about the run and hit, the slider, and pulled muscles, Petey."

"Little deaths," Petey said. "Tiny murders."

*   *   *

Back at the suite I put in a call to Wynton Mercer. Besides my own calling card, I dropped Al Bensmiller's name, and Mercer got back to me.

"Knew I wouldn't shake you," Mercer said.

I could just about feel the fat man's heat on the phone.

"You know Al B.? My buddy. Good copper," Mercer said. His tone was liquid now, decidedly different from the lip he had flapped at us in his office. "He says you catch bad guys. That boy killed in the Chicago stadium, for one."

"Wrigley Field."

"Yeah. Ain't never been there. So that's you, huh, Duffy House? You a gumshoe?"

"In my new life," I said. "Work for the commissioner of baseball when bad things happen in big-league ballparks."

"You're a busy man then. That sport's fucked up."

"With murder now?"

"Maybe."

"You got an autopsy?"

"In front of me. Lady got burned up pretty bad. Scorched any external marks on the body," Mercer began, then paused for his routine breath. "She wasn't shot or stabbed. They can tell that easy. You take your worst burn victim, I mean where they're brazed and then cooked like a roast in the oven, you still got insides, the organs and stuff, that are pretty raw." He gasped. "They didn't find internal damage. No bullet, stab wounds. No fractures." He gasped. "Leaves it up to the blood. She didn't have any carbon monoxide in her blood. You die in a fire, you suck in a lot of heat and fumes before you go down." Gasp. "Burns the esophagus, the lungs. And you breathe in carbon monoxide. Goes right in the bloodstream. Puts you down." Gasp. "But she was clean. No CO, as they put it. So she went down before the place went up."

He grabbed a mouthful of air.

"Got any ideas?"

Mercer cackled.

"Full of 'em," he said. "Lady coulda died of a heart attack just before the fire started."

"Next."

"You thinkin' dirty, huh, Mr. House?"

"That much I've learned."

"That's good. You're all right. We always think dirty in our

business. Even when we got no bullet, no stab, no skull fracture."
Gasp. "Coulda been laced. Lab'll tell us if she got poisoned. But
don't bet on it. Not in a fire." Gasp. "Leaves a choke or a blow
to the head, is all. Lady her size could've been choked to death or
knocked on the head real easy. Big guy could do it with one hand."

"You leaning that way, Lieutenant?"

"Put money on it," he said.

"Go on."

"Fire burns her all up. Burns off her hair, the eyelashes. Burns
off her fingernails. Skin fries like a sausage. Cooked all the
scratches and bruises away. Like any evidence she was, say, *choked*
to death. A man can shut off her windpipe and not break nothin'
for the coroner to find. But she's real dead."

I coped with all those images, seeing things in my mind as one
does when listening on the phone. Gruesome and easy this time,
what with Wynton Mercer's indelicate diction.

"Murder-arson?" I asked.

"Evidence says no."

"Whataya mean, Lieutenant? You just gave me chapter and
verse."

"No way, my friend. I gave you my twisted, homicide-dick
view of things," he gasped and, I think, laughed. "We got arson.
You can bank on that. Some cat took some time to torch that
place. We got a body weren't breathin' by the time the fire got to
her. That's all we got. Can't connect the two, my friend."

I chewed on that. Bensmiller was right about Mercer's brain.

"What does Al Shaw say?"

"Ain't sayin' shit. He's come in with his counselor. On a leash
so short, Shaw could hardly whimper," Mercer said. "Didn't tell
us jack shit. Why don't you try? Pull some of that commissioner-
of-baseball stuff on him and see what happens. Meantime, I'll lean
on his four-million-dollar, designated-hitter, green-grass ass."

"That I could do if—"

" 'So-kay. They callin' me here," he cut in. "Take this number.
Gets you to me. Don't be a pain in the ass, House, but you get
something, you tell ol' Wynton Mercer."

A call back to Marjorie at the commissioner's office got me the
name and number of Al Shaw's agent-lawyer. I was not looking
forward to talking to this sharpie. Sort of like addressing the tail
when you want the dog's attention. Fellow's name was Jack Edwin

Vander Male, and he was not happy to hear from me either. In fact, he told me to take a hike.

"If anybody in baseball is going to speak to Mr. Shaw, it would have to be the commissioner himself," Vander Male said, seemingly pleased with himself, or perhaps that was just his natural manner.

"I speak for the commissioner," I said.

"Not with me you don't," he said.

"It's Al Shaw I'm interested in, not you," I steamed.

"Mr. Shaw speaks to no one except through me or in my presence," Jack Edwin Vander Male said.

"Ah, yes," I said, "Must have been you arguing on his behalf with the umpire in the Yankee game last September."

"This conversation's over," lawyer Vander Male said.

I did not even put the phone down. Just direct-dialed Marjorie back in New York and told her I needed the boss. Needed his clout, really. She got right on it. Chambliss got right on it. An hour later a secretary in the law offices of Jack Edwin Vander Male rang my room and announced that I should be in Mr. Vander Male's inner sanctum the next morning at ten to meet with Mr. Vander Male and his client, in that order. She said the name three times.

Chapter

8

To MY SURPRISE, THE OFFICES OF AL SHAW'S BARRISTER WERE DOWN-
town in something called the Buhl Building on Griswold. *Surprise* because everybody in Detroit kept telling me that nobody
lived or worked in Detroit anymore. The city was a phantom.
You say Detroit, they told me, but you mean Southfield or
Livonia.

Nevertheless, Petey slipped into the cockpit of the Volvo and
aimed us toward Detroit. A truly quick study and a sure navigator,
she had bought a city map from a bookstore and mentally filed
every detail.

"What're we trying to get out of Al Shaw?" Petey asked.

"We make contact. Get his side of the story, for openers," I said.
"We don't know if he's a bystander or a player in this. Is he a nice
guy who bought her dinner and listened to her ballpark poetry in
the moonlight, or did those two have something going that went
all wrong?"

"I like the latter," Petey said. "I'm a romantic."

"No, you don't," I said. "This guy's life is at stake. If it's a
scandal, he won't survive it. Not with his past. So we learn what
we can learn. And use our charm and impeccable credentials to
convince the slugger that we're on his side."

"Piece of cake," Petey said.
"And tomorrow there's Kit Gleason's funeral," I said.
Petey took her eyes off the road.
"We going?"
"I am."

Finding a legal parking space downtown was no problem. Traffic on Shelby, Congress, and Griswold was light, the parking lots were half full, and only a few walkers dotted the sidewalks. A sleek, shiny car passed by on the new monorail overhead. It was empty. The whole center city of Detroit in midmorning had the feel of a big city—one situated in the Upper Peninsula.

Finding the Buhl Building was also easy, except that Petey preferred the Guardian Building across the street. What a beauty! Restored terra-cotta, glistening colored tiles, a red-tan brick, sharp angles, and Aztec designs, details everywhere, the Guardian was an architectural gem Detroit seldom gets credit for.

"Magnificent," Petey said, cemented to the sidewalk, scanning the stories. The building now housed the gas company.

While riding the elevator in the Buhl Building, I thought of Bob, that big right-hander who threw behind Warren Spahn on those fine Braves teams of the fifties.

The reception area of the law offices of Jack Edwin Vander Male were like those of law offices everywhere, except for the fact that Al Shaw himself was standing there. Shaw was an outfielder even in street clothes: tall, handsome to a fault, shoulders as wide as a truck, no stomach, and tapered trousers that outlined legs shaped like closed parentheses, hands like jai alai mitts. He wore black, the shirt open at the collar, a black sport coat out of some kind of suede that must have run him half a thousand. He idled there in all his mocha, Afro-sheened beauty, a cross between Lou Whitaker and Harry Belafonte. The receptionist, a young black woman with perfectly straight hair and lips glossed so red they screamed, ogled him.

It was a stunning, almost heroic sight, particularly if you knew what the darling of this young lady's swoon had been up to only a few years earlier. For back then, Al Shaw, the same guy preening here in clothes befitting a four-year, seventeen-million-dollar contract, had been in the big house. Stir. Southern Michigan Prison, the state's biggest and baddest, just down I-94 maybe eighty miles, in Jackson.

Shaw had been there for nothing special: theft, armed robbery, cocaine distribution and sale, the gamut of credentials that put people in those license-plate mills these days. In Shaw's case, he used the time to play baseball and lift barbells. The former was a God-given talent—he was fast and could hit a major-league fast-ball—and the latter was a prison fetish that kept him alive and put thirty pounds of gristle on his frame.

It did not take long for the Ron LeFlore hotline to get to Tigers brass. It was the circuit set up by Billy Martin back in his day when he took the time to scout inmate talent in person at the joint, and signed LeFlore to many good big-league years. Al Shaw carried on that tradition and improved upon it, becoming a bona fide superstar. He also became a hero to inner-city Detroit. He wore his freedom like a man reborn. He was rich, as all big-leaguers are nowadays, but spoke everywhere for no fee to let people, particularly young black males, know the difference between a prison yard and a ballyard.

Now Shaw, who knew trouble when he saw it, stood in the lobby of his lawyer's office with the clutched look of a rookie on his face. It was an expression, I thought, of dread.

"Al. Duffy House from the commissioner's office," I said.

He shook my hand, then Petey's. His was massive and moist. Not the hand of a comfortable man. He nodded at me as if we were casually standing behind the batting cage. He fish-eyed Petey, however, perhaps figuring her for a reporter, or a lawyer, or both.

"Tell me what you need, Commish," he said. "I'll cooperate. Give you what you want. I tol' the police down to Beaubien, I was with the woman, and I left the woman. Went home. That's it, sir. This is a frame, if you wanna know. Al Shaw don't start no fire. At Tiger Stadium? What kinda gump move is that?"

He rattled it off like a kid in the principal's office. Ten minutes more of this and I'd have everything I needed. Shaw was warbling.

"What the hell, Tonya!" came a shout from the inner office.

I knew who it was, and suddenly an imperially slim barrister in a pin-striped suit was upon us like an agent on a fee.

"Al, for godsakes! Get on in here!" he said lunging at his client and scowling at his receptionist. "Who's making him wait? Who—! You're House? Who're *you*?!"

He was staring at Petey, who was staring at him. Smoke came out of his nostrils. Petey was dumbstruck, never having seen a five-hundred-dollar-an-hour attorney going berserk.

"Miss Biggers," I said. "Investigator for the commissioner's office."

"No go," Vander Male said. "She's not on the list. She waits."

I exhaled. Al Shaw had disappeared into the inner offices. Jack Edwin Vander Male stood in front of Petey and me with a look he usually reserves for wasted time. In my time I continue to encounter pricks.

"Granville Chambliss—"

"No, Mr. House," Petey said, opting for the formal. "No need to block for me."

She nodded almost imperceptibly. A smooth, cagey move. I followed Al Shaw's flak catcher inside.

The outfielder was standing up, pacing really, casting pointed glances around the posh corner office he no doubt helped pay for. This one had a basketball theme. Vander Male was a Pistons fan. An orange autographed basketball lay on a corner étagère like a vandalized pumpkin.

"Sit down, Al," Vander Male barked.

Shaw stayed up. I sat.

"This is strictly a courtesy on my part, which is exactly what I told the commissioner," Vander Male began. "We have no legal obligation to the league office. Whatever was said outside this immediate office is to be disregarded."

No pleasantries. No grace. Just pressure. The kind of heartburn that made you hunt for your nitroglycerine tablets.

I studied Shaw. He wasn't paying attention. Vander Male had positioned himself behind his desk and suddenly was a head taller than I. The sonofagun had his chair on a platform. I've read about power offices and how a guy will attempt by furniture placement and other gimmicks to make his visitors feel small, but this was ridiculous.

"You may take notes, Mr. House—no tape recordings," Vander Male said.

As yet I had not done a thing but situate my wide behind on a narrow designer chair. I'd exhibited no notebook, no tape recorder. I had not even opened my mouth.

"What did you tell the police, Al?" I asked.

"That's irrelevant," said Vander Male.

"What's your story then, Al?"

"Very simple—" Vander Male began.

"For cryin' out loud!" I interjected. "I know all about how you're supposed to act, Mr. Vander Male. The TV and the movies are big on lawyers and how they all seem to want to squeeze the living piss out of each other. People seem to like that. But I don't. Let's say you give it a rest for a goddamn minute, okay, counselor? Be of service to your client, not a damn *impediment!*"

I had to take a breath.

Shaw grinned, a big, wide-body prison grin that revealed a lot of post-joint dental work.

"Fuckin' A," he said.

He snapped to, shortened up like a good hitter with two strikes on him, and aimed at me. He had perfect eyesight.

"Sparky," he added, "you're better 'n Sparky. Damn."

I accepted what I took to be a compliment.

"Here's what it is—"

"Hold it, Al," came Vander Male.

"Hold shit, Jack," Shaw said. "Commissioner can hear it."

"Al, can I talk to you a minute?" Vander Male said.

"No. Stay cool, Jack," Shaw said, not even looking at the man who took 15 percent out of his per-annum. "This ain't no *courtroom.*"

He said the word like a person who had been in several of them and did not particularly savor the memory.

"The lady was a friend and a business associate. First met her with social stuff on the Tigers. Off-season. The cruise, you know."

He spoke in a baritone, a true Paul Robeson with some fuzz around the edges.

"Then she made an offer to help me with *my* thing. EX-CON. Expanding Convicts' Options Now," Shaw said. He put a soft leather loafer on a chair. "Program for ex-cons. They come out of Jackson and come to us instead of fallin' back down. Counseling. Job placement. We got employers with us don't first thing look at your sheet. Drug abuse program. That kinda thing."

"I've heard of it," I said.

"Yeah, well, it takes a lot to keep it goin'. Lotta money, which

I can handle, and a lotta management. That's where the lady come in. She was on my board of directors."

"So you knew her. You had a business relationship."

"Oh yeah! That's why I was there! Her office is part of EX-CON. Share computers, software, telephones—Kit helped get us set up! That's in writing, man."

"You went out to dinner—"

"Roma's, near the Market. Nothin' to that. Check her calendar."

"It was only business?"

"Business."

"After dinner you went to the ballpark?"

He sighed on that. Wiped a hand across his face.

"Her idea. 'Let's go to Tiger Stadium, Al. I love the Stadium at night.' I said okay, that's cool."

"Unfortunate," I said.

"Damn unfortunate. Damn stupid, too."

"Still talking business? Nothing personal this time of night?"

"Don't answer that," Vander Male cut in.

Shaw reared, his closely shorn head snapping back. "I wasn't havin' no damn af-*fair* with the woman. I'm Al Shaw. Ex-con. Negro ballplayer. She Kit Gleason. Grosse Pointe, Caucasian lady. I got a wife, kids, and a lotta overhead. Al Shaw's cattin' days are over."

"You left before she did," I said.

"Yeah."

"Why?"

"Beeped. I was beeped, that's why. My home number. Don't nobody use it 'less there's an emergency, but there was no damn emergency. Turned out my wife wasn't even home. . . ."

I waited. He took his foot off the furniture. He punched a right hand into a left palm. It cracked like a bat breaking from a Jack Morris fastball. He was chafing now; I could feel heat from him. He was a monster, a physical specimen so raw and menacing even in his gentleman's togs as to convince ordinary people that we could never compete on his field, but he was in trouble and he knew it.

"We also had a row," he said softly.

It was a lovely word, and probably perfectly chosen. He had more.

"About the park," he said. "Kit wanted me to come out on her side. Go public to keep the stadium. Like Jimmy Casey. I said, 'Cool, baby. You know what that did for Jimmy Casey.' "

Vander Male sighed his displeasure, but he kept his mouth shut.

"We was up in the booth. TV-radio booth," Shaw went on. "She had a key. We sittin' there, open window, lookin' out on the field, and she say, 'Al, this place made you.' I said, 'Baby, ain't nothing made me but me.' "

"And you told her no? You weren't taking sides on Tiger Stadium?" I asked.

"Damn straight. Al Shaw may *feel* that way. Al Shaw's knees maybe feel that way. But he don't say it," Shaw said. "Michael Jordan tol' me once he didn't want no part of that new basketball stadium in Chicago. But he pulled back on that 'cuz he knew the stakes. Me too. I know the stakes."

It made sense. Al Shaw was a player, and old-fashioned in a way: He was known to sign a contract and live up to it. He showed up no matter whether the team played in a sandlot or Disney World. Never missed a game.

"And I didn't burn it down," Shaw said softly. "Come on."

"Why did you leave without her?" I asked.

"She wouldn't go. Said she liked to sit in the park sometimes till the sun came up," Shaw said. "That's my damn fault. I didn't *take* her out of there."

"Hold it, Al. Hold it," Vander Male cautioned.

"My own damn fault," Shaw repeated.

His words hung in the air like a eulogy. I let them hang.

"Nothing else?" I finally said.

He shook his head.

I reached into my jacket pocket and made a few notes on a pad I'd liberated from the Dearborn Inn. Nobody said anything, not even lawyer Vander Male. He sat tall and quiet in his chair, Lincolnesque one might say, except that Lincoln once suggested that lawyers should always seek to avoid litigation. Imagine.

In the silence, Shaw cooled down some.

"I talked with the commissioner last night," I said. "He may call you today and want to confirm all this. We're in your corner. He wants you to know that. I'll do what I can and the office will do what it can. In the meantime, cooperate as much as possible with the police. Be available. From what you've told me, you have nothing to hide."

Shaw acknowledged that and looked tired.

"Like to shuck this city for a good while," he said. "Press be camped out on my front porch."

"Don't, Al," I said. "Go to the funeral tomorrow. Kit would want you to be there."

Chapter

9

A<small>N OLD PROVERB SAYS THAT THE "BEST WAY TO GET PRAISE IS TO</small> die." That saw always nagged me whenever I attended the funerals of crotchety peers and fellow crumbums. The curmudgeons, rasps, scab pullers. Praise for these guys came only from clerics who never knew them. Closed caskets were a favor, for they relieved us of having to see eternity's scowl. That went for a few gals too. I knew a woman who owned minor-league ball clubs who was so loathsome, so ornery, so downright rancid in her view of life that death's cowl could only have brightened her gnarly mug.

And then there is otherwise. Almost a decade ago, I attended Bill Veeck's last rites. Old, craggy, fuzzy Barnum Bill, baseball owner, entrepreneur, philosopher, peg-leg. That ravaged body of his, with seventy-one years and three times the mileage on it, had finally made the last out in the bottom of the ninth. A lone trumpeter played "Fanfare for the Common Man." Rows of white flowers lined the altar. Pews were filled with the famous and the infamous, executive-box owners and vendors. Minnie Minoso, in his White Sox uniform, sat a few rows away and wept, the tears streaming down his purple-black cheeks.

I have felt similar emotions only in fleeting moments since

Veeck's death. The passing of Jimmie Crutchfield, that Negro League mite who played with Satchel, Josh, and Cool Papa, brought pause. And then I felt the same pangs at Kit Gleason's services. Petey and I were purely spectators, and only barely so, for the massive, stone Presbyterian church in Grosse Pointe was soon filled. We managed to grab two seats in the annex while the overflow crowd was forced to stand on the damp lawn outside. More than a thousand people paid homage and bowed their heads.

Apart from the explosion of flowers, many of them Tiger orange, there was mood indigo in this rich-man's church, a palpable agony, emotion apparent in people who, I'm certain, do not readily exhibit emotion. Atop the casket was an aerial photograph of Tiger Stadium, all green and full of fans, and next to it a photo of Kit in a Tiger hat, a smile as wide as center field.

Petey was moved, even teary. "I didn't expect this," she murmured.

"Neither did Kit," I said.

I attempted to bird-dog the crowd, and I recognized several members of the Tigers family, both players and executives. Joe Yeager and Sport McAllister made an entrance. Jimmy Casey sat up front next to Georgia Stallings. I spotted Kit's husband, the wealthy doctor. And Al Shaw. With a woman I presumed to be his wife on his arm, the outfielder strode in down center aisle. It had to have been a difficult walk, for if the public's scrutiny were a dagger, the back of Shaw's ink-black suit would have been cut to ribbons.

"Remember what you said in New York? At Rupert Huston's funeral?" I said, remembering well the memorial for the murdered Yankee owner.

"Tell me," Petey said.

"You said, 'He's here, Unk, the killer's here,' " I replied. "And you were right. So how about now. Feel any emanations?"

Petey's eyes narrowed. She stared off. I sensed her antennae extending. She held that pose for long moments.

"He's not here," she said without a grain of insincerity.

A somber, eloquent hour followed, after which we exited the church and chose not to join the cortege. As scores watched, fans bidding Kit *adieu,* the hearse drove off. We lingered on the suburban sidewalk, the sun high.

I felt a chin over my shoulder.

"Al Shaw. Our boy showed now, didn't he?"

I turned and realized where the chin came from. A black one, so scarred it had the surface of a potato. The rest of the face wasn't much smoother.

"I gotcha, Mr. Duffy House, Mr. Park Avenue investigator," the face said. "And you got me. James Holmes. Private operative. Holmes Security and Surveillance Services."

He said it under the cover of a wardrobe of black: loafers, slacks, turtleneck, a black leather sport coat, and a black straw fedora. His food of choice was probably licorice.

"You talking to me?" I said.

"Talkin' at ya," he said. "And also at this doll with a man's name."

He tipped a finger at Petey. She eyed him as if he were the reincarnation of Nat King Cole. He liked the attention. He was a skinny beanpole of a guy, with long arms that strained the limits of his sport coat's sleeves and sent his huge hands spilling out past his cuffs. James Holmes looked like he'd been raised in a time when fights were started with fists and ended with razors. And not always in his favor.

"Pe-tri-nel-la," he said.

Unctuous bastard, I thought, *like a crank caller who knows your name and the color of your sofa.*

"Okay, somehow you read our book," I said.

"Done more 'n that," he gloated. "I been in your closets. Tried on your sport coats."

"I smell a lawyer named Vander Male," I said.

"Wrong smell. I work for Al Shaw."

"Just what I said—Jack Vander Male," I said.

"Yeah, well, Mr. Jack signs the check. But you and I both know who's payin' the bill."

"To do what?" Petey said.

"What I always do for Mr. Jack. Tell him what he don't know. Make him look smart for his customers. In this case, make sure Al Shaw isn't framed."

"You a cop? Or were you?" Petey asked.

That got a laugh, a kind of chuff sound that you get from people who don't laugh much.

"Do I look like po-lice?" he said. "Did twenty years of peeper work that made Mr. Jack a rich man. I know every hotel room in the metropolitan area and a few in Canada."

Petey was puzzled.

"Divorce work," I explained. "Before Shaw's lawyer made his money off Al, he specialized in adultery. Snoop work."

Holmes noded at that, a kind of spastic head motion. By this time, the crowd had mostly dispersed, though the procession of automobiles continued. James Holmes, however, wasn't going anywhere.

"Big business, 'cept now I go both ways," he began. "Used to be only the ol' man. Slip the office for a nooner at the Ponch or maybe put the flooz up in a flat and catch a boff before the expressway. Easy stuff. But now you get the wives an' that afternoon delight stuff. They're sneakier. Cover they tracks better. Like this here lady. She wasn't dippin' Al Shaw no more 'n she was dippin' me. But she was stickin' *someone*. Oh, yeah! You can bet on that. James Holmes can smell it on 'em—"

"Give it a rest!" I said, and took Petey's elbow. "She hasn't even been buried yet!"

I liked this creep about as much as I did his boss. Al Shaw could do a lot better.

Holmes did shut up, then hot-footed it next to us.

"You told Mr. Jack you're on our side. That's cool," he said, the spigot still running. "Means we're sorta partners, even though, this bein' Detroit, I don't see how an ol' white dude and a twisty white chick can do shit."

He nodded at that, liking his own lines.

He went on. "We're both lookin' to make sure Al Shaw don't get accused of what he din't do. That's cool. That's good for Al Shaw. What's good for my man Al is good for baseball, you dig? Means we dog the department—no problem. Homicide, arson dudes I can reach out to. What say—you got the autopsy yet? No? I'll give ya a copy. Got it in my car."

I nodded at Petey. I wanted a copy of the autopsy, so we followed him around the block and down the street to his car. The crowd had made it impossible to park near the church. Holmes's ride was a black BMW 330 with those infernal smoked windows. It was a sleek number, and, except for the gold wheel covers, not showy. But the trunk, once popped, was a rummage: papers, attaché cases, cameras, golf clubs, clothes.

"This is it," he said, handing a copy of the postmortem to me. "More to come. All that lab shit."

"Saves me some time," I said.

"Damn right. More where that come from," he said. "You goin' after the ol' man? The doctor. There's a cat for ya. Kinda guy I love to roll.''

"He's on our list," Petey said.

"Then I know you'll be in touch," Holmes said.

He flashed a business card in front of our noses with the digits of a blackjack dealer. I gawked at it. He actually had his photo on the front, in color, which was mostly black, with Holmes in dark glasses and looking like he was wanted in three states.

Petey giggled.

"How many times 've you been mistaken for one of your kin-folk, name of Sherlock?" she said.

"Several," he said.

And I think he meant it.

Perusing an autopsy report, something I never did as a sports scribe, sickens me. Reading Kit Gleason's was almost more than I could take. Her body was badly charred, the extremities completely burned off, yet her organs were fairly intact. The contents of her stomach revealed a partially digested dinner. And to James Holmes's credit, there was no evidence of semen in her vagina. That was good news, of sorts, to his client.

The autopsy also confirmed earlier reports: that Gleason had died before the fire could kill her. One thing investigators look for with a body found in a fire is smoke in the nostrils. That much I knew. With Kit Gleason, there were no nostrils left. An immediate blood analysis, moreover, found no carbon monoxide within the blood. It was clear that she was not breathing when the smoke and fire consumed her. Yet her heart was in perfect shape. Her arteries were clear. She had not suffered a cardiac arrest or a stroke. The tentative cause of death was strangulation. There were no external marks or bruises, however, because there was no flesh left on the neck.

And that's when I vomited.

The next morning, which had turned overcast and gloomy, I called the S.O.S. Office. The second number, that is, and Georgia Stallings answered. Of course, she said, we could come on in and she'd give us every file she had. It was the kind of work I did not mind, but Petey seemed less than thrilled.

"Get used to it," I said. "This is how crimes are discovered."

"I'm a nineties type A, Unk," she said. "No patience; immediate gratification."

I grimaced, then saw the tongue in her cheek.

The S.O.S. office was an echo chamber of keening phones. They wailed and clicked on recording machines as Georgia Stallings unlocked the door to let us in, and locked it again behind us.

"Hello, Duffy," she said, glancing quickly over my shoulder down the hallway. "And you're the niece," she added with a handshake for Petey.

Stallings was stiffly dressed once again, in a navy suit this time, with an oxford-cloth blouse and a ribbon tie, low heels. And the caked makeup. A cigarette burned in an ashtray.

"How are you doing, Georgia?" I asked.

"I'm together. Maybe with Scotch tape and safety pins, but I'm hanging in there," she said. "Been here since six this morning. The phones haven't stopped. That's how strong people feel about this. If I weren't here, I'd be going nuts. And I gotta take my calls. My reporters have been good to me so far. There're just so many of them."

As she said it her phone rang, and she picked it up along with her cigarette. She dragged fiercely before answering. As a former smoker, a person who once sat in press boxes where the smoke was as thick as mist, I all but felt the nicotine rush. Petey made a face at the fog. She was raised in a smoke-free bubble, so what does she know?

Stallings motioned us toward the doorway to Kit Gleason's low-lit office. We walked inside and I stopped, even faltered some, for Kit Gleason's essence was still here. Her smell. Her spirit. The tiny mementos of her life. They had been untouched, and I felt like a trespasser.

"Uncle Duffy?" Petey said.

I shook myself and carried on. On a library table was a stack of files. We dug in. We lingered on back issues of *Bleacher Views,* the S.O.S. publication largely written and edited by Georgia. With the style of an English professor and the candor of a beer vendor, it bristled with indignation and scorn for anyone opposed to its cause.

"Evidence mounts that new stadiums are not catalysts to down-town redevelopment," it said, "but massive transfers of wealth from taxpayers to sports team owners." And so forth, with great chunks of research and grassroots testimonials to buttress its positions. Yet it was not without sarcasm and venom. It named names, particularly of city and county officials who, it was alleged, were clandestinely working to broker a deal for a new stadium. Issue after issue was filled with dollars-and-cents comparisons of newly built stadiums around the country, most of which, it claimed, lost money and burdened taxpayers. *Bleacher Views* was a true clarion, a one-issue stickler, a long syringe in the buttocks of Joe Yeager and Sport McAllister and others who would doom the beloved Tiger temple.

I paused over one of Kit's editorials.

"Joe Yeager earned his fortune the new-fashioned way: quick and leveraged. He expects to get a new stadium the same way. He will use other people's money—probably yours and mine—and erect the structure as if it were no more than a new chicken-and-pasta shack. With bleachers. I take that back. There won't be any bleachers. New stadiums do not abide cheap seats. . . ."

It was stick-it-in-your-eye prose, a one-note samba that was never dull, and I smiled to myself. The lady had been a tiger. I paged and read for a while, taking a few notes. Petey did the same.

Then I spotted something, in a Gleason editorial again, almost buried in a late paragraph. It read: "*Embarrassed* will be the word for Yeager, McAllister, and the rest of the front-office boys when some of their biggest players come out publicly in favor of Save Our Stadium. I'm talking about a *franchise* player, among others. . . ."

That was it. Dated only a month earlier. I scribbled a note about it, and underlined it.

We continued to work through the files. The din of phones in the other room continued, occasionally interrupted by Georgia Stallings's voice. At one point she popped her head in the door and asked if we wanted coffee. We did.

"Here's a read," Petey said a little later. "Kit Gleason's personal file. Her fan letters."

"True believers," I said. "Don't waste too much time with them."

"Wait a minute. Look at this," Petey said.

She passed a single page stapled to an envelope.

"Go back to Gross Point bitch," it read. It was badly typed on a machine with no spelling checker on a blank sheet of paper. "Tiger stadium sucks and so do you."

There were others like it, Petey discovered. Some scrawled, some cleanly typed, none of them signed. All aimed at Kit.

"Jesus," Petey said, handing me another.

"How about this: 'Burn down Tiger Stadium with you in it.' "

That one made me shudder.

There were also files on Joe Yeager and Sport McAllister. I grabbed the latter. An S.O.S. researcher had done a number on Sport, how he turned a sleepy south Florida college into an NCAA basketball giant by signing kids from Philadelphia and Chicago named Antwan and Deion and Philemon. How NCAA investigators came down on his program like fruit flies on a fig. How he abruptly left southern Florida and came up to Southern Michigan University and in two years, with the help of junior college transfers, turned that program into a national contender.

McAllister's file read like a *Sports Illustrated* exposé. I skimmed much of it, taking a note here and there. One name popped out of the pack. Doing McAllister's bidding in Florida and at Southern Michigan was a guy named Mickey Schubert. From all indications, Schubert was McAllister's bagman. Sport's players, the file said, referred to Schubert by his first name. I was sure they knew his private phone numbers. But there was not much else on him; good bagmen don't leave résumés. Schubert, the file did add, was known to be a golf hustler, a gift tht put him in some high-profile foursomes. That meant he took money from rich, but stupid, amateurs. I knew the type. I squirmed in my seat and underlined Mickey Schubert's name.

After a trip to the NCAA Final Four, McAllister had left Southern Michigan and his program's certain suspension to be Joe Yeager's general manager. S.O.S. howled. Yeager had hired "the Devil," they wrote. And then they really started calling him names.

The only file fatter than those on Yeager and McAllister was a three-inch-thick beauty entitled "Structural Survey of Tiger Stadium; Detroit, Michigan." It was loaded with official-looking documents that threatened to permanently cross my eyes. But it was important, I knew. It was an encyclopedia on the soundness of the stadium through an engineer's magnifying glass. The preparer was Gordon Olson Associates, an outfit located across the state in Grand Rapids.

One way to justify the scrapping of a stadium is to show it to be a "public danger," a structure unsuitable for public use. Just show that it's a wreck and somebody is likely to get killed just walking inside. Owners, legislators, and developers—many of whom are lawyers—love that cushion and use it often. By commissioning their own architectural study, however, S.O.S. could slap down anyone who said the old stadium was shot.

Much of the Olson Survey was a mishmash of drawings and calculations, the output of guys who were gnawing pencils in engineering school while I was plying locker rooms and viewing jock itch. My reading was helped by someone's yellow highlighting and margin notes. Actually two someones, judging by the penmanship, and I figured them to be Kit and Georgia.

The Olson people had scraped every girder and tamped every pillar, and used terms like *spalled concrete* and *iron fatigue*. Their conclusions were two: (1) the stadium was badly maintained; but (2) it was a tough old goat capable of lasting "indefinitely" if properly maintained. In so many thousand words, and, no doubt, for a handsome fee.

The survey was only a few weeks old, and I wondered how public it had become. I wondered if Joe Yeager had a comparable survey of his own, with contrary conclusions, of course.

Petey got up and read over my shoulder.

"These people have done their homework," she said.

"And made some enemies," I said.

Just then, Georgia Stallings walked in. She spotted what I was into.

"You got to the Olson Survey," she said. "It's our Bible."

"Is it credible?" I asked.

"They're known all over the world. Building and bridge appraisers. They do a lot of earthquake work. Experts. We were lucky to get them. We found out Gordon Olson is a Tiger fan, and we used it on him."

"Biased?" I added.

"As a matter of fact, yes. He said as much, so he sent his associates to do it. None of them had ever been in the park before."

"Two more questions," I said, now that I had Stallings talking. "What do you know about this Mickey Schubert?"

"Ugh," she snapped. "Mr. Sleaze. Sport McAllister's germ." She sucked the daylights out of her cigarette.

"Look at any sleazy college program or wherever," she quickly added, "and the Mickey Schuberts of this world come out of the cracks. From what we know, Schubert was a booster in southern

Florida when he met up with McAllister. That's where McAllister made his name, you know. Schubert was one of those friendly booster clubbers who love the action. A real jock sniffer. Sold cars or time shares or something like that. McAllister used him to get his players cars, stereos, spending money, steroids, you name it. Nickname was 'Keep 'Em Happy, Mickey.' "

"Where was the NCAA?" I asked.

"Day late and a dollar short, as usual," she said. "They went after McAllister and got his program instead. Probation, no tournaments, the usual slap. Mickey and Sport, meanwhile, ran up to Southern Michigan U., where they started right in again. And their hustle was the same. That's what gets me. They squeezed freebies from local business guys who wanted to sit behind the bench. McAllister got a bunch of illiterate semipro players from junior colleges, and suddenly SMU is a big college powerhouse. But don't get me started on the colleges. . . ."

She lit another cigarette off the one in her hand. She wasn't done yet.

"Long and short of it is," she said, "you don't ever see Mickey Schubert. Take that back, you see him on the golf course. He hustles big shots for big money. Two handicap. But you don't see him anywhere near Sport McAllister. No way. Nobody I know has ever met with Schubert. I know I never have. Nobody ever writes about him. But he's around. He's everywhere. Second question?"

"I forgot it," I said, still digesting her Schubert rap.

"No you didn't," she said. "Not you, Duffy House."

"Oh, yes, was Al Shaw on your side?" I asked. "Was he going to come out publicly in favor of keeping the Stadium?"

"Definitely," Stallings said. "He was the ace up our sleeve. We were going to make a video of him inside the park. He was going to say something like, 'After my wife and my mother, this is my favorite lady. I love this ol' place.' "

"He *said* that?" I asked.

"Right where you're standing now. Why?"

"He told me the opposite two days ago."

Georgia Stallings shook her head.

"Oh, Al," she said.

"He also said he was here on business with Kit—"

"EX-CON," Stallings said. "We're part of that. It was Kit's idea, her way to get Al involved with S.O.S., and it worked. I was against it. Lot of extra work—we do all their communications and P.R. We're like an auxiliary office."

"That cut into your time?" Petey asked.

Stallings lifted her eyes wearily at that.

"A *lot,*" she said. "Aside from a few college kids who ditto for me, this office is me. And EX-CON was getting that way. No disrespect intended, but those idiots over there can't order out for lunch and get it right."

"But it got Shaw involved," I said.

"That it did," she said. "EX-CON was his baby. He really feels for those guys."

"What's your take on what happened at the stadium that night between Al and Kit?" Petey asked.

Stallings ran a hand through her hair. She went over to Kit's desk and liberated a cigarette, lit it, sucked it home. She was a smoker all right.

"Kit could push," she began. "Kit had a way of seeing the world only in terms of her pet projects. She could squeeze people. Like shoving rats through a funnel. Sometimes she shoved too hard. Just way too hard."

"About what?" I said. "What'd she want from Al Shaw?"

"All or nothing," Stallings said. "She wanted him to hang his next contract on the stadium. Tigers stay, or he walks."

"Ridiculous," I said.

"Why?" Petey interjected. "Think of it, Unk. Like Michael Jordan, this Al Shaw. Walking franchises. Guys like that say they won't play, it'd give the owners fits."

"In fiction," I responded.

"Not in Kit's head," Stallings said. "I know she was going to go at Al with it, because she tried it out on me that afternoon."

"No wonder he left without her," I said.

"I wish he hadn't," Stallings said, her cigarette nearly spent. She lit another one off it.

We spent most of the day at the S.O.S. office. Just as we had hoped, the S.O.S. volunteers had done considerable research into the economics of baseball in general, and the Tigers in particular. They knew about every dime the team took in and every nickel it spent. The Tigers were "extremely profitable" at Tiger Stadium, according to the data, and would remain so if it were renovated.

Petey and I took extensive notes. The material was exhaustive and it exhausted us, but it was all here.

Georgia Stallings all but gave us a key to the place, inviting us to come back without notice at any time.

"I'm not going anywhere, I hope," she said.

Before leaving, I checked my messages back at the Dearborn Inn. One was from Al Bensmiller, and I called him back at Marilyn's on Monroe.

"Mercer's boys found an apartment. Thought you might wanna know," he said. "Leased to Kit Gleason. My man tells me there's Al Shaw all over it."

Chapter
10

"Now how'd you know that?" Wynton Mercer said. "Who's feedin' you, House?"

I'd called his number from Kit Gleason's office and got him right off. The man was always by his phone, always seated.

"We're in there right now," he went on. "Wanna go over?"

He gave me the details, including the detective contact on the scene, and I wrote them on a notepad from Kit Gleason's desk. The pad had KIT'S KOMMENTS in a cute typeface at the top.

"How'd you find it?" I asked Mercer.

"Like good detectives find most things—a tip," he said. "Blind phone call."

The place was on Brush Street, not far away, a high-rise building called Millender Center Apartments. It was a new place, a stop on the People Mover and built butt-to-butt with the Omni Hotel. All glass and chrome, thirty-three stories and one hundred fifty apartments. Another one of those in-city places outsiders don't think Detroit has anymore.

"This is getting interesting," Petey said as we walked over from the S.O.S. office.

"My outfielder looks bad," I said. She shot me a question with her eyes. "Shaw lied to me. Lied about his not coming out in favor of the Stadium. Lied about him and Kit being all business."

"Nobody's all business," Petey said.

"Is that right, Pete? Is there always something going on 'neath the table? Is anybody straight anymore?"

She turned and walked backward, facing me, her L.A. Gears picking up and putting down. She was skinny and athletic, the nip of the wind reddening her nose, and one false step and she'd land on her fanny.

"Biggers's Law of Interpersonal Relationships," she said. "If it's a contest between sleaze and no sleaze, go with sleaze."

"I didn't understand a word of that," I said.

"Adam always takes the apple."

"Adam makes four million a year—does he still eat the apple?"

"But you forget, Unk," Petey said. "The original Adam had it better than that. He had Paradise. Milk and honey, a great health plan, the lion lying down with the lamb. And he blew it. Guys are dumb that way."

"Uh, what's-her-name—Eve, that's it—didn't Eve have a little something to do with it?" I asked.

Petey shrugged.

"Perhaps," she allowed.

We could have taken the monorail to Millender Center Apartments—it ran right through a glassed-in corner of the building. At the front desk, we were met by a doorman who told us he let no one inside unless the person matched the photo on a Rolodex of occupants. He insisted that there were no exceptions. Biz Wagemaker, my loquacious septuagenarian doorman, would not have lasted a morning in this place. We waited while a Detroit homicide detective came down to get us.

He did it with a blank, almost hostile nod. We followed him, with no small talk whatsoever, to an eleventh-floor apartment, a one-bedroom, $648 a month. One step inside and I knew it was Kit Gleason's. She had furnished it with wood and crystal, silk flowers, wall hangings, Ralph Fasinella prints, and also with what can only be called Tiger Stadiama: photos, sketches, postcards, bumper stickers, hats, framed copies of *Bleacher Views,* and a signed cover of the Olson Survey.

I spotted photos of Kit smiling, tossing that head of hair in the wind, waving, wearing Tiger hats. Many were with players past and present: Kaline, Trammell, a great shot of Kit with Sparky, and, again, photographs of Kit and Al Shaw. Three of them. I couldn't take my eyes off them, including the one I'd seen in her office in which Shaw was wearing the rare old–time uniform with the head of the Tiger on the front. It was signed, "Token love, Al."

In all, the flat was an intimate extension of Kit's office, only without file cabinets, bulletin boards, or in boxes. An L-shaped sofa dominated the living area and faced a bank of stereo and video equipment, and a wall of books, many of them about Tiger baseball. It was a downtown home, a place where she obviously spent a choice amount of her private time. But with whom?

The answer, along with a cadre of cops, was in the bedroom. Petey went in first and let out a low, irreverent whistle. The object of her awe was a king-size bed, water variety, I learned, set on a mahogany base. Or maybe my salacious-minded niece was floored by the walls, which were totally mirrored. Mirrors floor to ceiling, reflecting every angle, every look. This was not a bedroom as much as it was a stage, an arena.

I noticed a copper eyeing me as I looked around. The jokes were unavoidable, and repeated, probably, for our benefit. "So she says to her date," said one detective, " 'Why it's just the four of us.' " The yucks went all around. "And he says to her, 'Hey, that couple's havin' more fun than we are!' " More guffaws. And the inevitable, "Hey, in the corner of that mirror it says, 'Objects appear larger than they actually are.' " And on and on without rim shots. Petey put a hand over her mouth and did a rotten job of stifling her amusement.

Two evidence boys were on their hands and knees. The bed had been turned down, and two others were fine-combing the sheets. A dresser, the lone piece of furniture in the room besides the bed, was covered with oils, unguents, several objects that resembled cucumbers, a blindfold, feathers, a black leather collar, black leather gloves, and a pair of handcuffs. The place smelled like a perfume counter.

We were kept back near the doorway, where we gawked.

"As I said," Petey whispered, "this is getting interesting."

"This paraphernalia, Pete," I said. "I'm lost. No map, no visa, can't even speak the language here."

"Then I know some books for ya, Unk," she said.

I was tapped on the shoulder by the detective who had ushered us up and told I had a phone call. I took it in the other room.

"Catch that pad, huh? That mirror shit. All those toys. God-damn!"

It was Wynton Mercer.

"I told the boys to leave everything be when they're finished 'cuz *I'm* gonna rent that place," he added, and gasped and giggled.

I waited for him to settle down.

"You guys are sure having fun at a dead woman's expense," I said. "And it stinks."

Mercer sniffed at that.

"Yeah, well, she ain't all what we're lookin' for," he said. "Our friend Al Shaw done some scorin' up there."

"Convince me."

"Pubic hairs, definite African-American sample. In the bed, which looked like it had some definite exercise on it." He coughed as if a doctor were probing his hernia, then resumed. "We got drinking glasses with prints. We got some other personal effects. Ain't had the opportunity to match 'em with Shaw yet. But if that boy wears Lagerfeld cologne, we're comin' at him."

"You got all that?" I asked.

"In the bags. And they ain't done yet, you can see that for yourself."

The crew was working over everything but the pictures on the wall.

"They're working away. Real comedians too," I replied.

"Hey, man, the job takes a sense of humor," Mercer said.

"Right. And you got on to this place with a tip?"

"We'd a found it sooner or later. Unless the ol' man found it first," he said. "It was leased in her name two years ago."

"Who said she didn't use it for business? Hospitality suite . . . and the like?"

"Ain't nobody said she didn't," Mercer replied. " 'Cept that bed . . . the handcuffs."

I gave him that.

"So now you know, House. Told ya I was your friend," Mercer said. "You keep in touch now."

"Just a second, Lieutenant," I said.

"What do you know about a sneak named James Holmes?"

Mercer coughed and garbled something nasty.

"Like to throw that nigger through a plate-glass window," he barked. "And that's all I'm gonna say."

*   *   *

Under watch of our moody silent detective, Petey and I took our own tour of the apartment, making notes, disturbing nothing.

"I wonder if her husband knew of this nest," Petey said.

"You don't see any signs of him. Mercer said he wasn't on the lease," I said, shaking my head and scanning the elaborate and costly hideaway. "This is going to hammer him," I added. "It would me."

"Nah," Petey said. "He probably has one of his own."

We left the apartment a half hour later and returned to the lobby. James Holmes was there, leaning on the doorman, trying like hell to get up to where we had just been. He was still Zorro today, with a black, thin-lapeled serge suite that had some years on it, a black shirt, and a black leather tie.

"Knew it!" he said when he spotted us. "The redhead and the ol' perfessor."

I'd never been accused of being Casey Stengel before.

"What say, Petrinella? What you got for James?" he said. "This cat won't let me up and the po-lice say they don't know me."

"Who are you?" Petey said.

Holmes gave her a dull-eyed look, then broke a grin.

"You're cool, baby," he asked.

He herded us to a far corner of the lobby.

"Cops put my man Albert up there?" he asked.

"They think so," Petey said. "Kit Gleason apparently had a rendezvous before she was killed. Drinking glasses with prints. Hair samples in the bed. The works."

Holmes made a face. "Do a *ron-day-voo* mean romantic?"

"*Romantic* is correct," Petey said.

"Don't hear that word much anymore," said Holmes.

"You may be hearing it a lot from now on," Petey said.

"Okay, I'm cool. My doorman puts Albert here at five and down at six. That long enough for romance? Don't matter, 'cuz they ain't got to Albert yet on this."

"They will," I said. "If the prints and the hair are a match, he's in trouble."

"Damn!" Holmes flared. He took off his hat and revealed a head shaven as clean as an egg "It's all bullshit. Man been framed."

"Says who?" I asked.

"Albert, that's who," Holmes said. "He wasn't havin' no ron-day-voos with this lady. He swore it to me, and he's straight. 'Cuz I know when it's happenin' and when it's not happenin', and with Albert it wasn't happenin'."

"Yeah, well, Albert lies," I said.

"He don't lie to me," Holmes said. He said it too quickly. "Ain't no sucker born can lie to me."

"How much do you know about the husband?" Petey asked.

"There you go! That's the cat I want," Holmes said. "He the mystery guest. I want him. My man Albert wants me to get to him."

"Your man Vander Male wants you to get to him," I said.

"Him too," said Holmes.

"And you can't get near him, can you?" I said.

The midnight peeper recoiled at that.

"Been near a lot like him, Jack," he said. "Up close. Looked in their wallets while they was in the shower. That's my specialty."

Once again I believed him. In the field of adultery spying, he was probably one of the best. Divorce lawyer Vander Male probably settled for nothing less.

That was enough of Holmes as far as I was concerned. As we parted, I got a whiff of his after-shave.

"Say, James," I said. "You know colognes? Men's colognes?"

"Smelled a few. Personally, I dab me some Dracker Nore," he said, which made Petey smile.

"What would Al Shaw wear?" I asked.

"Hell . . . Albert? He be a Lagerfeld man."

Chapter

II

THE TELEVISION STATIONS WERE ALL OVER AL SHAW THAT NIGHT. Forget about how many games he had won for the Tigers or how many high-fives he had inspired among the hometown fans; forget the goodwill he had spread with personal appearances or the ex-inmates he had helped through EX-CON; the Detroit news wasps were attacking in swarms. I flipped from channel to channel on my room's set.

They linked him with Kit Gleason in every possible way. They had tracked down waitresses, security guards, parking lot attendants, and anybody else who may have seen the two together the night of the fire or any night whatsoever. They quoted "unnamed sources"—always unnamed sources—in the police department who supposedly said Shaw was under intense questioning and would probably be charged soon.

And when they ran thin on the recent stuff, the reporters lurched into the past, which meant Shaw's stay at Jackson Prison. He had been a tough con, they said, the kind who got into fights and paid for them in solitary. Fellow inmates said he did thousands of push-ups, lifted thousands of free weights, and bounced a ball against a wall thousands of times. He was a visceral, rock-hard specimen nobody messed with. And when he came out, he was animal hungry, fast, muscled, and ready to play a game in which stealing was not only allowed but recommended.

To his credit, however, he had put on a smile and offered his hand to anyone who would take it. He had been conditioned in the streets and in prison to trust few people, to be casual and free with even fewer; yet upon his release and his newfound stardom, he was remarkably candid and forthright. "I could put on an attitude," he said, "and be angry at the world. But what's that gonna get me?" And he smiled a lot. With kids and dropouts, ex-cons and businessmen, Al Shaw had a winner's grin.

Not that it was easy. He once said that he felt like he was still on probation, because people were waiting for him to screw up. If you scratched him, his detractors said, you'd still find a con. "Let 'em scratch," Shaw said.

I digested the material like a father hearing about his wayward son. It was all too smug, too pat. "I know the stakes," he had said to me in his lawyer's office. I had seen the look on his face when he agonized over Kit Gleason's death. Now he was being publicly hanged for it. I wondered if Shaw, even if exonerated, could ever play ball in Detroit again.

Shaw, of course, had made no public appearances. Until they charged him, police would say nothing of their conversations with him. Television crews were parked outside Shaw's suburban home. One reporter ambushed Jack Vander Male in a parking garage, and the nicest thing Vander Male said was, "Nuts." James Holmes never appeared, which was too bad. Finally, none of the TV reports mentioned the Gleason apartment, even though all referred to the existence of "important new evidence." I figured that was standard.

Petey had changed out of her interview slacks and into jeans, from a print blouse back to her operating-room top, and joined me with two cans of cold Mexican beer, her choice. She hooted at a long-lost college roommate of Gleason's who said Kit had an affinity for black men. The implication was as distinct as the mike on the roomie's lapel.

"People will say anything on television," Petey said, as if she had just discovered that fact.

We watched until the hard-news segments gave way to even harder weather reports. I clicked around the channels looking for Sonny Elliot, Detroit's weatherman answer to Soupy Sales. No luck.

Petey turned to me and said, "You know, nobody said a word about Kit's husband."

"They didn't go after him," I said.

"My try," she said.

Petey went back to her room and worked the phones. I had given her Wynton Mercer's number, and she had James Holmes's card. The latter was pay dirt, as Petey described it later. Holmes wore a beeper and he got back to her within the half hour. He had the numbers for Dr. Cooper Nance's office and home. Neither of which answered. His car phone, however, which Holmes referred to with the envy of a man who spends too much time driving, was probably a better bet.

Every ten minutes or so for a duration of almost two hours, Petey dialed the number. It was an old routine, she told me, something she used to do in college when radio stations were giving away tickets to Grateful Dead concerts. When Dr. Nance actually answered, she admitted, she was almost too startled to be articulate.

Her approach was one part Commissioner Chambliss, one part feminine charm. She somehow convinced him that she was not a reporter. That was important, she sensed, for Nance seemed terrified of the news media. That she was an investigator with the commissioner's office, however, did not impress him. "Baseball isn't on my mind right now," he said. Still, he stayed on the line, detailing some of what he'd gone through with his wife's death. He seemed to want to talk about it, she said later, and she listened. Petey was a big-league talker, but she also knew when to dummy up and lend an ear. The doctor seemed to appreciate that, and he spoke with her for almost ten minutes.

"Meet with me," Petey finally said. "I'll drive out tonight. I won't take a lot of your time. If it's uncomfortable, just show me the door."

Nance agreed. He gave her directions to his home. Petey could not believe her luck. It was not the first time she had convinced a strange man to see her, but still she was amazed.

"I go alone, Unk," she said. "Nance won't see me if you come along, I'm sure of it."

"I don't like you going solo," I said.

"Nonsense. We can't blow this opportunity," she replied.

Petey is twenty-four, the possessor of a driver's license and night vision, and as much as I would like to fit her with a chastity belt and suit of armor, I am a fool to even suggest a crimp in her style. Sometimes, however, I wish she would just hang back a little. I wish she were married with children and raising Airedales on a farm in rural Kansas. I wish her ears were not pierced.

Having harrumphed all that, I must admit that I absolutely admire her pluck. We were in Detroit, however, a mean city in a country of mean cities. I told her to employ her street smarts before she went to anything she learned at Oberlin. I hoped she could still spot trouble from sixty feet six inches.

"Tell me, Pete," I also said, "what can we get—no—what do we *want* out of this guy? That the police don't already have, that is?"

"A face-off, Unk, for want of a better phrase," she said. "I want to meet him. Feel his pulse. Maybe spot a twitch or two. Is he a monster? Or a mope whose wife stopped washing his socks a long time ago?"

"He just buried that wife," I said. "Don't forget that."

"Okay. But I wanna get in there close. See what's under his skin."

"He has great skin," I said. "Keeping the surface smooth is what he does best."

She headed the Volvo out of Dearborn and onto the Edsel Ford Freeway, which took her on a diagonal across Detroit. At Alter, she got off the freeway and drove south to Grosse Pointe Park, the first of several lush Detroit suburbs along the shores of Lake St. Clair. It was dark, just after nine. The wind off the lake rustled the leaves of huge oak trees, the remnants of what was a great oak forest at one time. It does not take a big leap of fantasy to envision what the area must have looked like when Antoine de la Mothe Cadillac set up shop with his fellow French fur traders in the 1600s. And how many Cadillac owners know the heritage of their wheels?

Petey drove toward the water's edge at Windmill Pointe Park and turned onto a winding, nonchalant lane that featured some elegant, old-money properties. Circular driveways, huge lawns, brick fences, terriers, and Tudor-style mansions. These were estates whose deeds ran back to the days when Henry Ford was but a mechanic and five dollars a day was a hell of a wage.

Petey found the five-digit address and parked the Volvo next to a Chrysler luxury convertible. Wet down the asphalt, she thought, bring in Ricardo Montalban, caress the rich Corinthian leather upholstery, and start shooting the commercials for the Masters.

She was wearing a loose, navy blue, cowl-necked sweater and dark slacks. Over it was a soft, cocoa brown, waist-length leather jacket that must have cost her a lot of tips but was worth it. Her haul of red hair was pulled back in a ponytail that danced on the back of her neck. She shivered.

The doctor himself answered the door.

"Dr. Nance?" Petey said. "I'm Petrinella Biggers."

He nodded, dipping his silver locks.

"Come in," he said, then closed the heavy door behind her and led her through the house over hardwood parquet and Oriental rugs.

The place was quiet and low-lit, like a funeral parlor without the biers, and it reeked of furniture polish. There seemed to be no one else home.

He went to the kitchen, a huge, bright room with enough counter space to land a Piper Cub, sleek appliances, white wood cabinets, copper pots, and great clumps of garlic and red chili peppers. In the corner were a fireplace and sofa, littered with newspapers, which Petey thought was a nice touch, except that the newspapers were full of stories with deathly meaning for this house.

Out of the corner of her eye she spotted a half-eaten container of macaroni and cheese on the counter. It was a gourmet brand, Petey noticed, laced with spices and pimiento, but macaroni and cheese nonetheless.

"Something to drink?" he asked.

"No thank you. Maybe some of that macaroni and cheese," she said. "Just kidding. . . ."

Nance smiled feebly, making Petey wish she had not said it. He offered her a stool, then sat down on one beside it. He swiveled and faced her. He had the tanned, taut looks of an heir. His gelled, silver hair was combed back, leaving him with a lot of forehead. Skin was his trade, and his hide showed well.

"I'm not good company, I'm sorry," he said. He fussed with the collar of a starched powder-blue dress shirt. He was a great-looking man, and for an instant Petey marveled at the fact that men Nance's age could still pull it off. Except that he looked tired, like a man with manicured nails and Italian loafers who had been chased home by Dobermans.

"Don't be sorry," Petey said. "I mean, with what you're going through—"

"I appreciate that," he said. "You know, people have been great to me. They really have. This is actually the first time that I've been alone since it happened. Kit's family and all. . . ."

"And now I barge in on you," Petey said.

He nodded at that. "I was swayed," he said. "Your phone manner . . . you have a great voice."

It was Petey's turn to nod.

"Tell me again what you do," he said. "The commissioner of baseball—I caught that. The rest I didn't get."

"I'm an investigator for the commissioner's office. I work with my uncle, if you're wondering how I got the job. We go where there's trouble. L.A., Chicago—"

"When the Cubs pitcher was killed?"

"That was my first case," Petey said.

Nance exhaled heavily. "And now this. Kit," he said.

He had a precise manner, as if his speech had been tutored, but Petey could sense that he was edgy, frayed.

"Yes," she said tentatively. "Actually, my uncle is looking into the fire itself. The team owner, the situation with the stadium before it burned, that kind of thing. It was my idea to talk with you."

He shrugged.

"I'm not a cop or a reporter, Dr. Nance," Petey added. "I have no power of subpoena or arrest or that kind of thing."

"Good," he interjected. "The police have been jerks. I don't mind telling you that."

"I'll try not to be," Petey said. "I just want to bring the commissioner whatever can help him."

"Explain how I fit in. It eludes me," he said. "I wasn't involved in Kit's thing. You probably know that. I never really shared her obsession with the stadium. I never understood it."

"You don't like baseball?" Petey said.

"Not much of it. The Tigers, the stadium, the whole package," he sighed, "it never interested me."

Petey leaned forward. "How'd you handle it? Your wife's obsession, as you said?"

He smiled at that. "Role reversal, I guess," he said. "How do wives handle husbands who are sports nuts?"

"They resent them," Petey said quickly. "Probably," she amended.

"I didn't resent Kit," he said quickly, then added, "Put it this way. Two people sit in the same room. One reads a classic, the other reads trash. Then they get up, turn the light out, and make love to each other."

Petey smiled at that. She liked the idea, liked it a lot.

"I'm thirsty," he said, and went over to the refrigerator.

"Tell me, was she ever paranoid? Afraid?" Petey said. "I mean, did she ever communicate as much?"

"Afraid of what?"

"Of Joe Yeager, the whole stadium mess. It getting nasty."

"Not that I knew. Not that she told me," he said, pouring tonic water over ice. "But that was Kit. She wouldn't have thought that I needed to know."

"Not even if she was afraid for her life?"

"Not even if she was afraid for her life," he said. He placed a fizzing drink with a wedge of lime in front of her.

"Unspiked," he said. "Though I can change that if you like."

"This is great, thanks," Petey said, lifting the glass to her lips.

"But let me backtrack a few steps," he said. "Kit created that group. It was all hers. And it took off around here. It was like getting religion, like a cult. But I didn't join up. That was okay, she always said. She knew how I felt about baseball and she didn't push it. In the meantime, she had a new crowd, new friends, famous baseball players. She was quite the celebrity. In the papers. On TV. She enjoyed every minute of it."

"And you stayed in the background?" Petey asked.

"I did. I have my own work," he said. "It wasn't easy sometimes, I'll admit that."

At that, he took a long swallow of his drink. He eyed Petey over the rim of the glass. He had blue eyes, silver eyebrows.

"Look, if things were getting nasty or threatening over there, she never told me," he said, his voice weary. "I surely didn't know if she was afraid for her life or I would have done something about it."

As he said it, Petey thought she saw him tremble some. She was certain of it.

"I'm sorry," she said once again.

She stared at him. He looked away.

"Relationships are odd things," she said, and immediately wished she had not. It seemed corny.

But it worked.

"Kit was older than you are when I met her," he said evenly. "In her thirties. I'm guessing you're in your mid-twenties—if you're younger, you've had a lot of sun. She was in her second marriage. I was single. It's usually the other way around. I had money, looks, and the personality of a wolf—that's what she told me. She liked the first two, and she always said not to worry about the wolf part. From the first, she ran with me. No changes, no big battles. 'You live your life, I live mine,' she said. We hooked up at night and on weekends. She picked out this place and turned it into what you see. It was fine with me. I loved it. She did the same down on Marco Island. We went like that for six, seven years. We never missed a step."

At that, he finished his tonic. His eyes were watering now, and he dabbed at them with a napkin.

"Then one day she said she was bored out of her mind," he said.

"Boom," Petey said.

He wiped his mouth with the back of his hand. He exhaled.

"Out of the blue?" Petey added.

"To me, it was," he said, returning Petey's stare. "But I'm a cosmetic surgeon, remember. Skin-deep."

Petey blinked. A more cutting self put-down she had never heard.

"Let me put it this way," he resumed, "I was the one who was reading the classics."

"And that's when she started Save Our Stadium?" Petey asked.

He nodded.

"And you moved to the background," Petey said.

"Well, not at first," he said. "I wanted her back. I wanted the life we had back. I wanted her out of the crusade business."

He turned and leaned on the countertop with both elbows, his lush head only a few feet from hers. He had had this conversation with Kit, she was certain, and others even more strained.

"But the commissioner of baseball wouldn't want to know about this, would he?" he said.

"No," Petey replied, "but I do."

He raised a faint smile. He was dog tired. He wiped his face with the napkin again.

"How did you work it out?" she asked.

He dug the lime out of his glass with two fingers and chewed it.

"We let it ride. We accommodated each other. . . . that sort of thing," he said. "Kit was too busy fighting over there to fight me. And I'm not much of a fighter anyway."

"I am," Petey said.

"You're young," he said. "Don't take offense at that."

"Check," she said.

At that moment she wanted to ask him about Kit's apartment, if he knew about it, if it changed things. But she could not. She felt very sorry for him. She wanted to reach out and put her arm around him.

"The police showed me an apartment she'd leased downtown," he said.

Petey held her breath.

"A secret place," he went on. "At least it was secret from me. According to the police, she'd had it about two years. All decorated—like I said, she was good at that. You'll hear about it. Maybe the Detroit Police will even show it to you like they did me. They were real pleased with themselves walking through it. Real jerks."

He rubbed his hands together and looked even more wrung out than before.

"A city apartment," Petey said, "and you didn't know about it? A lot of people may not buy that."

"I can't help it," he said. "Would they buy it if I said I had known about it and still stayed together?"

He got up and paced the kitchen. He squeezed his hand into a fist. He looked like a manager at the mercy of a wild relief pitcher.

"But you're right," he said. "Common sense says I had to know. What husband wouldn't know, right? But look, I married Kit because I loved what kind of a woman she was. I still do. Even after walking through that apartment with a bunch of acned Detroit cops sniggering up their sleeves."

He looked away. Petey could feel his torment, the anger and the chafing. She drained the last of her tonic water.

"I didn't come here to put you through this," Petey said.

"I know you didn't," Nance said. "But it's all right."

"Look," he continued, "I'm not an emotional man. I'm a surgeon. I cut away excess tissue and leave spider-leg scars that literally disappear in a matter of weeks. I'm an expert at it. With Kit—look, what I'm trying to say is that she'll always be there. Somewhere in me. But if I want to get on with life, I have to let what happened between us heal over. And now with this apartment business . . . whatever comes of it . . . it won't be easy."

He leaned a hip against the counter and faced her. She lifted a trace of a smile, the kind a surgeon offers a patient's family when the chances are slim.

"I may be very out of bounds in saying this, Petrinella," Nance said, "but you're a very lovely woman. Stay in touch with me. Please. I'm worried about the police. It's their job to go after husbands of dead wives."

Nance extended his hand. Petey took it in hers, not certain if she should shake it or kiss it, knowing only that the soft skin of his palm was white hot to her touch.

She left a short time later. Nance was exhausted, and Petey knew it was time to exit. Had I been with her, I would have insisted that she return the way she came, up Alter and back to the Ford Freeway. But I was not with her, and Petey did what she damn well pleased. She turned left onto Jefferson Avenue, heading home via the east side of Detroit.

As it leads from Grosse Pointe Park, Jefferson is a wide, venerable street. It draws close to the edge of the Detroit River, where you can catch glimpses of Belle Isle and Belle Isle Park past stately, turn-of-the century, brick apartment buildings that line the shore. The buildings are elegant if preserved, seedy if neglected. In an earlier day, this was where you wanted to live if you worked downtown.

Petey plied the stop-and-go traffic, the lights, cars pulling in and out of what passed for roadside attractions on the avenue: a few bars, joints, convenience liquor stores, fillings stations where cashiers sat in locked booths. At each stoplight, she drew stares and leers and catcalls from teenagers wearing baseball caps backward and rheumy-eyed men who wondered what a redhead was doing on Jefferson this time of night.

At Meldrum Petey saw that the Volvo's low-fuel light was on, which meant it was running on fumes. At the same time she spotted a Purple Martin station and pulled into its wide driveway. Ahead of her was a delivery truck, a boxy thing with padlocks on the doors and *Farm Crest* written on the side. She didn't see the driver until she got out. He was standing in front of his open driver's side door, a chunky guy, maybe fifty, with gray sideburns prominent against the black skin of his cheeks. He wore a little cap, blue pants with a stripe down the legs, and he braced his arms against each side of the opening as if he were keeping the hordes away.

Petey saw it all in an instant, one of those American pieces of violence that flash out of nowhere. Two young guys, their heads nearly clean shaven, wearing team jackets over baggy pants, came up on the driver like snakes on a rodent, and socked him in the neck. It was bone on bone, and the driver, stunned, fell to his knees. He was kicked by one, then hit on the ear by the other. His hat flew off, and he struggled blindly to get back into his truck, to grasp the seat, to escape the blows.

"My God!" Petey screamed. She turned for help, seeing only the cashier sitting mutely in the armored booth.

One of the young men turned to her and glared as if she were a roach in a meat pie.

"Want some, bitch?" he said.

He came at her with quick strides and a fist in the air like a welterweight about to unload.

Petey screamed, and her would-be attacker suddenly went down. The driver had cold-cocked him in the neck with what looked like a taped length of pipe. But then the driver took another slug in the ear, a roundhouse from the second kid that put him down. He writhed on the oily pavement, still clutching the pipe. Petey screamed again as the kid stomped on the driver's wrist and went for the pipe. And then an explosion nearly raised her off her feet, deafened her, took her breath away, spun her around. Suddenly the second kid was also on the pavement, bawling and holding a knee that leaked blood like cranberry juice onto his hands.

"Take out yo' other knee next time, muthafuck," came a voice.

Petey, even in her trauma, knew the voice. She turned and looked into the face of James Holmes, the ebony op, Al Shaw's private eye.

"Hey, 'Nella," he said.

The two young thugs lay where they went down, one clutching

his knee and spitting, the other still out, lying there like a rag bag. Holmes offered a hand to the driver, who groaned but was lucid and who was still holding the pipe.

"What you got there, man?" Holmes said to him.

"My sap. My equalizer," the driver said, and he made a move toward the wounded kid. Holmes stopped him.

"Yo' what?" he said.

"Equalizer," he repeated, brandishing the pipe like a fungo bat.

"You almos' be equalized yerself," Holmes said to him. "What you got in that bakery truck? Cash?"

"Stale," the driver said.

"Hawaiian spice cake?" Holmes said, his tongue wet on his upper lip.

"All ya can eat, bud."

The driver reached inside and pulled out two boxes of snack cakes.

"My man," Holmes said, slipping the boxes under his arm. "C'mon, babe," he said to Petey. "We gotta cut. Let this pipe man clean up here."

Petey hesitated, estimating the sentence for leaving the scene of a felony, when she was pushed into the Volvo by Holmes.

"Follow me," Holmes said. "Don't make no turns. Stay close."

He slammed her door.

"You ain't goin' far 'cuz you almost outta gas, babe," he said, then trotted over to his BMW.

Her heart still pounding from the fracas, the crack of Holmes's gun still buried in her eardrum, Petey followed him several blocks down Jefferson until he pulled over in front of a Coney Island hot-dog joint near Trevor. He motioned for her to come over.

"Front seat, slick," he said, pushing open the passenger door.

She got in. Holmes was sitting there opening a spice cake. He was wearing a black nylon Raiders jacket, black jogging pants.

"Say hello to your guardian angel," he said. "You almost got slapped back there."

Petey gawked at him, her hands shaking. Holmes saw it.

"Calm down, baby," he said. "You gon' do this line of business, you gotta take some pops."

"Whatta you shoot?" Petey finally asked.

"Walther three-eighty," he said. "Don't leave home without it."

He grinned at that. "Slow down, honey," Holmes said, patting her knee. "Yo' adrenaline kickin' in. Mine just slowin' down. Happens."

"That kid came at me—shit!" she said.

Holmes fussed with the cellophane wrapper, tried to open it with his teeth.

"You were following me, James," she said. "Had to be."

She saw it all: Holmes had tailed her from the moment she left Dearborn. If he could not get to Cooper Nance on his own, she was the next best thing.

"Lucky for yo' butt I was," Holmes said. "So tell me, what the doctor tell ya? 'Bout his ol' lady and Al Shaw? And don't leave nothin' out 'cuz I saved yo' sweet cheeks back there."

"My black knight," Petey said.

"You got that," he garbled, his mouth now full of cake. He was as blithe as a baker. A good corner man to have on your side in late-night Detroit.

So Petey filled him in on Nance, gave him what he needed to know, and added a few personal insights. She owed him. The telling of it eased the filling station chaos from her mind. A half hour later, after Holmes had escorted her through a fill-up at another station, she was safely on the freeway headed back to Dearborn.

It was then that Petey started to shake. It was as if demons had crawled up inside her and were tap dancing on her bones. Her teeth chattered, she hyperventilated, her fingernails hopped on the steering wheel. Visions of the cake-truck driver sinking to his knees, the sound of the pipe on the kid's head, the smack and smell of the pistol shot. The scene raced across her mind and she reached in her jacket pocket for a piece of gum. Instead, she encountered a lump. She withdrew a spice cake Holmes had slipped inside. The sweet scent of it almost made her retch.

At the same time, I sat cursing the television in my Dearborn Inn. What I did not know about Petey did not disturb my evening, but the words of Joe Yeager, owner of the Tigers, leaseholder of Tiger Stadium, nearly sent me through the wall. In an impromptu press conference at his chicken-and-pasta office, he declared the end of the world.

"The stadium is uninhabitable and beyond repair," Yeager said.

"Impossible!" I shouted, hearing my own echo.

It was impossible for Yeager to make such a declaration, and

only hours after he'd coddled the commissioner and me. He had
no engineering reports. The rubble had not even been cleared.

Nevertheless, Yeager yammered on about fire damage and construction schedules and league obligations. Then he said the team
would play next season's home games in the Pontiac Silverdome,
an inflated bubble on the prairie. He prattled on about how heavy
his heart was, and I muttered something about how heavy his
head was. I checked for blood on his hands. This thing really stunk
now, reeked with a dank odor that carried from the black ruins
of the ballpark on Michigan and Trumbull to the green expanses
of the suburbs.

I was on the phone to Chambliss as fast as I could dial.

Chapter
12

I DON'T KNOW WHAT STEAMED ME MORE, JOE YEAGER'S CHUTZPAH or Petey's foolhardiness. Over good coffee and better danish in the Ten Eyck Tavern of the Inn, she tried to fuzzy up her night's escapade. She re-created the gas-station ambush as a kid might describe a Nintendo game. Fast, full of chops and shots, and none of it real. Except that it *was* real, with lethal punks who had as much regard for her existence in this world as do alley cats picking over a dead pigeon. Punks with guns, street violence as common as litter, I said to Petey. People are maimed, knees and spines turned into so much bone meal, or people die, dammit. This wasn't just a quickly flipped page in a paperback, I added, and she said no, it was not. She wasn't being coy; she said it took her until dawn to get to sleep.

"You haven't said anything about the surgeon," I said.

"There's plenty, Unk," she replied.

She shaded in the background, the house, the make of the refrigerator, the color of Nance's shirt.

"He was pretty shook," she went on. "Wounded, but not bitter. At least, not yet. The way he called it, they had a neat relationship, he and Kit. A little weird, he didn't dig her S.O.S. bit, but he didn't bum her on it either. What honked him was her star bit. Celebrity ga-ga. Lotta ego there, you could tell it. That was probably the only time his hooks came out. What hurt him the most, the way he told it, was that he lost his good life with her. There was no time for it, he said. And he was pissed that things had changed."

"You said he hated the whole stadium fight?"

"Not really. He just wasn't interested," she replied.

"Point against him, right? Neglected hubby resents the missus off on a crusade."

"I used that word, *resent*," she went on. "He said, no, he didn't resent her. He just wanted his marriage back. Then he brought up the apartment, which was convenient 'cuz I wasn't gonna. Just too moist, Unk. But he brought it up, was pissed at the cops for rubbin' his nose in it. Claimed on the Bible he knew nothing about it."

"And you didn't believe him?"

"I didn't say that," she said. "Put it this way. I kept waiting to disbelieve him all night. Looking into his baby blues. That tight skin along his jaw. . . ."

"Did he know he was a cuckold?"

"Great word, Unk. Leave it to you."

"He'd resent that."

"What man wouldn't? But mostly he was aching, Unk," she said. "This guy got punched in the gut. I really felt for him."

"Get over it, Pete," I said. "He's a suspect. 'A' list."

At that, she tightened her eyes like a person trying to read ingredients off a tube of airplane glue.

"You know, I can usually scope guys," she said. "Especially young ones, I mean, they all but have tattoos on their foreheads that say DO ME. Old ones are slyer. Gotta look harder, listen for code words. They usually say *Do me* too, but they're not as crass about it. With Nance, well, he's not just some guy with an act. If he was conning me about how he felt, about his marriage—this whole thing, well, then I need a lobotomy, Unk."

"Maybe he kept the ball hidden, Pete," I said. "Like a good pitcher. No high kicks. No telegraphs. Just snuck it by you."

"Tell me not," she said. "Tell me not."

"He's a suspect," I said.

"Right now, isn't everybody?" Petey said.

*   *   *

Later that morning we parted company. Chambliss wanted me
to talk to the engineers who had assessed Tiger Stadium's condition before it burned. As far as I'm concerned, engineers are like
accountants: Pay them well, and they can fry inspections the way
the bean counters can cook the books. After Yeager's statement
last night, I knew what his mechanics would tell me. I needed a
second opinion, and I called on Georgia Stallings.

"Yeager still has to make a solid case for relocating, as far as the
commissioner is concerned," I told Georgia.

She snorted. "Little Joe'll do it on the first ballot. The owners
will back him," she said.

"It's not a done deal," I said. "Not from what Grand told me
last night."

Stallings sniffed at that, exhaling the smoke of her ever-present
gasper.

"I like your boss—his head is screwed on right," she said. "But
he's a spear carrier, Duffy. The owners are tighter than ever. Yeager's case is a no-brainer for them."

"Not if Yeager's dirty," I said. "The fire was set. Kit was murdered. We know that. It's a scandal, and the owners won't cover
for it."

"Don't be so sure," Stallings said.

"Look, I need your stadium people," I went on. "Engineering,
structural analysis. Someone who can give me technical dope for
the commissioner to throw back at Yeager."

"Gordon Olson—our survey guy. Knows the place inside and
out," she said. "But he hasn't seen the damage."

"Will he talk to me?"

"Grand Rapids—he's there waiting," she said. "He called me
this morning. His people were threatened when they first dug into
their appraisal last spring, you know. They were told to watch
their step. Tell the commissioner that."

I could make it to Grand Rapids in just under three hours, and
I wanted Petey to come along. She could drive, she could chat,
she could stay out of trouble in Detroit. But she had other ideas.

"I love ya, Unk," she said. "But my idea of a good time isn't
talking to an engineer in Grand Rapids."

"Your alternative?"

"James Holmes."

"Cripes."

"James doesn't know it yet," Petey said, "but he's going to take me to meet Al Shaw."

"Good luck," I said. "Which reminds me. I want to know what the police took out of that apartment."

I called Wynton Mercer from Kit's office. One thing about a four-hundred-pound detective, he is always in. Planted in that chair like a potted palm.

"We got everything 'cept for full-color Polaroids, man," Mercer said. He sounded chipper. "Maybe find one of those too. Got a front-desk man puts him in the lobby. Got us a glass—a tumbler—with prints so good the boy must a stuck 'em on with Krazy Glue."

He drew a breath. I'd forgotten what a labor it was for Mercer to narrate.

"Got an authentic pubic hair from the sheets. Negroid. And that didn't come from the lady." Gasp. "We got that bottle of cologne except it's clean. So that don't mean shit. We got us a silk tie we like to think come right off Al's rack. But he'd beat that too. How's that?"

"Have you brought him back in?"

"Not yet. We gonna," Mercer said. "That lawyer prick of his gives me hives. When we take the slugger in, we gotta take him in big."

"Take your time."

Mercer snickered at that.

"You're holdin' somethin' out on me, Mr. Duffy?" he said.

"Wish I were, Lieutenant."

I hung up and called Petey again.

"So have a go at Mr. Shaw while he's still available," I said. "Tell him how the police all but have him on instant replay in that apartment. See what he says."

Petey said she would.

"And keep some space between you and that Holmes character," I added.

"James is cool," Petey said.

"Wouldn't trust him unless he was in traction."

"We make a good pair," Petey said. "He likes me."

"Forget about that, Pete," I said, and leaned on her. Rocky Colavito, that dreamboat Italian slugger brought over to Detroit from Cleveland in '59, used to point his big-barreled bat at the pitcher before he got set. Gave him a target. Gave the pitcher notice. If I'd had a bat, I'd have done the same to Petey.

"Get to Shaw, get him talking," I said to her. "But he's an ex-con, don't forget that. And we caught him in one lie already. Maybe that's a way of life for him, I don't know. But a very good cop on Beaubien Avenue is trying to put Shaw back in the hole. That cop sees him as nothing but a con, a fancy con with a bank account, but a con. He's accounting for every minute of the time Kit and Shaw were together, and he's thinking real dirty. It doesn't make sense to me that a guy like Shaw, who's had plenty of three-two counts on him, would blow it. Piss it all away. But I'm old and naive, Petey. You give it a shot."

So we split up. I took the Volvo and got on the Fisher Freeway over to the Jeffries Freeway, which was the start of I-96 heading west across the state. Say this for Detroit, it's easy to get in and out of. Too easy. You're never too far from an entrance ramp onto a fast road named after a car maker or a union boss.

I drove in the right-hand lane, at the speed limit, which meant that cars were flying by me. I felt like Lou Berberet doing wind sprints with Ron LeFlore. I drove without the nuisance of the radio. Following the flat highway, the expanses of suburban Detroit, then the outlying cornfields that were fast becoming treeless subdivisions, I saw the landscape but did not see it all. For I was trying to put faces on the crime.

Suspect those with the most to gain, the crime cliché goes. So Yeager and his cronies jump to the front of the arson hunt, no problem there. But would he do it? Would he have it done? Or perhaps someone who stands to gain from a new park, a suburban landholder, a city politician. That was more of a crapshoot, but there was motive there.

But murder? Kit Gleason? Who gained? Yeager and company getting rid of an irritant? Cooper Nance getting revenge on an unfaithful spouse? Al Shaw killing his lover? All or none of the above?

The miles heaped. The scenery was no more inspiring. Lower Michigan is green, mostly flat, good farmland and orchard country. And then I spotted a sign for Fowlerville. Oh my, the home of the "mechanical man," Charlie Gehringer.

Starting in 1926 when the Tigers' Frank O'Rourke got a late case of chicken pox, Gehringer took over at second base and played it just about nonstop for sixteen years. Damn near silent—he once asked a teammate why he asked to pass the salt when he could have pointed—and unbreakable, he scooped up everything in the field and sprayed line drives all day.

"Charlie Gehringer is in a rut," said Lefty Gomez. "He hits .350 on Opening Day and stays there all season."

Over the years he played with twenty-four different shortstops, although his teams in the 1930s were something. With Billy Rogell at shortstop, Marv Owen at third—it was Owen who started the fight with Ducky Medwick in the '34 Series—and Hank Greenberg at first, Charlie completed the infield dubbed the Battalion of Death. A little dramatic, if you ask me, but it was a hell of a quartet.

Charlie Gehringer. The kind of ballplayer I grew up on. You could count on him every year. Like a spring thaw, good topsoil, the prophet Elijah.

"Do I know where Albert is? Do dice have dots?" James Holmes whined.

"Then let me talk to him," Petey said.

Holmes buzzed into the phone, a blues number with good grumble in the bass. There was noise in the background, dishes, a bad saxophone, but nothing Petey could decipher.

"Talkin' to white women got Albert in grease in the first place."

"From what they took out of Kit Gleason's apartment, he did more than talk."

"What you got, Petrinella?"

Holmes said it with a long e and plenty of el.

"You got what they got?" he added.

"Take me to Shaw, and I'll tell you both."

"What a cookie you are. Where'd you get that redhead hair?" Holmes said.

"Got it from Aretha Franklin," Petey said. "She got sick of red."

Holmes liked that. He guffawed through something he was gnawing. Petey could just about smell the fat.

An hour later she was in the front seat of his black BMW, which smelled like window cleaner. Holmes was in black, of course. Beneath the black Raiders jacket was a turtleneck with *Sox* on the collar. Any team could claim his allegiance—as long as its togs were black. He also had on a pair of black chuckle boots that must have run a size thirteen. He was a skinny guy, the type who could slither through transoms. And on his slick head today was a black leather snap-brim cap that looked like something he had won in a hustle on the tee at Palmer Park.

"Had the scurrier hand-washed," he said. "Don' want a damn car smellin' like a chicken shack. This is my office."

"Where we goin', James? And don't start eating those spice cakes again."

"They gone. Long gone." He clucked his chops together like a bulldog. "But I'm gettin' more from the cake man. He owe me. Lifetime supply. Weren't for James Holmes kneecappin' that rapper, the cake man wouldn't be deliverin' no more spice cake."

"Is that a black thing?" Petey asked.

"That a Ha-*wai*-an thing," he said.

"Where we goin'?"

"Little here. Little there. Don' expect no grin when Albert sees you."

They rode freeways, the Edsel Ford, the Chrysler, with Holmes driving the left lane and never keeping more than a few inches between him and the bumper in front of him. The stereo played Buddy Guy. The sky was the color of concrete. Holmes dug into his teeth with a toothpick, and were he not so glad, he'd be Sad Sam Jones.

"Before this is all over," Petey shouted, "you've got to take me to the Motown house. Hitsville, U.S.A."

"You know about that shit?" Holmes said.

"I know everything, James."

"Know Lamont Dozier? I used to run with Lamont."

"Holland/Dozier/Holland," Petey said. " 'Where Did Our Love Go?' and other Motown dusties."

She did a passable Diana Ross pout.

"You got it," Holmes said. "Amazing! You got it."

Suddenly he jerked the car off the road into an open paved area. Traffic flew by in each direction. The sign said ACCIDENT REPORTING AREA. Petey had no idea where they were.

"You know where you are?" Holmes said.

"No clue."

"If you had a fastball, you could hit the Silverdome from here."

"New home of the Tigers," Petey said.

"That what the man say."

"How far are we from Birmingham?"

"Not at all. Why?"

"Ever read Dutch Leonard?"

"Not 'less he rates ponies.

"Your loss," Petey said. "Writes books. Lives in Birmingham."

"Yeah? You gimme a book, I read it. I read anything."

"What are we doing here?"

"There he is."

A huge white BMW pulled in off the expressway from the other direction. BMW 850i, biggest model the Bavarian Motor Werke puts out, smoked windows, license BENG AL, oozing major-league money all the way. It pulled up next to them, the drivers' windows across from each other. The 850's smoked window slid downward revealing Al Shaw at his menacing best. He looked past Holmes and locked on Petey. He was a great-looking guy, solid as a tree, but on edge, and she thought of the time I had told her about how Shaw had once checked his swing with such force that he cracked off the head of his bat.

Shaw nodded at her.

"C'mon," said Holmes, and she followed him around to Shaw's passenger door. They slid across the beige leather backseat, Holmes directly behind Shaw. The interior of the car was soundproof. Anita Baker teased from speakers in the doors. The car smelled like it was an hour old.

"How you doin'?" Shaw said, turning in his seat, his lids heavy.

"I'm fine. Wish I were better," Petey said. "I don't have good things to tell you."

I passed Lansing, the state capital, and moved into Western Michigan and the farmlands around Grand Rapids. The Dutchmen there used to make a lot of good furniture, but in the past few decades they've gotten more renown for making Amway products.

I personally knew of Grand Rapids, however, because of a correspondent. Back in the halcyon days at the Chicago *Daily News,* I received eloquent missives from a fellow named Homer Vander Mey. With such an apt first name, Homer was a high school baseball coach part-time and a literature scholar in the main. His command of the king's English could outdo Connie Mack and Kenesaw Mountain Landis put together, and I found his letters, all of them long, thoughtful analyses of baseball and issues I'd written about, a pleasure to read. I responded in kind, and over the years the two of us licked a lot of stamps.

On a swing through Michigan for some reason or another, I finally met up with Homer and sat in the stands one afternoon while he coached. He was a long drink of water with a longer jaw, and he exhorted his charges at every turn. I do not remember the outcome of the game, but I do remember Homer springing off the bench after a terrible call at home plate. He towered over the puffy, beleaguered man in blue, fixed him with a stare, and simply and elegantly intoned, "Ump, I think not!"

Homer Vander Mey seemed typical of Grand Rapids, albeit a good bit more well-spoken. Dutchmen, Poles, and blacks lived there, hard-working people who built a lot of churches. Gerald R. Ford was their congressman for decades before he became the president who terrorized people on golf courses. My directions dictated that I get off at the Twenty-eighth Street exit. I passed motels and car lots, every fast-food joint in North America, big shopping centers. I took a turn down the East Beltline and went by Calvin College, named after a smart but dour reformer—a school, I'd been told by Homer, that, apart from its prodigious output of pulpit pounders, had lately produced a number of literary pretenders.

I was headed for a street named Wealthy on the east boundary of the city, and I didn't have much trouble finding it. The Gordon Olson offices were part of a set of small shops a couple blocks off a charming little lake called Reeds. It was a pretty setting, though the day was gray and the rough end of autumn was in the air. I parked on the street, and as I approached the building, I spotted a broad bay window with a broad blond figure staring out. Olson was not a Dutch name, but the man checking me out looked like a Hollander to me.

He moved fast and was at the door before I could introduce myself.

"I'm Gordon Olson, welcome to Olson and Associates, and forgive me if I look like I'm glad to see you, Mr. House," he said, and he threw a hell of a handshake. He was in his fifties maybe, and sound of body.

"This isn't the baseball capital of the world, Duffy," he went on, "but we gave the Tigers Dave Rozema and Mickey Stanley. Stubby Overmire long before them. Phil Regan came from Wayland, Jim Kaat from Zeeland. How am I doin'?"

"Slow down, Gordon," I said. "I came here to talk architecture."

"We'll get to that. I spent two years at I.I.T., you know," he went on. "Illinois Institute of Technology."

"Oh my," I said. "That might've made you a White Sox fan."

"Grew up in Wisconsin. Braves. Spahn and Burdette. Then off to I.I.T. The Go-Go Sox of '59. Read every paragraph you ever wrote about them. Damn, what a season."

"And Nellie Fox?"

"Until he's in Cooperstown, Duffy, the Hall of Fame is a pretender," Olson said.

I needed a cup of coffee. I was in the hands of a degenerate fan, a horsehide historian, a veritable lexicon of line drives and late innings, a guy who could use the word *dinger* in a conversation with a straight face.

"Can you tell me anything about the ballpark that burned?" I asked.

Olson nodded, now game-faced.

"Every creak and groan," he said.

He led me down a hall, past other offices and drafting rooms with shirtsleeved young people poring over blueprints. His was the office with the bay window. He poured coffee and brought it over with a plate of cookies shaped like windmills. He was a big galoot, six-two, at least two-twenty, and the cookies were a nice touch.

"All out of Dutch Twins. Great cookie," he said. "Made right here by the Holland American Wafer Company."

He was a talker, and I like talkers.

"You played, didn't you?" I said.

A look of pure enamel eased over his face. He reclined in a fancy architect's chair and looked heavenward.

"I batted against two of the game's best pitchers: Satchel Paige and—take this—Eddie Feigner. Paige came through Wisconsin in the fifties. Played our town team. Threw me three curve balls. Each one a perfect parabola. I took the first, missed the next two by a foot.

"And Feigner—"

"The King and his Court," I said. I'd seen the famous softball barnstormer a few times. Played with three men behind him. Had an arm as thick as a utility pole, and windmilled a softball over one hundred miles an hour. The sphere was not an object when it came to the plate, it was a sound.

"Pitched from second base against me. I popped him up. Felt damn good about it," Olson said. "Paige and Feigner. After facing them, I knew I was going to be an architect."

"I have a feeling you could go on about this all day," I said.

"Often have," Olson said.

"I went through the Olson Survey for Tiger Stadium," I said. "Impressive."

"My life's work," he said. "My *Nightwatch*. My *Mona Lisa*."

"And up in flames."

"Calculated move, the bastards," he said, biting a windmill cookie in half. "Like raising ticket prices. They all but told us it was going to happen."

Petey did the opening monologue. She told Shaw what she saw in the apartment, from his affectionately signed photo to the mirrors on the bedroom wall and the toys on the bureau. She listed Mercer's finds. Petey has a remarkable memory and left out nothing. Even the cologne, which she thought she sniffed now. With each detail James Holmes fidgeted like a ferret. Shaw never even blinked. The tops of his irises, black as licorice, were partially covered by his eyelids, and Petey could not take her eyes off them.

"Evidence guys are good," she said. "If you were in that apartment, they'll find some of you. If you brushed your hair, drank from a glass, maybe clipped a fingernail."

"I was there," Shaw said.

"Shit, Albert," Holmes said.

"Was there a few times."

"Just you and her?" Petey said.

"Sometimes."

"Albert—!" Holmes squawked. "What that shit you tol' me?"

Shaw ignored him. Holmes took off his leather cap and slapped it against his thigh.

"Would you call it an affair?" Petey said.

"What do you call it if you never performed the act?" Shaw said. "Like if you touched the lady. She touched you. Got some heat goin'. But never scored."

Holmes snorted. "How you gonna do that, Albert? You do her or didn't you do her?"

"Calm down, James," Petey said. "Are you asking me or telling me, Al?"

Shaw wiped a hand over a damp face. He turned on some air.

"James," Shaw said, "call Jack and ask him what he gonna do with the cops. Then dial your ol' lady and talk some."

"Gimme your phone."

"Use your own. In your vehicle."

"Phone's gone, Albert, you know that. Let's don't go into it neither."

"Use that pay job over there."

"I'm goin'. I got the message," Holmes said, slapping on his cap and pushing out from the backseat. "Damn, Albert," he said as he got out, "this the kind a shit got you in this shit."

Shaw fixed back on Petey.

"I didn' have no sexual intercourse with the lady. I did not," he began. "Spent time with her. She could talk me down. She could run me. She did head games on me."

He turned and watched Holmes walk petulantly over to the pay phone.

"It got *bad*," Shaw said, about to elaborate, then letting it hang.

"What do you mean?" said Petey.

Shaw took a breath. His neck tightened.

"I was gone for a long time. Jackson. Thing you don't have in prison is women. Not just their sex—I mean, you don't have that first off. I mean, what you really don't get is that time when a woman looks at you with her cat eyes and reads your signals. Cuts you. You dig? Kit did that on me. She knew how to do it. She'd take my wrists, always on the wrists, pull 'em out in front of me and put her thumbs on my pulse vein—damn, you could feel it— and she'd gut me. She'd tell me who I was and who I wasn't and turn me inside out."

Petey stared at him, speechless.

"So," Shaw said, "in your book, does that say affair?"

"Worse," Petey said, repositioning herself on the seat and feeling the car's damp heat. "What did she want from you? What was going on?"

"Everything," Shaw said. "She used to play with me like that. Kit say she could make me anything I wanted. Say I got more brains than a CEO. Gonna make me one. Put me on top of a hunnerd-million-dollar company and let me run it. Say she can get the capital just with a phone call. Then she come on different.

Say I was a con. Black con. Lowest animal in the world. A termite. She used to say ex-cons are like termites. Was no way I could beat that. Soon as I stop hittin', stop the home-run trot, I'm every-body's worse nightmare. That's when she got sexy. Always on me. Took my shirt off once, raked her nails over my chest like bob wire. Scratch the hell out of me, get me so excited I wanna take her right on the floor. Then she pull off. Throw a change-up. Say, 'Put your shirt on, Al. That's just what I'm talkin' about.' That kind of thing."

"That kind of thing," Petey echoed.

"She leans over me," he went on without coaching, his eyes stapled to Petey's and yet, she noticed, unfocused, "and she plays with her tongue. Maybe blow on the skin some. And she says her ol' man hates ballplayers. Hates nigger ballplayers even worse. She says, 'Al, could he see me over you like this, he would kill us both.' That's what she ways. She loves this, she does, so sexy and close that she's turned on like a woman gets, breathin' like that, tense, and she asks me am I worth it? Am I worth it?"

Petey saw it all in her mind, felt Shaw's coiled tension, his hands like vice grips on the top of the seat. Sweat ran down his neck.

"Jesus," she said. "Why didn't you run in the other direction?"

Shaw shook his head and exhaled like a bear.

"I *was* runnin'," he said. "Fast as I could."

At that, Holmes returned. He knocked on the window.

"You two lovebirds done yet?" he said.

He was ignored.

"Who have you told this to?" Petey said.

"The missus," Shaw said, "and now you. The old man with you, the commissioner's guy, he said you and him was workin' on my behalf. Hope to hell you are. I didn't kill the lady. We had a thing goin' on. Now you know a little bit about that. And there's a lot more to know."

Petey sighed and managed a slight smile.

"You have my confidence," she said.

He nodded.

"Fuckin' *chilly* out here," Holmes barked. He hopped and slapped his arms.

As Petey let herself out, Shaw lowered his window.

"Mr. Jack tell me you a wanted man," Holmes said. "Gotta take you back down to Beaubien whenever you ready."

Shaw raised the window and left Holmes looking at his reflection.

"And you can kiss my pretty public telephone ass," bitched the detective.

A few minutes later Petey was back in the poor-man's BMW heading into town.

"He's a complicated man," Petey said, thinking out loud.

"Yeah, well," Holmes said, unamused, still cold, "he a lot more uncomplicated when he stops fibbin' to his chief investigator. And maybe keep his bat in his pants. That'd help too."

"Our commission was twofold," Gordon Olson began. "Determine the viability of the stadium, and propose a suitable renovation plan. We did both. First was easy. The place is built like a bunker. All steel and concrete. Good pilings, too many posts, enough pigeon shit to coat a battleship. But it's in better shape structurally, we found, than a lot of stadiums a third as old. Shea, for example. Concrete structure. Shea's not going to last."

Olson went on like that as he showed me pages of engineering reports, drawings, and photos. All were done independently by his associates, he said, because Olson did not want his personal credibility challenged.

"If the place had been built on a nuclear waste dump, I'd find a way to call it jake," he said.

"What about now?"

"I haven't seen the damage. They want me to. Stallings, the woman who's running it now, she called me about coming in. 'Course, the Tigers have got to let it happen."

"Couldn't you come in as part of the arson investigation?"

"Could I? It's a thought. The city of Detroit owns the place. I should be able to walk in."

"Georgia Stallings should be able to pull that. She's a grinder. Good lady."

"I'm available," Olson said. "For the time being, I've talked to people who've been inside. It's bad. Heat was so intense the steel buckled. Take as much time to dismantle it as to build anew. If they started now, got a mild winter, used precast concrete, maybe they could do it, maybe not, Duffy. They have to want to first. Yeager's got a good case to say to hell with it, we play in the Silverdome. God, I'm depressed at the thought of it."

"So the fire did its job," I offered.

"It usually does," he said.

"Backtrack, Gordon," I said. "You said you were all but told something was going to happen to the stadium."

"Good God, yes. First of all, they didn't want us there," he said. "No cooperation whatsoever. Some of our people were accosted flat out. Told us we were assholes. They had their own engineers, and they told them what they wanted to hear. And we got the phone calls and letters. 'Go back to Grand Rapids.' Got one said, 'What say we burn the place down with you in it?' Put that one on the bulletin board. Stuff like that."

"You weren't the only ones," I said.

"That's what Kit Gleason told me, God love her," he said.

"Take any of it seriously, Gordon?"

"When there's a couple hundred million dollars at stake, Duffy, you take everything seriously," he said. "I've been around a lot of old buildings. They can burn. If they get help, they can really burn."

I finished off the cookies, declined more coffee.

"Give me your hot-stove-league discourse," I said, knowing Olson, who could talk about stadium fires and ownership conspiracies and the designated hitter long into the night, had one.

"Think of it, Duffy," he began, knocking the mud from his cleats. "You want to dump the joint. So you either cook the books and show an operating loss, or you stop maintenance to where the place looks like a dump that lice wouldn't sleep in. But you got an Achilles' heel, a gadfly, a burr, a Diogenes in the person of Kit Gleason. She's smart, gorgeous, articulate, telegenic, rich, and she lives in the suburbs, where most of your fan base is. Couldn't have a worse foe. You see her in your sleep. You want to wring her Grosse Pointe neck. But you didn't get rich in fast food and customer service by being stupid, and you know that as much as you'd like to see the woman choke on her martini toothpick, you can't lay a hand on her.

"So if I'm Joe Yeager, I just plow ahead like a glacier. That's how Reinsdorf did it in Chicago. Ignored everybody until he could make his political deals, saying all along that Comiskey Park was unsalvageable when he knew it wasn't, until somebody somewhere comes up with a deal, a bond package, a state thing with obligations fifty years out. It may take years, but it'll happen. All the time I keep talking to other cities, especially St. Petersburg— *those* pooches talk to everybody—and leak little ominous threats to the local press, especially the Armageddon guys in the sports section.

"But I'm not Joe Yeager. I like my food slow, with plenty of courses and waiters and fresh linen and little Spanish guys who scrape the crumbs off the tablecloth before I take dessert. Joe Yeager eats with a stopwatch. The beep of the french fry machine is a symphony to him. So maybe he got impatient. Maybe he listened when one of his toadies who talked about all the bad wiring and insulation that could flame up faster than a fart on a Boy Scout campout. So maybe he took a chance because he's Joe Yeager and he's got more money than God, and he's never been nicked in his life. Or maybe he nods at his man McAllister, a nod that means somebody Sport knows might take a fly at it. Or maybe he says, 'Hey, don't come near me. Go see the guys in Pontiac who bought up all that acreage or the guys on City Council who got vacant lots up their ass. Put some bugs in their ears. See what they come up with.' Things happen. People look the other way. Hey, you smell smoke? I don't smell any smoke.

"But he's always seven layers insulated. He could easier be nailed for sodomizing a baboon in the Detroit Zoo than for torching his own ballpark. He lets Kit Gleason do her thing, but he ignores her all the time. Doesn't get too close to her. Says hey, you wanna save a barbecued ballpark, good luck. I'm outta here.

"But how does she get herself killed? Damned if I know. And Al Shaw—Jesus, Al!—what's he doing within five hundred miles of that lady in Tiger Stadium at midnight? *Good Lord.* And does the torch man run into her when he's spritzing charcoal starter all over the press box? Maybe? Or does he somehow get the word that she's up there and *then* he decides to start spritzing charcoal starter? We'll never know, Duffy. . . ."

I didn't say anything. I never cheered in the press box. I never interrupted a fan's lament.

"My dad once told me about the saddest day in Tiger history," he said, his voice subdued. "The saddest day in Tiger history, he said, was when Mickey Cochrane got beaned in 1937. Tigers had won it all in '35. Mickey'd had a nervous breakdown the next year, you know, but he was back as player-manager in '37. Had Greenberg, Gehringer. Schoolboy Rowe had a sore arm, but Roxie

Lawson was havin' a great year. Then Mickey got beaned. He had a triple skull fracture. Hovered between life and death for three days. Came back to manage but he never played again. Never. That's what Dad said was the Tigers' saddest day. Well, I'm glad my dad isn't around to see all this. I'm convinced we'll never see another roof shot, Duffy. Never see another one land in the overhang. The last best thing in Detroit has been turned to ashes."

Chapter
13

At first it was just an idea bandied about by the volunteers at S.O.S. Then it was echoed by callers. Then a radio talk show guy got wind of it and called up Jimmy Casey, and the two of them floated it over the airwaves. And faster than you could say Kit Gleason, a candlelight memorial was scheduled for a few nights after Kit's funeral.

The script was simple. A few hundred S.O.S. faithful would gather at Michigan and Trumbull and say a few hundred appropriate words, light a few hundred candles, and march a few hundred yards around the stricken stadium. TV Minicams would show up to make it official.

Georgia Stallings organized things, arranging for Casey and the deejay to appear along with a few sympathetic politicians—but not the mayor, a guy who was straddling the fence so staunchly on the stadium issue that his crotch was calloused—and a few former Tigers. None of the current players was available, for apart from Al Shaw, who was now forced to stay in the vicinity, all the millionaires of summer were bone fishing in Florida or golfing in Tucson.

"Let's go, Unk," said Petey.

I would have used the weather as an excuse to beg off, except that a front of warm air had moved up north for a day or so, and the night was mild enough to play nine innings. So we took another drive down Michigan Avenue. On the way down, I told Petey about Corktown, the neighborhood just south of the stadium. It is a grid of old, modest homes, the St. Boniface parish, with a lot of old-timers still hanging on. They kept up lawns, nurtured pots of geraniums on the porches, and painted their siding and trim.

As we approached the area, Petey spotted a sign on one of the few boarded-up houses which read: GET MAD! GET INVOLVED! STOP DEVIL'S NIGHT ARSON!

"A little late for that now," she said.

I've always thought that stadiums were good for the neighborhoods around them, even with the eighty-one days of hassle that they brought each season. They are sort of benevolent bullies, if you will, getting their way because of the crowds and money they bring in via parking lots, restaurants, saloons, and sidewalk concessions—yet bottling up the whole area in the process.

Which, much to my surprise, was happening that very night. People converged on Tiger Stadium as if the World Series were being played. Thousands of people. Police had been called out to direct traffic. Parking lot attendants appeared at a number of lots and began taking cash for spaces. There were even peanut vendors.

By eight o'clock, at least ten thousand people had shown up and were clogging the streets and sidewalks. The mob was so big that police convinced Georgia Stallings and her fellow organizers to move the event from Michigan and Trumbull over to Al Kaline Drive on the other side of the stadium, just in order to keep a semblance of traffic flow on Michigan Avenue.

The proceedings were the usual, but bordering on moving. Stallings pushed things along with a portable bullhorn. I got the impression she kept one in her purse at all times. Jimmy Casey brought the crowd to cheers and raspberries with a bevy of *faux mots* aimed at Joe Yeager. There was the moment of silence, of course, and no shortage of genuine sentiment. Kit would have been proud.

Then, just as things were wrapping up and people were about to light their candles—and it was remarkable how candle vendors appeared out of nowhere—the overhead stadium gates suddenly lifted.

"We've been invited inside," Stallings announced. "Amazing!"

A cheer went up.

"A nifty countermove by Little Joe," I said.

"His nemesis is gone," Petey said. "He can afford to be gracious."

By the glow of the security lighting, we drifted into the ballpark along with the others, an impressive processional. Once inside, I turned and looked up into the right-field upper deck. Sure enough, there was a clump of men, Yeager and his brain trust no doubt. They were looking down on the horde and realizing, I hoped, that it was the essence of the franchise.

Once inside, people moved from the aisles and grandstands onto the field itself. The infield was soon filled, then much of the massive outfield area. Stallings and the others stood atop the Tiger dugout along third base. Behind them, of course, was the blackened, ravaged remains of the fire. Most of the crowd had never seen it close up, and they were stunned by it.

"Maybe we shamed him into this," Stallings announced, and the crowd applauded and whistled.

But no more was said about ownership, or the stadium itself. A young lady was helped onto the dugout roof and with no sound amplification but with a set of pipes that likened her to Aretha in her gospel days, she sang an a cappella "Abide with Me" that stirred us all to our bones.

Then we lit our candles and shielded them from the breeze. It was a hell of a sight—the dark, shadowy interior of the damaged ballpark lit by thousands of flickering flames in tribute to a single individual. And nobody said a word.

Even this naysayer was impressed—with the feeling, with these fans, with Detroit.

Later that night, Petey sat me down in The Snug, out of earshot of the lovely Monica, and we tried to make sense of it all. I was used to this kind of thing. Once in a while when the moon was blue and children stopped laughing at the old pull-my-finger joke, I used to pause and write a thumb-sucker on who got along with whom on a ball club. And who did not. And whether or not it mattered. The kind of thing today's toilet-trained sportswriters do every other day.

Mostly I stayed away from them, the piss-and-moan columns,

that is, the touchy-feely, communication-is-a-two-way-street jobs. Simple reason was that they usually made as much sense as a family feud. If the combatants patched it up the next day, or if the moaner went four-for-four, then whatever you wrote was moot, whatever great psychological insights you served up were whacked out of the park.

Mostly, however, Petey peppered me with what came out of Al Shaw's mouth in that humid car of his. I could only sit and marvel like a Ubangi listening to a missionary rave on about the Apostle Paul. I heard every word and could fathom but a few.

"What was she doing, Unk?" Petey said. "What was Kit Gleason up to?"

She decided to answer herself.

"I look at Al Shaw and I like see this level-eyed power hitter, okay? Measures every pitch. Knows his strike zone. You know, Unk, I always thought big-league ballplayers were older than me. Okay? Every pitcher was Tom Seaver and every slugger was Hank Aaron. Old guys. But now they're not. Al Shaw is twenty-nine. Maybe five years on me. Take away the five years he spent in jail, and he's my age."

"Maybe not," I said. "Those years aged him."

"In one way, yeah, I'll give you that," she said. "On the other hand, they retarded him. Stunted him. He doesn't know how to interact with people. A woman like Kit Gleason tied him up in knots."

"Are you overthinking this?"

"I hope so. I'm reaching back into my Psych 101 bookbag for everything I can get."

"I still don't see what could have cracked him," I said. "Shaw's no rookie. He spent five years in one of the worst prisons in the country. And some dame sets him off?"

"*Some dame.* Listen to you, Unk," Petey said. "You don't get it. You didn't sit two feet away from the guy and feel the heat."

I gave her the back of my hand. Comments like that made Petey sound very young. Then again, maybe I was too old.

"Two men in Kit's life," I mused, "and you've met them both."

"And I'm not sure what I think of her anymore," she replied.

"Al," I said to Bensmiller, "who knows Shaw? I mean way back. Somebody who's not an agent, no brown-noser. Somebody without varnish."

I'd reached the Greektown restaurateur after his lunch rush. He scolded me for not bothering him sooner.

"I heard what the evidence people pulled out of that apartment," he said. "I know those guys. They smell blood."

"So who's out there, Al?"

"You goin' after Shaw, or you after the torch, Duffy?" he said.

"Both."

"Hell, Duffy, Al's no torch," he said. "Go after the fire setter. Let Shaw wiggle out of his own jam."

"How good is your arson-homicide unit?"

"I don't know how good, but they're busy, and they need all the help they can get. Arson for hire is a hard pinch to get."

"Are there pros available?" I asked, "or do you grab the first guy with a gas can in his hand and send him to Tiger Stadium?"

"There's pros for everything, Duffy," Bensmiller said. "Stay in that bullpen, why don't you. I personally think Kit Gleason would be dead now even if she hadn't been in the fire. Maybe the guy who lit it knows who killed her."

"Where should I go?"

"Let me work on that. In the meantime, try Deacon. Deacon McGuire. If you can cut through his bullshit, Deacon can help you."

"James knows him," Petey said. "He's talked about a Deacon McGuire."

"Holmes knows everybody," I said. "He's a black version of a Doc Greene. Nifty sportswriter who used to run about this town before dawn."

"When everybody else was just getting out of bed, right?"

"That was Doc. So ring up Holmes. See what he can do for us."

Holmes worked fast and got us an intro to McGuire, community organizer, hell-raiser, and self-promoter. McGuire's headquarters were down in Corktown, near the stadium.

"And I got another date," Petey said. "Dr. Cooper Nance. He called and wants to get together again. He liked our talk the other night."

"And you did too."

"I'm on base, Unk," she said. "Makin' things happen."

How about that, I said to myself.

"Don't let him catch you leaning, Pete," I offered.

*   *   *

I spent longer than usual getting ready that morning. I know there are guys who bolt from the sheets at dawn, run three miles while listening to a French language cassette on their headsets, then grill bacon and eggs on the hibachi off the balcony. Not I. The bed felt good, and when I left it, I felt like shit. The five hours in the car yesterday had not done my spine any good. My head hurt from Gordon Olson. After the cookies and coffee, he took me out to lunch and convinced me to imbibe bruised gin. The best kind. Not to mention that the flinty Michigan weather was to my circulation what locks are to the St. Lawrence Seaway. And I was constipated. Staying in motels for too long will do that to you.

So I did not sing the body electric, or any of that other good morning stuff. A lot of guys my age are dead now, as Casey used to say, and is it a bad sign when you find yourself quoting Stengel? I decided to let Petey drive and manage the ball club for a while. She had the legs for it. She had no vices that I knew of, at least none that left her clipping the hair of the dog in the morning hours.

She drove us down Michigan Avenue again, toward downtown and the stadium. Near the stadium, we took a right onto Sixteenth Street at the first historic sign for the Corktown district. Straight ahead of us was the giant, scorched Union Station of yesteryear as we rolled along the west border of the park. This was the dilapidated side of Corktown. The businesses along Michigan were mostly boarded up; homeless transients wandered the green of the park; and to our right was a field of weeds.

We took another right at the first corner and came upon a classic red-brick, tall-steepled church. This was Deacon McGuire's Soweto House; the cornerstone said it was built in A.D. 1872. Neglected eaves and bricked-in rose windows testified to the changes it had seen in its century and a quarter.

We parked out front, right behind James Holmes's hand-washed and gleaming BMW. Our Volvo attracted little attention. Holmes's Bavarian car had a tipsy old gentleman with oily pants and red sneakers sizing it up from the sidewalk as if it were in his future.

"That's a car," he mumbled as we passed.

The inside of the center was part gymnasium, church, campaign headquarters, and day-care center. A single, high-ceilinged room lit by epilepsy-inducing fluorescent lights contained a jumble of tables and chairs, an ornate pulpit with Latin carved into it, tumbling mats, televisions, toys, and a long bowed shelf of what looked like *Reader's Digest* condensed books. Old men played cards at the tables, toddlers in plastic diapers whacked at the toys, the televisions went full blast with no viewers, and the condensed books leaned on one another.

"Hey!" came the voice of James Holmes from somewhere in the depths. He appeared in a charcoal suit, his knit shirt just as black and buttoned at the collar. His bald dome was an eight ball with two eyes.

"Pee-trin-ella, my sweet child," he said like Duke Ellington announcing the A Train. He gave her a cupped hand in some kind of ritual hand pump. "And Uncle Duffy House, my good man," he added. "Hey, you catch an old rubby-dub keepin' eyes on my wheels when you came in?"

"He was staring the paint off it," said Petey.

"Good. Nothin' but thieves around here."

He led us into a carpeted rear office, a paneled den dominated by a wide and cluttered desk. Around the perimeter were shelves full of boys'-baseball-league trophies. Below them were plastic lawn chairs. JOBS NOW! DRUGS NEVER! read a poster on the wall. GUNS FOR JOBS! read another. Mounted around them in dime-store frames were the usual office glossies, most of them black men and women at banquets and ceremonies, all including a particularly stern-looking fellow in snug-fitting sport coat or golf shirt whose hair style through the years went from the bushiest of Afros to smart skull cuts. The fellow was sitting behind the desk now. He'd filled out some, but he still looked like he could play some ball. Maybe forty-five. Age had not been good to his hairline. No smiles.

"Here they are. Right on time, Deacon," Holmes said.

McGuire got up and offered a hand first to me, then to Petey as Holmes introduced us. Then the detective swept the lawn chairs of newspapers, record jackets, and menus so we could sit down.

"The commissioner of organized baseball," McGuire said after he'd sat down in a squeaky leather chair. He had good pipes, a Lou Rawls voice that must have detonated microphones. "I've had mayors, congressmen, senators, and presidential candidates come to me, but never representatives of the commissioner of baseball."

"Your lucky day," I said.

"He wanna sell that ash heap down the street?" McGuire said.

"Ouch," I replied. "Actually, the commissioner likes Tiger Stadium right where it is."

"Don't make me crack up," McGuire said, true to his word. "Baseball's wanted outta this neighborhood ever since Ty Cobb retired. This place here is called Soweto House because this city is as close to Johannesburg as you'll get in this hemisphere."

I sniffed. My age permitted me that.

"How about you? You want it out of here?" I asked.

He leaned forward and plunked both elbows on the desk.

"Good question, Mr. House. The stadium puts some of our people to work. We *love* sellin' peanuts and parkin' those cars and draggin' that infield. 'Course our people don't get the management jobs or anything close to the executive suite. And right now, there ain't no games so the stadium and all these vacant lots around here sit cold and empty and don't do us a damn bit of good. So you got me there, Mr. Commissioner."

I ran my tongue around my teeth. I had had a feeling this guy was not going to be sweetheart, and he did not disappoint.

"But who we shittin' here, folks? There's a master plan and we ain't a part of it," McGuire went on. "We were never asked and never considered. This fire 'of suspicious origins'—" his voice aped that of a television anchorman— "is just a new shot been fired. Surprised even me, and I don't surprise at nothin'."

"Say it, Deacon!" James Holmes snapped.

I coughed. The placed smelled like french fries. Petey crossed her jean-clad legs.

"Next thing you'll tell me," I said, "is that Magic Johnson's virus and Muhammad Ali's Parkinson's disease are conspiracies."

Petey's eyes widened at that. *What the hell,* I thought, *why should I take this guy's hogwash?*

"Sounds about right," McGuire said, rubbing his hands and going through a few third-base-coach motions. "Before you start with that white man's snicker, lemme give you a little short course in how things are done around here.

"I call this story 'St. Boniface and the Tigers.' You see, the wine maker sells the Tigers to the new man a few years back, check? Good Catholic individual, he always made a big deal about that. Now you got St. Boniface right across the street. I know those cats. Work with 'em. All those good Catholic people in that church volunteer to park cars during ball games in the church lot. Raise good money. One hundred fifty large in good money every year.

They give all that to the parish. Got two schools it ran. Good schools, teach our children.

"But when the new owner comes in, check this, he makes a deal with the bishop to buy the church. Buy the got-damn church. And all the property with it. Just the two of 'em put it together. Nobody in the parish even knows a damn thing about it until it's a done deal. Then the bishop announces the church is gonna *close*. Schools along with it. Everything but the communion wafers he sold to the Tigers. Hell, they closed some fifty Catholic churches in Detroit so far, so what's one more.

"Now the people scream and yell enough to the cardinal so he flips and keeps the church open. For the time being. But the schools are gone, and the money for parking all goes to the Tigers. The bishop, hell, he got hisself transferred to Rome, where he eats spaghetti and gets his feet washed in the Vatican every day or so and we ain't heard from him since.

"And that's the story of St. Boniface and the Tigers. And you come in here and tell me I'm *dreamin'* some conspiracy?"

"I hear ya!" chorused Holmes.

I wished Petey could have shoved one of those Little League trophies down his throat.

"A very dedicated woman was killed in that fire," I said.

"You got it, man!" McGuire shouted. "I'm cool with that lady. Nice white suburban lady comes down to my neighborhood to save that ballpark. Thank you, darlin'! I knew her. Shook her hand. Gave her a kiss on the cheek. Told her while she was busy savin' the ballpark, maybe she could help save the got-damn neighborhood!"

"Damned if she does and damned—" I started.

"Don't give me that shit!" he cut in. It was his floor and he ran it. "Everybody on that committee of hers lives in Bloomfield Hills or some damn place. Tiger historic ass Stadium is all they care about. They got all those white memories inside, and they don't wanna lose 'em!"

"Okay, okay, okay, Mr. McGuire," I said. "You're gonna win this debate no matter what—"

"Damn right," Holmes said.

"Shut up, James," Petey said.

"Which is okay," I continued. "No matter what you think, I came to you for help. The fire was set. The woman was murdered."

McGuire leaned back. When in doubt, stroke the guy.

"Ain't seen any Detroit police," he said. "Only detective ever comes around is James here. How you get my name?"

"Police," I fudged.

"No shit?"

I waited.

"Okay. Get out the notepad," he said. "Stop thinkin' black. Fire happens around Devil's Night, everybody says some nigger did it. Hell, niggers is burnin' down everything else. That's racist bullshit. Because the stadium ain't no crack house with the back door swingin' open. It's got security, Jack, steel gates, cameras, security guards. Give 'em that. Anybody get in there, he got to breach that security. And that's an inside job. Like when you knock over an armored truck. Always got some fool on the inside.

"I heard there was somethin' on the street to start a fire," he added. "Ten large. That's what I heard."

"Heard it too," said Holmes.

"That's the lottery to these fools," McGuire went on. "And wasn't no one took it up cuz no one can *do* it. They gonna *jump* the damn wall with a gas can on their back? Shit. Start lookin' to Yeager's people. Man in the restaurant business needs a lotta labor help. Labor in Detroit, you dig? Same cats put Jimmy Hoffa to sleep. Put him in a football stadium. That ring a bell?"

"Or look at Sport McAllister's roster," Deacon continued. "He's got some shady character for a sidekick that's done work for him since he was at Southern Michigan . . . name's all wrong, like a baseball composer or somethin'."

"Mickey Schubert?" Petey suggested.

"That's the one. Word is he golfs bigtime with some heavy land cats in Romulus—where they want a new stadium built. Word also is, the man can get the job done, whether it comes to basketball points, kneecaps, or Molotov cocktails."

"Was it an arson-murder contract, or the other way around?" I asked.

"Does it matter?" Deacon countered.

"Matters to Al Shaw," I said.

McGuire recoiled at that and cocked a finger at James Holmes.

"My man," Holmes said.

"Your headache," McGuire said. "Man deludes himself. Don't know where the ballfield ends and the real world begins."

He turned to me.

"You know how Brother Shaw got snagged? Write this down too. Wasn't in that lady's bed. He's a fool, but he ain't *that* kind a fool. He bought her program, that's what. Her *program*. I know 'cuz she come in here with it. She wants to help out the Soweto Center. Give us computers. WATS lines. Tutors. I said, 'Shit, lady, give us cash!' "

"Damn!" Holmes said, and slapped his seat.

" 'Oh my,' she says, and backs off real quick," McGuire went on. "She put the same move on Shaw with his thing. The EX-CON thing he got. Bad idea in the first place. Cons are cons. Bring 'em all together's like breedin' piranhas. Shaw oughta know that."

"Bad idea, huh?" Holmes said. "How many guns you take out, Deacon? I don't see no thugs linin' up to give you their pistols."

McGuire snarled at him. It did not take a genius to surmise that his guns-for-jobs program was not knocking corporate Detroit for a loop.

"What'd you say, James?" McGuire said.

With that, he reached inside his desk drawer and pulled out a gun. It was an angry, long-barreled thing with rubberbands wound around the handle.

"Forty-five," Holmes marveled. "Shit, Deacon."

"Boy gave it up yesterday," he said.

We all gawked at the gat.

"Boy got a job yet?" Petey asked.

We left the Soweto Center with Holmes, who erupted as soon as he hit sidewalk.

"Goddamn!" he howled.

The man he had hired to watch his car was sitting in the front seat. Holmes jerked open the door.

"Get your wine-drinkin', lice-infected, wet-pants ass out!" he yelled. "How you get inside in the first place?"

"The fuggin' door," the old sentry grumbled, making a pained face as he swung his unlaced sneakers out of the driver's well. He was thoroughly insulted.

Steam rose from the top of James Holmes's head.

Back in the Volvo, which had remained unwatched and untouched, I stared out the window.

"Reedy's, Unk," Petey said. "You want to grab lunch at Reedy's?"

"Fine," I said.

"So let me hear it while it's fresh," she said, pulling away from the curb.

" 'Cut through McGuire's bullshit,' Bensmiller told me," I said. "And something hit me when he was knocking EX-CON. Put all those guys together—"

"Like breeding piranhas," Petey finished.

"Or creating your own labor pool," I said.

Petey glanced at me. Knowing exactly what I was driving at.

Chapter
14

We drove back to Dearborn via Michigan Avenue, our usual route. The more familiar that wide street became, that old Chicago Road, the more I began to see in it. At nearly every traffic light kids and adults wanted to wash your windshield, sell you peanuts, flowers, or newspapers, or they just plain panhandled. The blight, the struggle, the almost Third World ache became unavoidable. What I did not witness firsthand, I read about in the Detroit papers or saw on its ambulance-chasing television news reports, and gradually, like the wearying motions of a scoreless extra-inning game that will never end, the data of Detroit began to mark me.

One day a city official seriously suggested leveling large parcels of vacant and abandoned city properties, fencing in the land, seeding it, and turning it into pastures. Displaced persons would occupy the estimated seven thousand vacant houses owned by the city in more populated areas. Another day someone mentioned that the city had lost eight hundred thousand residents since 1950, when one million eight hundred thousand lived there. Or that nearly 50 percent of the city's children live in poverty. Or the fact that suburban Southfield has more commercial office space than downtown Detroit. There is no department store in Detroit, and there has not been one since Hudson's on Woodward Avenue closed in 1983.

Then there was the fellow working in the police chief's home who was hit on the head by a packet of twenty thousand dollars in one-hundred-dollar bills that fell from a ceiling panel. The chief had embezzled over two and a half million from a police fund. Another day the city's aged, irascible mayor all but convicted and sentenced two of his city's police officers accused of beating a motorist to death. And he was running for reelection with literature featuring neighborhoods with lush trees, a riverfront aquarium, more monorails, and a new Tiger Stadium with a retractable dome.

As the old Tiger Stadium lay amoldering.

Did it matter that I was sifting through the ashes?

"Keep sifting," the commissioner told me that night. "I can't force Yeager to stay, but I can make his seat hot if it looks like he's even tickled that the place went up."

In need of a little hand holding, I'd reached Chambliss by phone.

"He's sent the league formal notice that he wants to play in the Pontiac bubble," Chambliss went on. "That's his option. But the league has to decide if baseball can be played there."

"Oh boy," I moped. "Baseball was played in a football field in Los Angeles when O'Malley bolted. They played in Parc Jarry in Montreal. Hell, Grand, you can play the game anywhere."

"There's sentiment among the owners to lean on him to stay in the old park," he said.

"Come on," I said.

"Well, there's sentiment from *me*. And I got allies. Get a good structural engineer to say the place can be rebuilt. Make a case for it."

"That I can do, Grand."

"Then implicate the sonofabitch, Duf," he said. "We'll force him out and get somebody in there who wants to stay put. Maybe a pizza mogul or some other civic-minded soul."

I let out some breath.

"Detroit does not rhyme with civic-minded souls," I said.

"Nothing does. You have to put a gun to their heads."

"They do that well here."

"I don't envy you," he said. "You want a raise?"

"Of course. But save it. Give me a bonus if we bring you a scalp."

"Get some sleep, Duffy."

I couldn't sleep. I went over my lists, my sources, my angles. I spotted Del Howard's name. He was my Chicago FBI pal, and he had given me a Detroit G-man I could tap into once the ashes had cooled. They were cool. I made the phone call to a beeper number. It was nearly ten at night, but Howard said this guy was a member of the Mayo Smith Society and he knew I wanted to talk to him. That spiderweb-thin net that snags fans never ceases to amaze me. I once had a twenty-minute conversation with the great actor George C. Scott, an audience with a man who did not gab with just anybody. It was not a discussion of Method acting or *The Cherry Orchard,* but of the Detroit Tigers, of whom Scott was a slavish fan.

Ten minutes later he called. His name was John Cronin, and he had been so primed by Del Howard that I had to cut through the thick accolades just to get a word in. We spent a lot of time talking about old Tigers like Jake Wood and Jim Bunning, whom Cronin told me had become a congressman from Kentucky. Cronin held his breath when I reminded him that Lou Gehrig ended his consecutive-game record right here in Detroit. It was in May of 1939, and Gehrig was dogged by the disease that now bears his name but about which he knew nothing then. He took himself out of the lineup that day for the first time since 1924, changed clothes, and went down the street to Ed Shea's Restaurant, which is now Casey's, and sat there drinking coffee while the Yankees thrashed the Tigers. In the stands that day was Wally Pipp, the very man who had had a headache the day Gehrig replaced him in '24, who had come in from Grand Rapids to watch the game. Two weeks later, after Gehrig had been diagnosed at Mayo Clinic, he returned to the Yankees, but in the eyes of fellow players like Hank Greenberg, he had been sapped of his will.

Cronin savored the story like a collector. Then I steered him to the fire.

"We're not officially in it," he said. "No authorization for the Bureau to come in. ATF is in, and they usually come to me. Arson is a specialty of mine, even though I'm not an official expert. I just know a lot. Washington's got a whole unit does psych profiles and patterns if the arson is interstate. But between you me and the wall, Mr. House, personality profiles never pinched anybody. In a case like the Tiger Stadium job, you get an informant or you get nothing.

"I know what they got as far as evidence and witnesses are concerned, and believe me, they need an informant bad. The more time passes, the more it looks like they won't crack this one."

"You been inside?"

"Oh yeah. I wouldn't miss it. That's my ballpark. And it was hard to take at first. Hell of a fire. But by the second day, it was just another char for me. But a tough one."

"Then backtrack for me, John," I said. "What'd you find?"

"This is just for you, right, Mr. House? Just background. No media, no official league report? I mean, Mr. Hoover is dead, but we have rules. And anything with FBI and Detroit will come right back to haunt me."

"I don't even know your name, John," I said.

"It's Cronin," he said. "So where do I start? They been in there with dogs. Found good evidence of accelerant in several places. Burning was low. That's always a sure sign. Pour patterns, flash points. As bad as any fire is—and this was a hot one—you can usually get a feel for what happened. Problem is, fire runs where it wants to run. Throw in wind and air currents. Just figure the height of that place and all the crazy angles. Gives you a mixed picture.

"Biggest thing, you probably already know, is ignition in three different places at once. Multiple origin: Arson, capital *A*. Thing is—and this is what pissed me off—here was a guy who wanted the heart of the park to burn. All the front offices are in right field, you know, and they didn't even get warm. I mean, this guy set a fire that would hurt the players, the press, the vending offices, the real operations of a game. Sweetheart, huh?"

"Anybody know how he got in?" I interjected.

"Probably walked in. I mean, there are no signs of a break-in. I don't think you could crack that place if you tried. Most of the park gates are overhead steel doors. There's one small steel service door on Michigan. Then you got security. The guardhouse at the player's parking lot on Trumbull and the freeway. The front lobby on Trumbull. The cameras, once he's inside. But he got in some-how. Past security, maybe at the guardhouse, maybe the lobby, nobody knows. But a couple hundred bucks can go a long way nowadays.

"The security guys on duty have some years on them. They're cooperating. Lie detectors, the whole bit. They think he had keys, 'cause when he got inside, he still needed two different keys for different locks going into the clubhouse and the third-deck suites. The locks are Best, which are the top of the line. Only special machines can cut those keys. Can't be done at the hardware store.

"No, this guy was a pro. I'd say Jimmy Barretti, except he's been in Jackson for three years. You have to know what you're doing because if you start spreading accelerant all over hell, it can go up at any time. Like gasoline. Most of the arsons you get are some asshole dousing a stairwell with gasoline. You take a closed area like the Campbell box in right field, you spread accelerant in a place like that, and you're creating a bomb. One spark, and the fumes could blow and send your ass fifty feet in the air. This guy knew that.

"Looks like he spread a slow burner, maybe a charcoal lighter, not straight gasoline, something that'll light but not explode. He lit it and it went slow, got some heat, and because you're talking about a place with corridors, once it got going, it really went. Corridors are like giant cylinders—the fire has no place to go in them. The air superheats to incredible temperatures and keeps sucking in more air—it's a hell of a sound, Mr. House—and getting hotter, maybe two thousand degrees hot where things start exploding. Things ignite instantly. Glass, plastic, even steel becomes molten.

"This guy knew that, or he was just lucky, I don't know. After he did the third deck, he got the hell out and went down to the clubhouse level and started that going. Went inside the Tigers side on the third base and moved around to first. Hit the carpets, the wooden partitions, and it went up fairly quick. In fact, by the time he was around to the visitors' side, there was probably a hell of a vacuum being built up by the heat upstairs. That could have caused him real grief, maybe trapped him. But by then he was gone.

"Probably left the way he came in. As I said, security's got nothing. Monitors got nothing. When the third deck went up, they all scrambled up there and left the store. He could have strolled out. The player parking area behind center field, I'd say.

"And the police and arson guys did what they usually do. 'Cept this is a lot different than a back-porch job. Not like a house or a garage that goes up and people say, 'Hey, we remember this guy or that guy hanging around.' Happens a lot. Then when the fire is going like hell, the guy who set it is in the crowd watching. Lots of times the guy who called in the fire is the guy who set it. Or he's helping the firemen. You get a lot of pathetic assholes who set the fire and then act like volunteer firemen, work the hoses, all that. I remember a pyro who worked board-up. He'd start the fires, and then he'd get back there a few hours later with a contract to board it up.

"I could go on forever, Mr. House, and none of it would be relevant to the stadium. If I had a thousand hours of free time and absolute access, I'd turn Little Joe Yeager's shorts inside out. I'd comb every ledger book and run down every guy with a Bic lighter he ever had a cup of coffee with. Tiger Stadium was set on fire, Mr. House, and he owns the ball club.

"Then I'd tie into McAllister. He's the new face in town, and his knock is that he's not a true baseball man either. But I'd get into his jockstrap too. Look at the moves he pulled in that dirty program back in college. And look into a sidekick of his—I can't remember the name—a gambler and fixer."

"Schubert," I said. "Mickey Schubert."

"That's him. McAllister's pilot fish. Look into both of them. If I had my way, I'd be a shadow they couldn't shake."

I grunted approval at the whole notion.

"And if you were me?" I said.

"How much access does the commissioner's office give you?"

"As much as the club wants to give. Or as little."

"That's what I thought," he said. "Then again, there're some big differences."

"Such as what?"

"You're good, for one."

"John, John. Don't take the Mayo Smith stuff too far."

"Hey, I know your dossier," he said.

"Thank you, and I'm flattered. You said *differences.* Plural."

"They maybe don't expect you. I mean, arson, homicide, even ATF—we all think alike. You don't. You didn't go to our schools. You come at them from a different angle."

"I hope so, I really do. One more thing, John. Whataya make of Al Shaw?"

It was his turn to grumble and mutter.

"Like everybody else—in with a broad," he said. "Messy affair. Both of 'em should've known better. But let's say he socked her, panicked, started a fire to cover it up. People do that. Except security has him leaving the park long before the place went up. Long before. And he never could've set the ground-level fires. So he's not high on my list. He's high on my list of all-time dumb asses, but that's another story. . . ."

"What was the name of the guy in Jackson?" I asked.

"Jimmy Barretti. Jimmy the Match. Mob torch. Restaurants. Trucking firms. Gay movie houses. Could do it all. But he's in the hole, and don't think we didn't check to make sure. I mean, this is a crazy world."

"Jimmy Barretti," I said.

"Gargled with lighter fluid," Cronin said.

It was after eleven. I was tired, and I thought Cronin was talked out. But no, he asked me about Mayo Smith—any good stories, a good line or two. I truly scoured my brain. Mayo was Mayo. There are few nuggets out there, mined or unmined about him. Cronin seemed stung.

The doctor was serious, Petey said over oat bran the next morning. Kit Gleason's widower wanted to meet her for lunch. Dr. Nance suggested she make a return visit to the house. She suggested they meet someplace with a maître d'. First, however, Petey wanted to do some background on him.

"Don't you think?" she asked me.

"I sure do."

"Go to the well?" she added.

"Georgia Stallings, of course," I replied.

First I made a call to the lady of S.O.S. myself. Agent Cronin's remark had stayed with me through the night. "You come at them from a different angle," he'd said. I liked that. Let Petey and James Holmes clamp onto Cooper Nance—and good luck to them— but I decided to work backward. If the fire was set by a pro, then talk to a pro about it. This guy Barretti in the state pen.

Georgia answered on the first ring. She always picked up quickly. She was always on the job.

"Who do you know at Southern Michigan Penitentiary?" I asked.

She was taken aback.

"No one," she said curtly.

I had a chuckle, trying to humor her. She was in no humor.

"Let me try again. With EX-CON, Al Shaw's program—"

"I understand."

"Did you touch base with anyone from the prison? Some liaison, or whatever?"

She made some sound in her throat. It was early, and her day did not sound pleasant.

"First of all, I don't have anything to do with EX-CON outside of straightening out the mess they call an office system over there," she said. "I never got involved with the program. And I never wanted to."

"Except for Shaw."

"Fine. Except for Al," she said. "As far as I know, they worked with an assistant warden. He was on the letterhead."

She gave me his name and his office number.

"Why?" she asked.

"Hunch. A trail . . . a goose chase. Pick one," I said. "I want to talk to an inmate, a professional arsonist. See what he can tell me."

"Good luck," she said. "Personally, I have no use for those people. What I've seen of them depresses me."

"I thought you had nothing to do with EX-CON."

"I don't. I never did. But I know what goes on over there. It's enough to put a big distance between me and them."

I whistled. "I'd hate to see you on my parole board."

"You would," she affirmed.

I chuckled again. I was a jolly guy. Her end of the line, however, was a cold pond.

"My niece is going to stop in for a talk," I went on.

"What about?"

"Dr. Cooper Nance."

"Oh?" she said.

The receiver warmed a bit.

"I'm here," Stallings said. "I'm always here."

My contact with the assistant warden at the Jackson prison was direct and efficient. EX-CON was a magical acronym: The second-string warden was a member of the steering committee. He said he was also a good friend of Al Shaw's, but he had a warden's opinion on what was happening to the outfielder. You could take the kid out of Southern Michigan Penitentiary, but not vice versa. Which kind of surprised me.

Before bending his ear, I was all prepared to pull a ruse to get in, to put on my journalist's hat or dig out some pastor's credentials. Prisons are regularly penetrated by clerics, and ordination is hardly a problem since just about anything in God's or Allah's name qualifies nowadays. But I did not have to go through the fuss. The assistant warden said a key to the prison awaited me. Jimmy Barretti, whom he seemed to know well, had become something of a model inmate, a prison lawyer who liked to talk to strangers. He'd set it up. That afternoon was fine.

"He's in for arson, you know," he added. "He can probably give you an earful on Tiger Stadium."

Of course, I said to myself. The idea was suddenly so obvious I considered abandoning it. How many detectives, reporters, and TV crews had already beat me to Barretti?

"None," the assistant warden assured me.

Invariably prisons are built in small towns and burgs far away from the scene of the crimes. It was no different with Michigan and its big house in Jackson, which claims to be the world's largest walled prison. In a world full of prisons, that's some bragging right. Again I traveled west out of the Detroit area, this time on I-94, the highway that cuts across the lower half of the state. It was cold, and a crosswind blew sand against the windows. Forty miles out I passed Ann Arbor, which is mostly the University of Michigan. That's where Bill Freehan played his college ball—along with Ted Simmons and quite a few other pros—and I just read that the bald and brawny Tiger catcher through most of the sixties is now the U. of M. baseball coach.

Another forty farm and woodland miles down the road was Jackson. I pulled off the highway right after seeing a sign that read: PRISON AREA: DO NOT PICK UP HITCHHIKERS, and headed into the countryside. As any felon in Detroit will probably tell you, the joint is easy to find. The prison is a complex of new and old buildings, mostly one- and two-story, arranged on several acres of rural land. Were it not for the high fences and the barbed wire, the towers and the cautionary signs, you would have thought you had stumbled on a vast agricultural college. Except that the matriculates were serving sentences, not parsing them.

I registered, showed my driver's license, was cleared, searched, cleared, searched, and the back of my hand was stamped with some exotic but invisible ink. I passed through an electronic metal detecting device, was patted down, and then my hand was scanned by a turnkey in a little glass cage. Finally the door buzzed open.

I was taken to what looked like a cafeteria without food service. Plastic chairs, small tables, vending machines. If you are visiting a minimum-security inmate, you don't have to talk through Plexiglas. Jimmy Barretti had apparently been a good boy. Other visitors sat at tables with inmates, most of them wearing nondescript prison clothes and U. of M. sweatshirts. The atmosphere was dull and lifeless, but not morose. There were no tin cups or manacles.

Now my two favorite Italians on the Tigers were Reno Bertoia, a slim, banjo-hitting tapioca infielder from St. Vito Udine in the Old Country, and Don "The Sphinx" Mossi, the pitcher who made a basset hound look cheerful and who was once described as having "loving cup" ears, but who also was a pretty good lefty. Barretti reminded me of neither. Suddenly appearing at the table with an accountant's armload of manila folders, not more than five and a half feet tall, maybe weighing a hundred twenty-five pounds, Barretti looked like a batboy from Sicily.

"You . . . hey," he said, sitting and running his files on the tabletop like a blackjack dealer does his decks. "You're a writer, and I'm a writer. I got articles here all written down. Got the word count right on top. Don't need no editing. Facts all checked."

"I'm Duffy House, not Swifty Lazar," I said.

"Who's that?" Barretti said.

"Agent. Gives big parties."

"Hey, I need an agent. You know this guy? Give 'im this one. Constitution guarantees a minimum-square-foot area per prisoner. Got a class-action suit on it. Go ahead. Take it."

I didn't dare look at the copy. I feared the slightest bit of interest would make me Jimmy Barretti's Maxwell Perkins.

"Who told you I came to see your portfolio?" I asked.

He reared at that, hitting the back of the chair and putting a scowl on his face like *Il Duce.*

"Hey, Warden told me," he said. "Said you're a writer. So am I. So what's the problem?"

"Editors."

"Fuck 'em."

"It's been done. They're still a problem. They publish what they want to publish."

"Hey, you ain't shittin' me, pal. I got turndowns comin' outta my ass," Barretti said. "I get out I'm gonna go see 'em. Say, 'Hey, I'm Jimmy Barretti. 'Member me, chump? You sent me this letter said you liked my stuff but it wasn't right for your needs.' And I pull out a nine-millimeter automatic and say, 'So now tell me if this ain't just right for your needs at this time.' Make 'em shit."

"Every writer's dream" I said.

He came back to the table, both elbows on the Formica.

"Hey," he said. "I'm just kiddin'."

"Good," I said. "You write anything about EX-CON? Al Shaw's program? *That* I could do something with."

"Hey, that's nothin'. How 'bout this one on conjugal visitation rights for the criminally insane?"

"Cripes."

He laughed at that, a sort of crooked-face guffaw.

"Shaw been charged? They stick him yet?" he asked. "Hey, it won't happen 'less there's another chick. Maybe the ol' lady. Come on, nobody gets time on crime lab bullshit. Take it from me. I gave crime labs their lunch. FBI, all those fungolas. They never got shit on me. My ol' lady fingered me."

"You know about Tiger Stadium? The fire?"

"Whataya think?" he said.

"When it went up, the cops said they checked quick to make sure you were still down here."

"Those jackoffs," he said, grinning.

"But they're right, huh?"

"Coulda done it in a walk."

"That easy?"

"I didn't say that," he said. "I didn't say *easy*. How you gonna make the place 'less you got help? Gotta get in. Gotta move around. There's good security and there's cameras. Security does a twenty-minute loop. That kind a thing."

"You been there?"

"Hey, I used to like baseball."

"You know what I mean."

"Let's just say there's levels of security, you know what I mean? Things are the same all over. Trick is gettin' inside. Once I get inside—and there ain't no place I can't get inside—it's easy. Nobody's payin' attention 'cept to the offices. Payroll, computers, and shit. Meantime the place is lit."

"I heard there was money to be made."

"Hey, pal, there's *always* money to be made. We're talkin' Detroit. People wanna leave that shithole. A nice blaze can help things. Last thing *I* heard, the Tigers wanted to leave."

"Was there money to be made?" I repeated.

"Heard there was. Fifty pieces."

"Know anybody who could do it?"

"Besides me?"

"Besides you."

"No way. I'm your man. And hey, I got an alibi."

"Okay," I said, scratching my knobby head. I pushed the folders around on the table. "Now where's the one on conjugal visits?"

"Right here. Hey, what about the agent?"

"Lazar. I'll give you his number. So who ya got out there?"

He smiled and leaned back in his chair like the diminutive, lethal, antisocial, pyromaniac bug that he was.

"Why should I finger anybody? What's in it for me?"

"Me," I said, not hesitating.

He seemed to like that. I was probably the first guy without a tattoo to visit him out here. I reeked of the gentlemen's profession of publishing. Or maybe Barretti was just dumb.

"There's Freddy Malchow. He works in a crew, but he could do it. I heard Leo Rugendorf was workin.' And Jackson . . . Billy Jackson. Clyde Miller. He's done some work. You writin' these down?"

I did so in pencil on the back of the manila folder fat with dubious pleadings on behalf of horny psychopaths.

"Who are these guys?"

"Cons. Some good inside men. Cat burglars. Some setters."

"Where are they?"

"Hell do I know. They ain't in here, that's all."

"Would EX-CON know?"

"Hey, go fish. I tol' you too much already."

I nodded, finished writing.

"The fire bother you? The Tigers and all?" I asked.

"Oh, yeah. Hey, I was awake all night," he said, and stuck his tongue in his cheek like a chaw of Red Man. I wanted to tear the eyebrows off his forehead.

"Okay," I said. "You helped me. I'll do what I can for you. Your address on this?"

"All the numbers," he said.

We both stood up. Barretti picked up the rest of his ramblings.

"Hey, if you're shittin' me I'll find where you live," he said. "Pay you a visit with a penlight one night. Maybe wake you up just in time so's you can see your living room go up."

He laughed, and walked off, then turned back around.

"Hey, just kiddin'," he said.

Chapter 15

CONSULTING GEORGIA STALLINGS ABOUT A MAN, PETEY CONFIDED in me later, seemed like asking the queen of England about mud wrestling. Petey was in her twenties after all, a member of a generation that marketers have put an X on for lack of anything more descriptive. From what I read, this group of baby boomer babies believes that love stinks, work stinks, and life is not much better. And while I always thought Petey to be ageless—certainly much older and more savvy than her whiny, chilled, meandering peers—she was still occupying a body with just more than two decades of rings on it. Next to Georgia Stallings, a woman in her fifties who probably grew up writing on a slate tablet in grammar school and who appeared to hold disdain for all things sexual, Petey was a guppy.

But she was a learner as far as Dr. Cooper Nance was concerned, and Stallings, she felt, might be a mentor. While I had driven off to Jackson and the prison, Petey cabbed into town and the S.O.S. offices. Stallings in uniform—the gray worsted business suit and prim beige blouse—awaited her. Her frosted gray hair was curled just below her ears, and the ever-present cigarette glowed. The word *spinster* vaults to my mind, except that I no longer use that word unless I'm in male company in a soundproof ice fishing shanty in Northern Wisconsin.

Petey, for her part, had slipped into a dress, a high-necked, navy-blue belted number that tastefully adhered to her sleek form and stopped just above her knees. She added hose and a pair of blue heels that made her even taller than normal. Her hair was pulled back and draped over one shoulder. She was business and allure, not sure which one would come in more handy for her luncheon date with Nance. As for Georgia Stallings, it was business or nothing.

The S.O.S. secretary was alone, the phones now quieter, and the office door unlocked. She talked while sitting on the edge of her desk. Smoke leaked from her mouth and nostrils on its way to yellowing the walls. Petey stood across the room.

"I'm not sure what you want from me," she began. "Your uncle didn't really say."

"Kit's husband," Petey said. "Dr. Nance."

"You've already met him. What's the point now?" she replied.

"We had a talk. It was a bad time for him. And he was wary, I think."

"Wary?" Stallings said.

"Suspicious of me, I guess."

"He's suspicious of everybody. And for good reason. How did you get to see him in the first place?"

"Beeped him on his car phone. He couldn't resist."

"And?"

"We talked. I drove to their home. It's beautiful. He was subdued, but intense in a way. It's hard to describe."

Stallings blew smoke at that.

"He's a remarkable surgeon," she said. "The papers say 'cosmetic' surgeon, but he is *not* just some plastic surgeon doing eye tucks and skin peels on worn-out socialites. Not Dr. Nance. He is an expert in facial reconstruction. He's taken horribly disfigured patients—mostly children—and literally rebuilt their faces. Birth defects, deformed eye sockets, mandibles. He's a miracle worker, really. The before and after photos will make you cry, he's so good. He's on staff at Children's, at U. of M. He's in great demand as a consulting physician."

"How long have you known him?"

"About ten years," she said. "People don't understand surgeons.

Surgeons see problems and they attack them. They go in while the rest of us are still fidgeting about it. That's Dr. Nance. One of his colleagues once said about him, 'He may be wrong, but he's never in doubt.' "

Stallings liked that quote, and savored it with a draft of tar and nicotine.

"So it's not easy for him to deal with people looking over his shoulder," she continued. "This whole thing has laid him wide open. The police. The media. Even people like yourself, like it or not. It's difficult for him to face that."

A phone rang and Stallings ignored it, leaving it to the electronic message. She smoked.

"What was their relationship like?" Petey said.

"I don't know. I'm not a prying person. Before he married her, medicine was his whole life. He would operate at dawn and be in his office until eight at night. Six, seven days a week, whatever it took. He's a dedicated man. He's been that way all his life."

"How'd Kit squeeze herself in?"

"It was her third marriage, the doctor's first," Stallings answered. "She met him at a benefit while she was on the arm of her second husband."

"He was how old—fifty-some when they married?" Petey said.

"Fifty-two. She was thirty-five. Two teenaged children. She gave her ex-husband custody and moved in with Dr. Nance."

She recited the details like a manager giving his lineup.

"I take it you weren't too hot on the relationship?"

Stallings waved through a cloud of smoke.

"It wasn't any of my business. I worked for them and they never once asked my opinion. I don't think I'd be paid more for it either."

"Did you take sides?"

Stallings stopped the bellows at that.

"Look, I can see what you're doing," she said. "You're a good digger and that's what you're supposed to be. But include me out, as the saying goes. I worked for Dr. Nance, and when he closed his office I came here. Everything's changed now. I don't know if we can survive here much longer. There's a lot of anger out there. The calls I'm getting. At first they all were about the fire. Now all they want to talk about is Kit and Al Shaw. That's very upsetting to me, and it's not why I'm here."

"Should I be careful of Dr. Nance?" Petey asked.

"Careful? Why? He called to see you again, is that right? I mean, *he* made the overture to *you*?"

"For sure," Petey said. "He said he thought he'd been short with me the first time around."

"Well, good for you," she said. "He's a nice man. I feel awful for him. In a perfect world, nothing would take Dr. Nance away from his work."

"But nice men aren't always nice men," Petey said.

"Don't be silly," Stallings said.

A phone rang again, and this time Stallings answered it. She seemed interested in the call, certainly more interested than she was in Petey's inquiries. Petey took the opportunity to wave and slip out.

Her Swatch watch told her she had a half hour before her rendezvous, so Petey decided to prowl downtown Detroit. It was clear but cool, and she put on a pair of Ray-Bans. She was wearing a trench coat, and she was glad she was. Walking down Shelby to Congress, she turned the corner and a spear of reflected sunlight caught her eye. She quickly looked over her shoulder to see a golden wheel cover and a rumor of a black car body, then it was gone in traffic. Almost immediately, as if she had expected it, she smelled a tail. She crossed the street and animatedly motioned for a taxi.

She found one, a boxy new yellow cab driven by a young black, and she hopped in the backseat and told him to take off. But where? The hack drove like a tourist down Larned, over to Randolph. The stick was up and the meter ticking. Petey looked through the back window and spotted the black BMW, the Glo-Coat doing its stuff in the midday sun, about four cars behind hers.

"The produce markets, okay?" she finally said. In Chicago one of her favorite places was the Randolph Street markets, the wholesale produce, fish, and poultry outlets. Every big city has a version of it, or so she hoped.

"Eastern Market. No problem, ma'am," the hack said, as if Petey looked like she was in the mood for a crate of burpless cucumbers.

He swung over to Russell and then past streets named Riopelle, Dequindere, and Napoleon. He drove into a labyrinth of railroad tracks and warehouses with giant overhead doors and loading docks stacked with pallets. Forklifts moved around farm trucks and semitrailers parked at odd angles. Everything from abalone and eel to artichokes and zucchini choked the sidewalks. It was bustling and smelly and alive with yelling, burly guys in yellow hard hats. The whole place was as vital as downtown Detroit was moribund, and maybe just right for Petey's purposes.

She cast a quick glance in back of her once again. The area's busy lots and haphazard traffic provided some cover for someone wanting to stay hidden, but Petey could not miss James Holmes's ebony scurrier. Gawking at the loading docks, Petey mentally scrambled to come up with something, to somehow ditch Holmes. The cabbie slowed, clattering over railroad tracks and potholes, moving past the various terminals, when Petey realized that the sprawling buildings had front and rear entrances on opposite sides of the block. That was it. Time for the oldest dodge in the book.

"That building—the one with the pistachio sign—does it cover the whole block?" she asked the cabbie.

"Huh?" he said.

"Is it open inside? Can I pass through it to the other street?"

"If you wanna. That's Central Market. Indoor," he said.

"Check. Hang a left and pull over," she said.

The taxi was now on Gratiot. Fuchs's Religious Goods stood mystically on the corner. Across the street was the long white facade of the Gratiot Central Market and its mural picturing meat, fowl, and fish.

"Market's got a door on the freeway side, right?" she said, making sure.

"What is this, a test?" the cabbie said.

"Keep the meter running. Be there in five minutes," she said.

"Without nobody on my ass," he said, looking her in the eye.

"Smart guy," she replied, and made an elaborate show of paying the hack.

"Later," she said, slamming the door and strolling across Gratiot without looking to her right or left.

At the Starfish and Seafood Co. door she turned inside the market. It was redolent, a live fishhouse; young black clerks in earrings and with forearms wet and scaly called out prices and threw live, flopping fish up on the counters. Red snapper, buffalo fish, bullheads, trout—all were clubbed, scaled, beheaded, eviscerated, sprayed, wrapped, and handed to customers in a matter of strokes.

Petey paused for a moment. In her heels and trench coat she looked like a banker who had lost her way. Standing by the ice-gorged fish case, she could scan Gratiot Avenue, where she saw Holmes's BMW parked at a hydrant, allowing him a clear view of the market. They were now glomming each other, something, Petey remembered, from the "Spy vs. Spy" cartoons in her old *Mad* magazines. It's easy to dog somebody when he doesn't know he's being dogged, she also thought. Holmes probably worked with that advantage most of the time.

This was otherwise, and she quickly moved around the fish-mongers, past the Asian woman selling baseball caps. She took a right turn down a walkway between Joe Wigley's meats, where rabbits, hams, and ducks were hung for review, and Ronnie's Meats, where a hand-lettered sign told her Ronnie's ribs were NO. I. She kept going toward a far door straight ahead.

The smell hit her as she exited. Outside the door was a seven-foot-high stack of live chickens, ducks, and turkeys. From their wire prisons they clucked, quacked, gobbled, shat, and generally raised unholy hell in the few moments they had before they met their executioner.

Through the veil of stink Petey saw the taxi waiting a couple of doors down to her right. She hustled to it.

"You're cool," she said to the hack.

He grinned and bobbed his head, and lurched into a slightly illegal left turn toward the freeway entrance. Petey looked from side to side.

"The black beemer," the cabbie said. "Still idlin' back there."

Petey stared at him, then let out a laugh.

"Get me to Windsor," she said. "Whatever that takes."

In no time they were on the Chrysler Freeway heading for the tunnel. Petey settled, sighed, and stretched out her long legs the length of the backseat. A half hour, a toll, and a customs check, and they were in Canada.

It took the cabbie only a few minutes more to find Au Berge de la Bastille, a quiet, French country restaurant so removed from the grimy commerce of the Detroit markets as to be in another country. Which it was. She tipped the cabbie heftily, and he grinned and bobbed again.

"That black beemer," he said, as he added the bills to his clip, "ain't your problem."

She fish-eyed him.

"There been a silver-color Lincoln on us since we left the market," he added.

"What?" she said.

"Wasn't cool about it," the cabbie said. "White guy. Pulled up 'bout a block back."

Petey exhaled, now not sure of what was going on.

"Town car, case you interested."

"Thanks," she said.

"Whatever you into, babe," the cabbie said as he put the taxi in gear, "be some kind of popular shit."

She did not respond, and the cab pulled away. Moments later she was perched at the bar working on a smug Chardonnay.

At noon the doctor walked in. You couldn't miss him, and nobody at the front of the restaurant did. Not the thick silver hair combed back from his forehead. Not the tanned, clean-shaven, blemish-free skin or the Redford chin. Not the black, double-breasted Donna Karan suit or the white, collarless crew-neck shirt that he casually wore beneath it. Not the Rolex that slunk on his wrist or the four-hundred-dollar hand-stitched alligator shoes. He went six-two, no more than one eighty-five, and if you did not know what had befallen him in the past week, you would have taken him for a Gary Cooper in his *High Noon* days.

He sidled over to Pete like a rake in progress. Smiling, a grasp of her hand, instructions to the barkeep for a martini stirred, not shaken, no olive, and he slid onto the cushioned stool. This was hardly the same troubled, morose surgeon Petey had encountered in the Grosse Pointe Park mansion. She smiled back, played with her hair, and madly tried to reshuffle her game plan.

"Navy looks great on you," he said.

It was a good opener; where was she?

"I'm not sure if I was decent to you the other night," he went on, "and I wanted to apologize. That's why I invited you here. Not only that, but before you, I'd never met a woman named Petrinella."

He joined his glass to hers and bit into his martini. He'd chewed them before. He'd been in bars with beautiful women before. Petey flashed on Kit Gleason, mother of two, wallowing in a second bad marriage, and getting the same toast. In no time she was a woman run mad.

"No olive?" Petey said.

"Never," he said.

"Smart," she said.

"Hmmm?"

"Sherwood Anderson, the novelist—" she began.

"*Winesburg, Ohio*," he said.

"Yes. . . ." she continued. "He swallowed his martini's toothpick, developed peritonitis, and died."

"Is that right!" he said. "I *must* remember that."

Petey congratulated herself. She'd never used the Anderson nugget before. Not many people drink martinis nowadays.

"Okay, smarty," he returned, "do you know of your namesake?"

"Petrinella?"

"Uh-huh."

"Eleanor of Aquitane's sister," Petey said, having gone to Oberlin for good reason.

"Indeed. She started a war you know, or, at least, an incursion," he said.

Petey lifted her eyebrows.

"She was about nineteen, a frisky lass to say the least, and she carried on with Count Ralph, who was thirty years older and married with children. Eleanor had Louis the Seventh get the marriage annulled, and Petrinella got her man. To make a long story short, an enemy of Louis, Theobald, if I remember correctly, prevailed upon the pope to set aside the marriage and excommunicate Ralph and Petrinella. Louis the Seventh promptly invaded Theobald's villages, set them on fire, killed hundreds. All because of Petrinella's lusts. . . ."

"Ralph must have been quite a swordsman," Petey said.

"I'm sure. Whatever, another pope came along and reinstated their marriage. Petrinella had three children with Ralph, two girls, and a boy, Ralph junior. He was a leper and died in his twenties."

With that, he finished his martini. Petey was awed. She had been told many stories in bars before, but never one like that.

"You *do* read the classics," she said.

It was his turn to lift his eyebrows. They were also silver gray, but trimmed.

"I dabble," he said.

They sat down, with the doctor next to her instead of across the small table, and ate very thin slices of veal. It was a wonderful lunch. With more martinis, he did most of the talking, and though most of it was about himself, he was excellent company. Almost too excellent. Petey finally wedged a few words in and asked him about reconstructive surgery.

"I've done some of that, but not really very much," he said.

"The technology is almost impossible to keep up with. My bread and butter has always been cosmetic work. Liposculpting, dermabrasion, spider- and varicose-vein removal, collagen injection. Interested?"

"Should I be?" Petey said.

"Your skin is like silk," he said. "But it won't be forever. You might consider lip enhancement."

His hand went over hers, the one with the Rolex and a diamond ring worth more than most cars. He had not mentioned Kit once. Petey did not dare.

She pulled her hand away and took a slug of water. Two glasses of wine, she knew, could buzz her right into Dr. Nance's lap. Just then she swallowed an ice cube. It hit her throat and burned like they always do. She pressed her napkin against her mouth and swallowed madly. It was awful until it passed, or melted, or whatever happens, and her eyes watered some. Her brain also cleared.

"Do you miss your wife?" Petey said.

"Terribly," he replied, and took some water himself.

"So would I. I would just miss this person so much I'd be crazy with grief."

"You can't really know how you'll react," he said. "I don't think it's hit me yet."

"I'd stay busy," Petey said. "Clean the house, work around the clock. For sure, I'd stay away from people who reminded me of her."

"What are you trying to say?"

"I don't know, but I'm not sure I'm comfortable with your hand there," she said.

"Scared of me?"

"Terrified," she said.

He patted her hand once again.

"My whole life has been devoted to putting women at ease. I'm usually good at it. I remake them. After I'm done, they look in the mirror and they like what they see."

"Let me try on my own," Petey said.

"Just a professional courtesy," he said. "I see a beautiful face and I want to improve on it. It has great potential. Or maybe it's my way of grieving."

Petey wasn't sure she heard that right.

"You mean, you keep busy, is that right, Dr. Nance?" she said.

"Yes. I do keep busy," he said. "And now promise me this:

Let's not talk about my wife anymore. There's no place to go with it."

Then he put his hand on hers once again.

I was able to get back to Dearborn by midafternoon. Messages awaited me. One was from Marjorie on behalf of the commissioner. He wanted an update and I gave him one. He listened impatiently.

"Is all this going to tell me if Joe Yeager burned down his own ballyard, Duffy," he finally blurted, "or are you just jerkin' off?"

I told him to calm down.

The next call was from Jimmy Casey. He had not heard from me and he was getting antsy. I decided to give him some homework.

"Name of Mickey Schubert keeps popping up," I said.

"It should," Casey replied.

"How well do you know him, Jimmy?"

"Know *of* him. That's all."

"Help me out," I said. "See if you can find out what he's been doing lately. If you can, tell me what kind of car he drives. That sort of thing."

"I'm your man," Casey said.

Then I phoned Georgia Stallings.

"EX-CON keeps a file on its clients," I began.

"If you can call it that," she quickly replied. "Their records are a disaster."

"But a roster—they must have a roster of the men who come in or who they work with."

"They do."

"Can I see it?"

"I imagine. Why?"

I told her about Jimmy Barretti and his list of burglars and fire setters.

"It's a stab, but I'll take it," I said. "At least I'd like to know who's been around. I bet Al Shaw would too."

She seemed to buy that, and gave me a contact at EX-CON. She even offered to call ahead and tell them what I wanted.

"It's three o'clock," Stallings said. "They're probably out of there by now. The office, I mean. You wouldn't believe the hours they keep."

"The place closes at three?" I said.

"Well, not the center. That's open twenty-four hours. The office people, I mean."

"Tomorrow then," I said, and rang off.

I was tired myself, and quite ready to call it a day fit only for neutral spirits, cashews, and a loin chop or two, when my niece rang my phone. She was still downtown, having pried herself loose from the doctor, and wanted to know my plans. If there was anything to be done downtown, she'd meet me there. I told her about EX-CON and my list.

"Strike while you're hot, Unk," she said. She always ran my legs up and down the block with ease. "I'll cab there. We look at the books, and grab chow at Monroe's. You know, Bensmiller's place. After my encounter with Dr. Nance, I sort of feel like Marilyn."

"You're on," I said, and sighed.

EX-CON occupied two stories of a wide three-story building that fronted on Michigan Avenue just down from the stadium. On the corner was Lou's Pawnshop, jammed floor to ceiling with guitars and golf clubs, power tools and stereo speakers. On another corner was the Corktown Mini Station, a sort of convenience police post. The three establishments made for a lot of action, women and kids in the Mini Station, diamonds and high-interest loans bought and sold. Not far away was Deacon McGuire's community house, not to mention Tiger Stadium and the abandoned Union Station. I was getting to know that area real well, even considered running for mayor. The seat of the Volvo had scarcely cooled when I aimed the red bread box in that direction.

The front door was open, and Petey and I walked past clumps of scarred men and a few women whose glassy eyes watched television programs about serial killers and child rapists. Complete with toll-free numbers in case they had information on the whereabouts of the perpetrators. Apart from the droning of the televisions—and there were televisions everywhere—the center seemed little more than a joyless hotel lobby without rooms upstairs. But there were several makeshift cubicles with phones. A jobless person, we were later told, particularly one just out of prison with a less than stable home life, needs a phone and a number where a potential employer can reach him. Most of the activity in the cubicles, we were also told, occurs in the morning.

Right now there did not seem to be anybody else around. There was not much in the air. For a place that catered to ex-convicts, people who ate their young, the center seemed as sedate as a friary. Petey and I found the office in back, two young black women who were both named Felicia and who had fingernails like talons, and two golden retrievers that had the run of the place and nearly licked our sleeves off. There were dog hairballs the size of tumbleweeds on the floor. The Felicias seemed happy to see us, almost as if we brightened their day.

"Love that," they cooed at Petey's outfit.

They didn't say anything about my duds. But they were taken aback when I told them I was happy to see them still at work.

"Say why?" they said.

I mentioned Georgia Stallings, but soft-pedaled her opinions.

"She don' like us," the Felicias said.

We told them who we were, and what we were about, and they thought it was all keen. After a little hunting and collating, they handed us a folder full of printouts. Each contained row after row of names of ex-offenders who had come into the center. Many of the names were handwritten, as if stuck in as an afterthought, along with vital statistics and the date they left prison. But there was not much more. Few names had addresses, and those that did, the Felicias said, were probably unreliable. Perhaps the most significant piece of information with each entry was the name and address of a relative.

Sitting in folding chairs, Petey and I combed the lists. EX-CON had only been up and running for two years, but more than five hundred ex-offenders had come in looking for some kind of leg up. It took us an hour before we got three bingles: two Billy Jacksons and one R. Clyde Miller.

After some more hunting, some impatient finger slaps at a computer console, and a lot of rummaging through multicolored folders, the Felicias dug up the expanded files on William Buford Jackson, a Caucasian male from Ypsilanti; William "Billy" Jackson, a black male from Detroit; and Roscoe Clyde Miller, black male from Garden City. Georgia Stallings was right. The record-keeping in this office was as disciplined as the golden retrievers, and the pooches, at the time, were chewing on each other's ears.

"Any photos?" I asked.

"Used ta," the Felicias said. " 'Cept police come around after them shots 'cuz they were recent. We stopped doin' it. You think a dude come in here get his picture took so the police can have it?"

"I'm curious," I said. "How much does your office have to do with the S.O.S. office?"

"We're all tied in. Phones, fax, computers. Got a job line," they said. "She set all that up. That lady you mentioned."

"Georgia Stallings."

"Don't say her name."

"Mr. Shaw come around much?" Petey said.

"Did 'fore his problems. We miss him. He's so sweet."

We left as unheralded as we came in. The two Felicias waved. One of them pointed a finger at Petey and said, "Gon' do my hair red, girl."

Chapter 16

A THIRD-BASE COACH, A GOOD ONE, THAT IS, KNOWS WHEN TO PUT
his hands up and stop a runner who is motoring into third looking
to score. The coach is old and savvy, he's been there before, and
he is paid to disregard the heat of the moment and the fury of the
runner and be as prudent as a diamond cutter. In a split second or
so. Better alive at third than dead at home. Then again, a coach
must have something in the gut that tells him to wave the runner
on, push it, throw on another shovelful of coal, and hope the
flames get white hot and this dervish thundering around third will
pick up speed and force a bad throw or the catcher to shy and,
against the odds, he will score.

So I told Petey. She was sprinting around the bases and she
wanted to score on Cooper Nance so badly I'd have to tackle her
to make her stop. I'm not much of a tackler, and she was in full
steam.

"He was just so different, so mellow, so goddamn brilliant,"
she fumed. "He knew everything his wife was doing, Unk, I'm
certain of it. He's too smart not to know. He just oozes it, like
the wise-ass kid who sat behind you in seventh grade and knew
every answer and shot spitballs and never got caught.

"Like in that old Sting song, Unk, 'every step you take.' I'll bet he knew her every move, every breath, what she had in the bottom of her purse and when she lost an earring. I bet he knew every number that appeared on her car phone's printouts and which one she dialed more than once.

"He's so gorgeous, so suave, so articulate, so delicious that he can get away with it. He was like a wolf—he said Kit called him a wolf. Just waiting for her to mess up, to slip up or go overboard or make a fool of herself or get crazy or get in too deep with the wrong people.

"And then he did it. I know he had her killed, Unk. Think of it. He hates baseball and he hates S.O.S. and everything Kit's gotten involved with. She's got a new life and he's not part of it. He flips out when he finds out that Kit and Al Shaw are squeezing it, and he hires someone to get rid of them both. And drop a few kerosene-soaked rags while you're at it."

All that came after Petey had set the background music to her Windsor lunch with the physician. We were in Marilyn's, which was minus Al Bensmiller, who had taken the night off.

"He just put his hands on yours, right?" I recapped. "Just an affectionate grasp? Not a grope? Not in tandem with an under-table squeeze of the thigh or a pinch of your butt?"

"What's all that supposed to mean?"

"The conclusion you're leaping to," I replied.

"He was so oily, Unk—"

"Of course. That's his profession. But you act as if he lit your hair on fire."

"He killed his wife," she said.

"Maybe so, maybe no. Husbands of dead wives are always prime suspects and always should be," I said. "But what do we have on him?"

"Just wait," she said. "First off, I'm going to the state physician's registry," she went on. "See if they can tell me what complaints have been made against him. If he's ever been sued, that kind of thing."

"You mean malpractice?"

"Among other things."

"That does not a murderer make."

"But it will lead me to people who don't think he's so wonderful. Right now I need those kinds of people."

"Talk to your friend Holmes," I said.

"I spent half the morning trying to ditch him," she said.

"Maybe that's not so smart. If you want dirt on someone—and I'm not sure that's going to do any good here—he's the shovel."

She sniffed. Her exasperation level was as high as I'd ever seen it.

"In the interest of candor," I ventured, "and with the risk of getting disemboweled, this wasn't a pitch of woo gone amiss, was it? His advances, I mean?"

She glared at me.

"You *should* be disemboweled for that," she grumped. And she chafed and squirmed. "Look, Unk, he's a beautiful man. Edible. Like right out of *Vanity Fair*. Push me over. One pinky. But hey, wait a minute. This guy just buried his wife and he's mashing on me! Calls it grieving! I call it sleazoid."

I searched for a piece of asbestos to put between us.

The next morning we synchronized beepers. As long as Petey wanted to beat the bushes on Dr. Nance, I'd let her go her own way. I was on my way to Wynton Mercer with my names. We'd keep in touch with these little belt contraptions.

"What are you going to do for transportation?" I asked.

"A BMW," she said. "James Holmes's wagon. I took your suggestion, Unk. Called him, told him I was going after the doctor. He said right on."

"You mention his tail yesterday?"

"No. I'm saving that."

"Bad." I said.

She grinned. "Geez, I almost forgot," she added, erasing her smile. "Stupid of me, but I didn't tell you about another tail. Cabbie said a silver Lincoln followed us to Canada. He was sure of it. White guy driving. That do anything for you?"

"Nothing good," I said, trying visualize the automobile. "Silver Lincoln. Detroit car."

"Land yacht," Petey said.

Holmes was soon out front with his tail wagging, and Petey drove off with him. I've had better feelings about her consorts, but this would have to do.

I hied me to Lieutenant Mercer. They were starting to get to know me down on Beaubien Street.

"Barretti. Jimmy? The arsonist. I tell you about him? How'd you get onto him?" Mercer said. His words were punctuated with his little gasps again, although now I was used to them. And he was in a chair. I'd still not seen him stand. Wearing a dashiki top that looked the size of a pup tent, he had already broken his morning sweat.

"Member of the Mayo Smith Society told me," I said.

"Say what?"

"Somebody in another agency."

"Feds. Doesn't matter, I ain't jealous. What you got?"

"Probably nobody your guys haven't already pulled in."

"Don't be so sure. Names are names."

"Malchow—"

"Freddy Malchow? He's dead. Broke outta prison in Pennsylvania." He gasped. "Jumped off a bridge rather than get taken in," he said. "Last words were 'Oh shi-i-i-i-i-i-it!' "

With that, he had a conniption. I thought he'd need oxygen.

"Guy named Leo Rugendorf."

"Leo? The old mobster. He's dead too. Died in his sleep. For a hoodlum we call that *un*natural causes."

Again he rippled. Mercer the jester.

"That's a hell of a list you got there, Duffy," he said. "Sounds like Barretti pulled your chain."

"Okay, try these three: Jackson, Jackson, and Miller."

Mercer looked at my paper.

"This William Buford Jackson cat sounds familiar. Miller. Roscoe Miller. Know him too. Lemme see what I got."

He swiveled over to his computer, and with an effort akin to swatting a fly with a beach ball, he tapped at the keyboard. His gelatinous arms extended in front of him like melting tree trunks.

"Hey, Wynton," I said as he worked. "Why don't you lose some weight?"

He stopped midpeck and scowled at me.

"I like bein' fat," he said.

A few moments later his printer started sputtering with arrest records. We both looked at the results.

"All three're bad guys," Mercer said. "I'll give ya that. 'Cept that this Billy Jackson's in Ionia. The other state pen. The other Jackson, Buford Jackson, is this one. I 'member that redneck. Bit a copper's finger off and swallowed it. Last pinch was three years ago. Means he's back in Oklahoma or he's dead. Maybe that finger killed his ass.

"And then this Roscoe Clyde Miller. Barretti say 'Clyde Miller'? I'm thinkin' this is Roscoe Miller. Male, black, eight-eleven-fifty-three. Five-ten. One sixty-five. Light-skinned dude—I know him."

Miller's sheet ran two pages, starting when he was twelve years old.

"Gang banger. Burglar. Jewel thief," Mercer read on. "Pretty good thief. Carries." He gasped and wiped his brow with his palm. "Used to be two kinds of burglars, Mr. House. Ones that didn't carry weapons and ones that did. Miller carries. Put a gun in a baby's ear once 'til the mother gave up her rock. Family guy. He's comin' back to me now. Junkie. Was he a junkie? Lessee . . . no junk here. See this one? That one he whacked a security guard in a food store. That one right there. Took him in July eighteenth, '87, and got nothin'. But he did it."

"What sent him away the last time?"

"December '90. Armed robbery. Don't know the details. Unless there's a homicide it doesn't come in here."

"Your man say Roscoe does arson?" Mercer asked. "Don't say that on him here neither."

"No," I said, "Barretti said Roscoe could get inside. Said once he's inside, he could do it all."

"I'll buy that. A stone hoodlum. I'll call up a mug shot for ya. He's outta Jackson last June. We aint' run into him, but that doesn't mean he's not workin'. Guy like Roscoe works or he doesn't eat."

I scanned Miller's printout, the tables of dates, arrests, street stops, and convictions that amounted to a lifetime of mayhem and a total of eighteen years in prison. Some of the notations made sense, some did not.

"What's this?" I asked Mercer, pointing to a puzzling entry.

" 'Sentence adjustment. S.M.P.' Means Roscoe pulled some shit in the pen. Maybe put a shiv in a boy's ribs. Got him some more time. Happens a lot. They bring up charges against cons like everybody else."

"Coals to Newcastle," I said.

Mercer nodded.

"State prisons got a whole department does nothing but investigate inmate crimes, you know that?" he said.

"No I didn't," I said, folding Roscoe Miller's sheet. "May I have this?"

"Yours," Mercer said. "But look, Duffy House, leave Roscoe alone. He'll kill ya."

"You going after him?" I said.

"Why not?" Mercer said.

He wiped his face and arms with a hand towel.

"Where's Al Shaw stand right now?" I asked.

Mercer gulped air.

"On a bubble. On thin ice. Between a rock and a hard place. How's that for ya? There's a prosecutor stackin' a case against him. Says he's got a witness'll say Al was puttin' money on the street for some work for hire. Says Al's missus knew about his dippin'. That kind of thing."

"Whatta you think?"

"Always think dirty, remember? Shaw isn't right on this and he never has been, you dig? He come in here like he's Sid-ney Fuckin' Poit-ee-ay. I wanna say, 'Hey Al, look in the mirror. You're an ex-con. Give me some answers.' "

He'd lost his merriment.

"Personally, I think he hit the bitch," he said. "Hard. Mighta killed her. Then you got the rookie factor. Rookie prosecutor gonna make a name against the pro, dig? That kid down there— some *L.A. Law* woman from Wayne State—wants to make herself a name on baggin' Al Shaw. If she does it, she gotta name. Bank on that."

As I turned to leave, a uniformed officer entered with a breakfast tray. A stack of bagels and danish, a quart of orange juice. Mercer waved it in like a valet calling in a limo.

"You doin' some grade-A detection work, Duffy House," he said as he slathered an onion bagel with chive-laced cream cheese.

"Be good now," he added, pushing a bagel into his chops like a gardener feeds saplings into a wood chipper. "Don't go sniffin' after a felon. He got nothin' to lose. And you do."

As Petey was to tell me later, James Holmes was her eager Watson. He snapped up her offer to put a new press on Cooper Nance. He arrived hatless and sporting in a black jogging suit, a smart number that made him look like Sugar Ray Robinson about to do some roadwork. Or a cat burglar. Holmes could pass for a cat burglar. He was full of chatter and ideas, and he let it slip that if he didn't get something that would lessen the heat on Al Shaw, he might be out of a job.

"That gives me gasotoria," he said. "Bad case."

"Gasotoria?" said Petey, and hooted. Holmes put a Junior Wells tape in the deck and scooted into traffic.

"You got to the doc twice, huh, Petrinella?" he asked.

Petey nodded.

"I ain't got to him once," he said. "Sat on his ass a lot. He don't do much. Hangs at his club. Plays tennis. Got him a machine tan. I thought that was bad for a skin doctor. Likes martinis. Ladies. That kinda routine."

"You got him where you want him, James," Petey said.

"Shit," he murmured.

They headed back to the Millender Center, the site of Kit Gleason's hideaway flat. Holmes had reached out to a night security guard, and Petey wanted a shot at him, perhaps buy him breakfast. But when he saw Holmes, the guard did not glow. His eyes, behind dirty glasses, checked his flanks. He was maybe thirty, a heavy, humorless man who overate in the lonely early morning hours and had trouble with his shirttails because of it.

Holmes leaned over the counter and mumbled some wisdom to him. Then, after glancing quickly at the lobby cameras, he guided Petey over near the door.

"Man needs twenty."

"Okay, give it to him."

"I'm a little thin."

Petey dug a bill out of her purse. Holmes took it, rolled it up tightly, and stuck it in the sand of a freestanding floor ashtray. A few minutes later the doorman came out from behind his post, collected it along with a few cigarette butts, then returned to his station. Petey admired the intrigue, decided it was all for the benefit of the lobby's security cameras, and awaited her cue. Holmes waved her over.

"This is Larry," he said.

Larry, who had a narrow gold pin on his lapel that read LARRY, nodded. It was close to the end of his shift; he looked tired, and was not smelling very good.

"Detectives been all over him, so be cool," Holmes said.

"I'll make it quick," Petey said.

Larry nodded.

"You know the doctor? What he looks like?"

He nodded again.

"He came here? To her apartment?"

Another nod.

"How do you know he went to her apartment?"

"I know. Got my ways," Larry said.

"That's right," said Holmes.

"You sure?" Petey asked.

"Couple times for sure," Larry said.

"Al Shaw too?" she asked.

"Don' know 'bout him."

"How's that?" she said.

"He came in alone. Every time. Had his own key. I never talked to the man. Never talked to me."

"And you never saw him with Kit Gleason?" Petey said.

"Never once," said Larry.

"You got that straight," said Holmes.

Petey considered.

"Run it by me. Did he show up alone? She come along afterward? Before? What?"

"You never know," Larry said. "He'd go up. She show maybe an hour later, maybe two, maybe not. Sometimes she be up already and later he come in. Wasn't no routine to it. Not to them, but there was to me."

"You sure he went to her apartment?"

"Nope, never said that," Larry replied.

"Shit," Holmes said.

"Police did," Larry added. "They asked everybody on the floor. They all seen him."

"They say they saw the doctor too?"

"Don't know. I seen him. That's good enough for me."

"You're only here eight hours. Other times you don't know, right?" Petey said.

"I know," Larry said. "I know what the other guys know."

"When was the first time? First time the doctor came here?"

" 'Bout last summer. Maybe July."

"You can remember all that, Larry?"

"Man with his look, it ain't so hard," he said. "Plus, it pays for me to remember."

"You got that, Jack," Holmes said.

"How about Kit Gleason? You ever talk to her?"

"All the time. Nice lady. Generous lady. Every day is Christmas."

"But you never saw her come or go with the ballplayer or the
doctor?"

"Nope."

They left Larry to a shift change.

"He square?" Petey said in the car. "Or is that just twenty bucks
telling us what it thinks we wanna hear?"

"My man Larry?" Holmes said. "Three years square. Doorman
sees all."

"And tells nothing," she reminded.

"Yeah, right," Holmes said.

From the Millender Center they got on the Lodge Freeway and
headed out toward Southfield. Petey had located the Michigan
State Office of Professional Regulation. It was a division of the
Public Health Department and it kept a registry of physicians.
More important—and a fact little known outside the medical
profession itself—the office kept track of all actions taken against
physicians. That included malpractice complaints, suits, settle-
ments, and anything else that might be on a doctor's record.

Petey wanted to find somebody, she had told me, who did
not wear blinders when it came to Cooper Nance. And being a
cosmetic surgeon, she said, there had to be people out there who
did not like the results once the bruises healed. I cautioned her,
told her not to get caught up in a Nance-bashing campaign for
no reason other than she did not like the guy. Told her that she
could spend a lot of time and a lot of legwork chasing down
disgruntled liposuctioneers who could not shed a spear of light
on whether or not Cooper Nance killed his wife. But she was off
anyway.

The state agency was like most other bureaucracies that were
housed in antiseptic, airless glass buildings that made their em-
ployees sick, hummed with flourescent lights and video display
terminals, and were cauldrons of carpal tunnel syndrome. Other
than that, it offered Petey a clerk who apparently needed some
pathos in her life. Over the phone she asked if Petey had been
"victimized," a word that buzzed, and Petey replied with a the-
atrical quiver in her voice that she thought she had. The clerk said
her name was Kim and she would personally help her so long as
Petey did not show up on her lunch hour. Petey did not. James
Holmes stayed in the car listening to his blues.

According to Kim, the file on Dr. Cooper Nance was not ex-
traordinary. "I mean," she said, "we got that Dr. Death in this
office—the suicide doctor, you know? Next to him *everybody* looks
good." She was a mousy, acne-scarred woman of twenty-some-
thing with enormous yellow hair and enough eye makeup to put
her in a chorus line. She had spit up a printout of Nance's file,
and navigated through it for Petey with a sparkle-covered fingernail. Nance had never been brought up on malpractice charges,
but he had been sued twice in the past ten years. The latest was
three years ago, and, according to Kim, the suit had been with-
drawn, "which means he paid 'em off."

"Boy, that name sounds familiar," she added, injecting the eraser
end of her pencil five inches into her hairdo in order to scratch
her scalp.

"I can get the plaintive for ya," she said. "I can get anything."

Petey urged her on.

"What'd he do to ya?" Kim said.

"You don't wanna know," Petey said.

Kim lifted her eyes and made a face as if she already did. She
returned more paper, the identity of the plaintive—a woman with
a tricky Polish surname who lived in Livonia—her attorney, and
a history of the filing. Petey said it was just what she needed, and
she reached over the counter and squeezed Kim's hands.

"Go get 'im," Kim said.

She returned to Holmes, who was doing the hand jive and bongo
variations on his steering wheel to a new Junior Wells tape he had
just picked up in a sound store across the mall.

"Pay dirt," Petey said.

With the help of directory assistance, the woman in Livonia was
not hard to find. Petey called from a phone in a Laundromat and
got an answering machine. She called every ten minutes for an
hour, but never connected. It might go that way for the rest of
the day, she said to Holmes.

"Fact of my life," he said. "Lotta time I be sittin' and waitin'.
Gotta have tapes to get ya through."

On the floor in back he had a case of fifty, a rhythm-and-blues
hall of fame.

"Roscoe Clyde Miller? Ever heard of him?" I asked.

John Cronin, my FBI agent, drew a blank. He went to the

computer, found a dozen Millers in it, and called me an hour later.

"Hard *not* to be in this machine," he said, "but I can't give you much on Roscoe Clyde Miller from what I see here. I got a book on a guy named Floyd Miller. Ran a hell of an airline scam before they put him away, but not much on your Roscoe individual."

I tried Al Bensmiller. He was warmer, and he did not even have a computer to go to.

"Light-skinned, squirrelly prick. Jewel thief. Home invader."

I read to him from Miller's sheet.

"That's the creep. Woman had a diamond ring—"

"Miller put the gun to the baby's ear," I interrupted.

"Oh, yeah. He's comin' in strong now," Bensmiller said. "Mercer got him?"

"Not yet," I said.

"Don't you try," he said.

"If I do, I'll call you, Al."

He laughed. "Hey, Duffy, you do that. I'm serious. I'm bored as hell in this place. Still got a license to carry. I'd love to help you out."

"You serious?" I said.

"Think I am," Bensmiller said.

There was a loaded silence on the line.

"By the way," Bensmiller finally said, "was Miller in Jackson with Al Shaw? Be interesting to find out."

That was easy, and after I hung up, I checked Miller's printout. From what it said, and from what I knew of Shaw's background, their stretches at S.M.P. overlapped by six months. That intrigued me, and for the next hour I dialed my way through the Michigan state bureaucracy until I found someone who directed me to the office of prison investigations. It took several calls before I got to the voice mail of the gentleman who covered Jackson, but it finally happened. His name was Jerome Cheech, and after he gave his message, he thanked me for calling him and wished me a "nice day in freedom." I guess toilers in the penal colony tend to think that way.

Petey got bored and beeped me. She and Holmes were reluctant to leave the suburbs without making contact with the woman in Livonia.

"James wants to talk to you," she said.

"Say, Uncle Duffy," Holmes started in, muffled. He spoke as if three guys were trying to listen in. "My lady Petrinella here says you seek a cat named Miller. That be Roscoe, then I heard of the man. Run across him. Think I know him. Can't be sure."

"Which is it, James?"

"You know the Pennant Bar? On Lafayette? You don't know the Pennant Bar," he said. "Used to be my office. Man at the bar took in goods, VCRs, Bulovas, you dig? Cats brought him stuff. Man named Roscoe used to come in. One time I said to him, 'You ever know Roscoe be what gangsters used to call a firearm?' He say no, he didn't know that."

"Thin guy? Light-skinned?"

"Sounds cool."

"Pennant Bar still there?"

"Yeah. The goods man ain't. He went on vacation to Jack City."

"Whataya suggest, James?"

"Deacon?"

"McGuire?" I said. "Great, I've been dying to visit him again."

"Up to you, Uncle Duffy. Deacon used to run with those cats." I hemmed.

"What's this *Uncle Duffy* stuff, James?"

He made some bemused noises.

"My attempt at racial harmony," he said. "Then again, don't get a big head. I call all cats uncle."

"Take care of my niece," I said.

Near ten o'clock that night, Petey finally got a human instead of a machine on the line in Livonia.

"Who told you about me?" the woman said. Her name was Dziedzic, and after a few tentative replies to Petey's inquiries, she let her tongue fly.

"I have a friend who's a hairdresser—" Petey began, having rehearsed the line.

"Oh, Georgette, of course," the woman said. "I thought Dr. Nance was retired. The news, I mean, you know what happened to his wife? Wasn't that awful? I don't feel sorry for him, the asshole. I feel sorry for *her*. But they all said he was retired."

"My case was last year—" Petey offered, but she didn't have to.

"Takes *forever*. You don't have to tell me. And the lawyers get it all. It was really my daughter's case, you know. Emily was eighteen. She's twenty-three now. He did a chemical peel. She nearly died right on the table. Went into shock. Let me tell you, he was just damn lucky."

Petey let Mrs. Dziedzic spout. She'd tapped a gusher.

"What'd he do to you?" she went on. "Let me guess. Liposuction. I mean, pardon me, 'cuz I've never seen you, but he was big on liposuction."

"Liposculpture—"

"Yes, yes! That's what he wanted to do on Emily, that asshole. Liposculpture. It's really gross. Like they use a vacuum cleaner. Pathetic. We settled because my attorney said it would take eight years to go to court. Eight years! He could be dead in eight years, that asshole. Maybe not. He takes care of himself. He's real good-looking. I don't have to tell you. Liposculpture, huh?"

"He was so highly recommended," Petey said, trying to move fast. "And—"

"He's an asshole. He had an assembly line in there. Women came in there like cattle. Girls. He was doing all that stuff. Liposculpting. Like Michael Jackson does. He made a fortune. We settled for three hundred thou. He got off easy. I tried to get on *Oprah* about him, but they weren't interested. Maybe now they'd do it, what with his wife. You think he was involved with that? We were talking about it at work. They all asked me. I said, 'Girls, that man nearly killed my daughter and he didn't even know her. I wouldn't put it past him with his wife!' Her having an affair with Al Shaw! Can you believe that! What a winner. Those two deserved each other, the assholes."

"Did you deal with him personally?"

"Sure did. I used to be his patient. I'm forty-seven now, that was thirty years ago. That's why Emily went to him. Same office on Woodward. He had the same secretary, same everything. I seen that woman on television—the one who's big in the Tiger Stadium club. What's her name? She was his secretary for years. I remember her. I had real bad acne when I was a teenager. So what's acne when you can do chemical skin peels? Or better yet—liposculpture!"

"You mean Georgia Stallings. The S.O.S.—Save Our Stadium—" Petey said.

"Yeah. She worked in his office way before she went there. I remember her when I was going to him. Real know-it-all. Always called up the day before your appointment like you were too stupid to remember. And now she works for his wife. Or did. I don't know how she can stand the two of them."

Mrs. Dziedzic would have gone on like that, Petey was certain, long into the night. Petey finally said thanks, that she really was glad to hear she was not alone in her mixed feelings about Dr. Nance. Mrs. Dziedzic told her to sue the asshole for millions. She volunteered herself and her daughter as witnesses. And she asked Petey if she knew anybody connected with Oprah.

I was settling into the evening news when Petey knocked on my door to run down her day and compare notes. She actually had a reporter's notebook. She'd stolen it from me. Petey was dressed in Tiger sweats, a jazzy blue-and-orange-velour number with tiger stripes on the pants. Must have set her back a hundred bucks. She sat on the divan and drew her legs beneath her like youngsters and contortionists do as casually as the rest of us sneeze.

"Legwork. Legwork. You call, you talk, you try to figure out who's lying and how much," she said. She was run in, not sure what her day's work had given her.

"Gives you a case of gasotoria," she said.

"What?" I said.

She laughed, and mentioned James Holmes's malady. I did not want to know the details.

"Georgia and Nance go way back," she added. "Wonder if those two ever had a thing."

"And Jimmy Barretti is their love child," I offered.

"It could happen," Petey chimed.

I did not disagree. This was Detroit, the city turned inside out.

When the phone rang, Petey got it.

"He's here," she said, and covered the receiver. "Ever heard of a guy named Cheech?"

"Indeed," I said, motioning for the receiver.

It was my prison investigator, and a man who actually answered his phone mail. After explaining who I was and what I was about and how I thought he could help me, Mr. Jerome Cheech had a good laugh.

"Roscoe Miller, eh?" he said, and kept laughing. "That little weasel. Ordinarily I'd say, can't help you, sir. This time I can.

Buy me breakfast—I live in Romulus, not far from the airport—I'll tell you a story about Roscoe and Al Shaw."

"Tomorrow. First thing," I said, suggesting the comforts of the Dearborn Inn.

"I'll be in the lobby," he said, and started laughing again.

Before he signed off he said, "You made my day."

Chapter

17

At just after eight in the morning, a brilliant autumn sun sliced through the maples and oaks of Dearborn. Now in the second week of November, the sky was high and the air cold, and people blew in their hands for warmth. If you had some corn still in the fields, it was a good day to harvest. I made a note of it just before I showered.

Jerome Cheech called my room from the lobby at the appointed time. Romulus was just down I-94 maybe ten miles, so the Inn was no great detour for him. I invited Petey along, but she took a pass. I wish she had not, because Cheech turned out to be an albino black man and a sight to see. White skin, freckles, pinkish eyes—though he wore tinted glasses—beneath white eyebrows, kinky hair as yellowish white as a wool sweat sock.

He started chuckling from the time he spotted me, and offered his pale hand to me like a lost cousin. The girl at the registration desk was staring at him as if she had never seen such a sight. Cheech seemed at ease with the situation, for as we turned to walk to the Ten Eyck Tavern, he looked at her and said, "I get sunburned too, baby." It gave him a laugh.

I did not know anything about that, but if this guy still had a sense of humor with the crazy apples that grew on his DNA tree, then I'll be damned if I wasn't going to laugh right along with him. About forty, average height and weight, Cheech wore a tie and a herringbone sport coat, and looked like he paid taxes. On the way to the Ten Eyck Tavern, he said he'd been with the Department of Corrections for twelve years. Went to prisons all over the state.

"I'm surprised you found me," he said, grinning still.

"Can't miss you," I said, which gave him a charge.

"Damn nice of you to come to me," I added.

"I like this place," he said, "and you're buying."

He ordered eggs, hash browns, a side order of waffles, and a bowl of fruit salad, and in no time he was cutting and chewing and smacking away. He was a public employee and probably ate in cafeterias way too often.

"Roscoe Clyde Miller is one of my favorites," he began. "He juked more scams in the joint that any five cons put together. Everybody owed him shit. Everybody on his pad."

He went on to detail Miller's hustles, all of which were fascinating, but didn't answer my question. He got to that once he finished the waffles.

"He hung close to Shaw. Set him up, did business with him. You see Al, you'd see Roscoe. So they were in the weight room one day. Shaw's an animal, you know. He'd press free weights for hours. Roscoe, I don't know that he was lifting, the skinny little bastard, but he was in there. Anyway, something went down between Shaw and another con named Jiggetts. Jiggetts was one big swingin' dick. Doing triple life on homicide. They had words or something about con shit that built up over time. Always does in the joint. And one day Jiggetts just picks up a twenty-pound free weight and he throws it clear across the room at Shaw's head. Al's on his back bench pressing and never sees it coming. Woulda hit him in the head and woulda killed him or turned him goofy. Roscoe sees it coming and he throws his arm out like this and deflects the thing. This is twenty pounds of pig iron now. Busted Roscoe's forearm almost in two. But it missed Al. Weren't for that skinny shit's arm, the Detroit Tigers are out a big star. And Al knew it.

"That's the inside story. I spent a lot of time on it. You ask Shaw. That's why I had a laugh when you asked about Roscoe and him. Not too many people know the story I just told you. And you know, when I read about the trouble Al's in now and knowing Roscoe Miller's been out of the joint for a while, I think two and two is four. Just my opinion.''

He started in on his fruit salad.

"Food's great here," he said.

"Story's great," I said.

"Thought you'd like it," he said. "Know what happened to Jiggetts?"

"I know you're gonna tell me."

"They ate him. Yeah, he's gone," he crowed. "Word was they took him down, ground him up, and put him in the stew. That's what I heard, and whatever I hear in the joint, there's some truth to it. I only know Jiggetts's gone. There's a warrant out for his arrest, but he never broke out. They *ate* him."

A rippling Cheech chuckle consumed his last sentence, and he nearly spilled his fruit salad on his pants. An albino black man with a great personality and a choirboy's laugh. And the busboy from Lebanon stared at him in disbelief.

Jerome Cheech's story transformed me from a third-base coach to a base runner. Roscoe Miller was taking on a life of his own in this thing, and I wanted a crack at the guy. I dialed EX-CON. Miller had touched base there, and maybe the Felicias could tell me more, could tell me that they loaned him money, or set up housekeeping with him, or that he was selling Toyotas out the back. But it was not the Felicias who answered.

"How may I help you?" the voice said.

"Georgia?" I asked.

"Yes. Duffy?" she replied.

"Did I dial wrong?"

"No, no. EX-CON switched over here," she explained. "The glamour girls are out again. Don't get me started. We're tied in on a call-forwarding arrangement. Kit set it up. Except that I'm stuck with fielding two offices whenever those two skip out. Just what I need."

The tone of her voice could have fried bacon.

"Then I won't bother you."

"No, please. What's happening?"

"Some headway. Learned of one of Shaw's prison friends who may have done some damage. EX-CON client. That's why I called."

"Who? What's his name? You need his file?"

"Got that, but I need anything else I can get. These guys are hard to find. Thought maybe those two could help."

"Forget them, Duffy. I'll get you what you need. If you tell me what that is."

"Roscoe Miller. Roscoe Clyde Miller. I wanted to run him past the girls at the desk."

"Miller?" she said. "Roscoe Miller? You sure? I mean, I'll ask the sisters and comb the files and get back to you."

"No trouble?"

"Not for you," she said. "I want to be in the loop, Duffy. I'm isolated up here, remember? I need to know what's afoot."

"Save our stadium, Georgia," I said. " 'Sail on, O Ship of State.' "

She sighed. "It may be on the rocks, Duffy."

I kept working the phones. I did it all my professional life, and it's what I'm good at. I tried to reach Deacon McGuire but got no answer. I tried James Holmes and got a very angry woman who said I'd never see him again if she got to him first. I even rang up the Pennant Bar and got a fellow who told me he didn't know no Roscoe, but he just cooked up a fresh batch of boneless chicken legs. I hung up and wondered when I'd last eaten a good, cold hardboiled egg.

Then Petey knocked.

"I met an albino who told me a hell of a story," I said.

"Great lead, Unk," she said. "You gotta use it sometime."

Then she listened and was suitably impressed.

"It's the best we've got so far," she said, "but I still see Nance in there somewhere."

"We need a smoking gun, Petey. This Roscoe looks like he uses one. Graduated from the right school."

She ran her hands through her hair, which was loose and wild. She was wearing jeans and a T-shirt with something in French on the front.

"Should I see what Al has to say?" she asked.

"If you can."

"What do you mean?"

"If I were Al Shaw, I might not want to talk about old prison IOUs."

"Let me give it a shot."

She went off to make connections. I phoned Deacon McGuire

once again. This time he picked up. I could hear the noise of the community center in the background. Somebody was bouncing a basketball on his desk. He grunted when I mentioned Roscoe Miller.

"Still thinkin' black, aren't you?" he said.

It was my turn to grunt. Good old Deacon never met a white man he didn't think was Jesse Helms.

"My friend, the police captain, also a man of African-American heritage, I might add, calls it 'thinking dirty,' " I replied.

"Yeah, well, some brothers talk funny when they put on a uniform."

"Black, white, green, he just wants to pinch an arsonist and a murderer and maybe both. So do I."

"Why not capture the *souls* of black brothers instead of incarcerating their bodies," he said.

I inhaled and waited for the *amen* from the gospel choir. I never met a community organizer who didn't think he was Jesse Jackson.

"Roscoe Miller," I said. "I heard he ain't worth your rhetoric."

"Thief."

"Seen him lately?"

"If I see him, I hurt him."

"So much for capturing souls," I said.

The basketball bounced again. Deacon was practicing his Curly Neal routine.

"Ain't seen him since he got out," he finally said. There was not an ounce of timbre to his voice. "He's got a boy. Maybe ten. Lives with his aunt over on Lakeview, just off Kercheval. East Side. Her name's Doby. Find her, find the boy, you got Roscoe."

I nodded and rubbed my neck on my end of the line. People like McGuire were ball crunchers, scufflers, Punch and Judy hitters who fouled off everything you threw them. Then they hit one fair.

"Owe you one, Deacon," I said.

I am not a coward, nor am I foolhardy. Which means I may be in the wrong business. When Grand Chambliss first asked me to snoop around the ballpark, I asked him what would happen if some hoodlum put a gun in my nose and asked me if I felt lucky. That's a lot of asking. Chambliss said something to the effect that bad guys are not interested in ventilating old sportswriters. I did not buy the answer then, and I do not buy it now. Nevertheless, in this era of random carnage, I do not own a firearm. I hate the damn things. Petey totally disagrees with me, and she packs. It's a macha thing, I tell her. She agrees.

But I'm in Detroit now, Toto, a place once dubbed America's Murder Capital—though it has since been overtaken in the carnage sweepstakes by several other lovely municipalities—and numbering my days any more than necessary seems about as appealing as listening to old George Romney speeches. So I opted for company in rooting around Detroit's East Side in search of Roscoe Miller's relatives. My options were two: Al Bensmiller, the former cop who probably knew the turf but, alongside of me, made for a very Caucasian front seat; and James Holmes, whom I didn't much trust but who was pepper to my salt, knew what Miller looked like, and had demonstrated in the service-station parking lot with Petey that he knew how to think and shoot and at the same time. I had to go with Holmes.

James found me.

"Heard you called. Talked to the ball and chain, huh?" he said.

I told him my needs, firepower and otherwise.

"Wise choice," he chirped. "We find Roscoe, he ain't gonna ask us in for Hawaiian spice cake."

Petey stayed back at the Inn. She had not yet reached Al Shaw, but was close. I didn't want her with us anyway. Red hair, good target.

Holmes showed up at noon in his boxy little foreign car. It was polished outside and in, the leather seats looking like they'd been massaged by eunuchs. Holmes himself was in his black jogging suit again, black Converse high-tops, and a black leather snap-brim hat. He reminded me of a pro golfer named Calvin Peete, a nice guy with a withered arm who never missed the fairway.

"Anybody ever tell you you look like Calvin Peete?" I said.

"Always," he said. "Walk into Kmart, people say, 'Hey, Calvin.' "

Okay, it was wise-ass day, which was fine, because it meant James's brain was firing. His stereo brayed with some goof who sounded like his foot was caught in a lawnmower.

I shouted, "Got any Lawrence Welk? Liberace?"

He cut the tape.

We were off the freeway and hooking around downtown Detroit, past the refurbished Pontchartrain Hotel and then past Cobo Hall (built on the site where Bailey had his first circus, I'd been told) and the Joe Louis Arena with its huge sculpture of the pugilist in the lobby. A sign in front said that the National Evangelism Movement would be there next week, followed by the Nation of Islam the week after that. Kind of gave you an idea about Detroit.

On another one of Detroit's great traffic arteries, Jefferson Avenue, we passed the tunnel to Canada, the Mariners' Chapel (where wives of seamen lost on the Great Lakes mourned their dead), and the towering silver cylinders of the Renaissance Center. Floating along East Jeff, as it's called, we had the river on our right and across it, a full view of the skyline of Windsor, Ontario. Along the riverfront stood some nicely developed properties that spoke of an earlier, more prosperous Detroit.

"You know the East Side?" I asked.

"Know all the sides now," he said. "Grew up in Rouge, though."

"River Rouge. What was that like?"

"Ever run your finger on the inside of a kerosene lamp?" he said. "That's what. But we were all right. My momma worked the Rouge Plant. Lived in a house, had dogs and cats. Shoot, my brother Fennel had a monkey."

I figured he could go on and on, so I let him. It was his car and he'd shut down his music, so he had my vote. Not only that, but as we continued down East Jeff, he started in on Detroit. How it was the marvelous city of his youth, how his family went to Belle Isle, and how, as a young man, he ventured into the city to lose whatever innocence he still had. He and two buddies, he said, in an old Chevy, driving up and down John R and Brush Streets, ogling the whores who stood in the doorways, watching out for cops and pimps. The whores, he said, all looked beautiful, with giant Afros and exotic eyes, like the Supremes. Out of fear, or poverty, or both, James said, they did not partake, except in their dreams. And then they walked up and down Washington Boulevard, going into the Book Cadillac because that was where the teams stayed and maybe they could catch sight of Reggie Jackson or Frank Robinson.

"And you know who we saw one time?" he said, "Standing on the corner by the Book. All alone, like he was lost or something. It was Joe Louis. Thought of that just now when we passed the arena. I said, 'Damn, that's Joe Louis.' My buddy Kenny says, 'Shit, that's just an ol' man.' 'Ol' man'll whup yer ass,' I said. My daddy used to put Joe Louis on top of the pile. A hero to our people. Said when his fights were on radio, you could walk down the middle of the street in Rouge in your bare feet, 'cuz there weren't no cars on the road to hit ya. And there he was standin' there. All kinda gray, lookin' hangdog, and I'm too stupid to shake his hand or have him write his name on my cap. A car drives up, big T-bird, and Joe Louis is gone."

If I had a dime for every story I've heard like that, I'd be a change purse. Holmes's was the Joe Louis version, which I'd not heard before, and it was just as sweet.

Right after the domed edifice of the Conner Creek Pumping Station and Chrysler's enormous Jefferson Avenue assembly plant, Holmes took a left on Conner, went up to the first light, and turned right on Kercheval.

"Now here's a famous street. Street shot the hell out of my sweet innocent youth," Holmes said. "You don't 'member the Kercheval Incident, what they called it. August in '66. Changed everything for me. Cops came down here to take in some sucker on Kercheval. All of a sudden, people on the street gets pissed as hell and starts riotin'. Wasn't Watts, but it set the rules 'tween us and the pigs. Man, that was just a warm-up. Main event came in Ju-ly next year. Pigs raid a blind pig on Twelfth Street. People went nuts. Po-lice and brothers had running firefights. Lasted a week. Streets on fire. Shit, that was somethin'. Governor called in the National Guard. President Johnson sent in fuckin' army tanks and paratroopers. You got forty-five, fifty people killed, most of 'em brothers. White folks scared as hell, movin' out. Left Detroit a fuckin' bombed-out war zone. Ain't no more bombed-out city in America, Uncle Duffy, L.A. included.

"And you know what? We didn't learn a got-damn thing. Twenty-five years later, we got that Rodney King shit and that cat Malice Green right here—same po-lice brutality. Look at this damn Kercheval. Nothin' alive on this street but the crack man."

As I looked around me, I could see James was right. On the neighborhood streets running off Kercheval, I would see only one or two buildings on each side, separated by fields of weeds where houses once stood. Fields of broken dreams. Nature had through the years covered over the scars of the destroyed homes and gouged-out lots with its greenness, the uncut weeds running riot in the empty lots. But those who lived there at the time, like James Holmes, remembered. It was not a story with a happy ending.

"Whataya shoot, James?" I finally asked, nudging him into the present.

"Nine-millimeter semi," he said, snapping out of his reverie. "Packs fifteen rounds."

"You sharp?"

"Shoot the nuts off a squirrel," he said.

"Leave the squirrels alone," I said. "What are we going into here?"

"Don' know 'til we get there. Roscoe could be waitin'. Could be no sight of him."

He inhaled.

"You got Roscoe's talk fee, 'member? Two bills. No less," he said. "I go in. you stick your butt to the front seat 'til I come get ya. Kids devil you, tell 'em you Santa Claus doin' some advance scoutin'."

"Won't the kids be in school?"

"You never know. Whatever, Roscoe's gonna take your money. What he give back is your problem."

"Al know about this?"

"Hell no. Roscoe's my find. Or yours."

He smiled real quick at that. Too quick.

He drove with his eyes in a thousand places. This was the ghetto, sleepy at noon on a brisk fall day, few cars, few live faces. People tell me I'm supposed to be terrified of these areas, but all I see in the broad daylight is an old tired neighborhood and a few folks with bad backs carrying laundry bags.

"Dope dealers be sleepin', that's why," said Holmes, reading my thoughts.

At Lakeview we were at our block, and after a couple of lots that were a scrabble of busted concrete slabs, stinkweed vines grown amok, piles of tires, and a burnt-out hulk of a pickup truck, we were at our address. It was the only house on this side of the block: a faded red-brick, two-story with a long porch that had plastic on the windows and a storm door that had not weathered storms too well. An old white stove stood on the porch, and white-painted trim on the windows and the porch steps showed some attempts at keeping it up.

Holmes parked and got out, paused, and adjusted his belt and whatever was holstered under his jersey. He was not smiling, and there was no jive or fingersnaps. His eyes, those limpid black beauties, were working overtime, jumping, scanning, missing nothing. He skipped up the steps of the porch and tried the bell, then knocked on the door. Dogs barked. Tough, eat-your-throat-out barks. Still, Holmes got nothing. There were no heads in the windows, no stirrings.

He left the porch and peered around the side of the house. A white picket fence, thigh-high on James, lined the front and went around to the back on both sides of the house. A sign on the fence said: BAD DOG. STAY OUT. He went in anyway, which impressed me, but not before he had grabbed a tire iron from the automotive detritus in the front yard. On his left sat a gutted Chevy Suburban, everything stripped but the metal frame. In the back was a patch-work plywood lean-to that seemed to function as a kind of pathetic carport. Three more vehicles lounged cheek by jowl with the carport. The dogs barked again; they really seemed pissed this time. I figured they must be chained to the carport.

He was not gone three minutes when a woman the size of a dirigible came out the front door. She took her porch steps side-ways, one at a time, her caftan draping nearly to the wood. If I were not told differently, I was looking at Wynton Mercer's female twin.

She made the steps, huffing away, and then came at me. She was mad, her doughy black face chewing and scowling. The car windows being electric, I had to open the door to hear what she wanted from me. And she wanted something.

"Suckah in back gon git shot less he come out," she railed, pointing a finger the size of a fat date at me. "Po-lice come. I tell 'em shoot, they gon' shoot."

"Hold everything. Don't call the police," I said. "We're okay."

"Prowler back there ain't okay," she growled, her face wound up tight, her hands clutched. She was barefoot.

At that Holmes reappeared.

"Say Momma," he said.

"Don't you *Momma* me," she snapped.

Holmes pulled back, like he'd just had his fingers spattered with grease.

"We're looking for a boy. Maybe ten—"

"Be Tenille. His aunt live there," she said. "What you want with him?"

"Keep him in school," I said. It sounded good.

"Thas' what he need!" she said. "Thas' it!"

It looked like Tenille Miller and this lady had had some set-tos.

"His daddy around now. Tenille stay by him on Drexel, two blocks over."

"Got a number?"

"Ain't but one house on that side of the street. What's yo' problem?"

"Dizzy," Holmes said. "You make me dizzy, dizzy, dizzy."

I gawked at him. The woman turned and waddled back toward her house, mumbling as she went. " 'Dizzy.' Silly nigger gon be dizzy, I show him dizzy . . ." was all I could make out.

Back in the front seat Holmes grinned at me, then yawned.

"Don' make no ugly woman yo' wife," he said.

Since Tenille's address was just two blocks west of the fat lady's, Holmes decided to drive his immaculate BMW through the gravel alley strewn with glass and sharp metal objects. He drove very slowly, cursing the potential damage to his car as we crunched along. As we approached Drexel, we had a large field of weeds with a mountain of discarded tires on our right, and the back end of East Detroit Towing, a junkyard, on our left.

Holmes stopped the car in the alleyway with another curse about his tires, and then we stared directly at the joint facing us across Drexel. It was a massive Victorian structure of some past elegance, painted yellow over red brick with splotches of the original red leaking through. It was high-shouldered and square with a two-window dormer way at the top, turrets, balconies and porches, three chimneys, and dark-painted trim that had some artistic relief to it. The building went back so far that it almost seemed narrow from the front. I could see two or three windows boarded up on the south side of the house; the rest of the first-story windows were barred, and gutters hung off the eaves like windsocks. The phrase "the glory hath departed" kept coming to my mind.

A carport that had probably seen days when it housed Essexes, Packards, and an Auburn now held a couple of old vans, one with a flat tire, a hot-looking red Camaro, and a motorcycle with a sidecar, of all things. Grounds that looked like they once hosted croquet matches were patches of shrubs and tall grasses. A damn ailanthus tree grew on an angle from the north foundation. In all, the place probably had twenty rooms, and judging from the clutter of mailboxes in front, they were now cut up into a dozen flats. Down the street, in front of another field of weeds, stood a lonely plywood basketball backboard and rim mounted on two-by-fours, standing at about the right height and right on the street.

"This be the place, same MO," Holmes said, patting his waist.

He swung out of the front seat and clicked the locks before he slammed the door. I felt like someone's invalid uncle, sitting like a boiled shrimp in the front seat while the children forged my signature on my Social Security check.

Because the house stood alone on the street, with nary a garage or a coach house in sight, Holmes's approach was anything but covert. And this time he did not go up the front, which made me wonder. There were two side doors that I could see, and more in the rear, no doubt. He went around by the carport, past the vans, limp walking like a carefree meter reader, and was out of sight.

I waited, growing sleepy in the warm interior of the Bavarian motorcar. But I kept my eyes open, scanning the grand home and letting myself imagine what a sight it once must have been. I could have grown up in a house like this: Mother's literary club meeting on the front porch in gay weather, Father returning from his office in the Chrysler headquarters in Highland Park, the *Free Press* spread out on the floor of the parlor as I read about Charlie Gehringer and listened to Harry Heilmann call a day game over the RCA Victor.

The big house remained lifeless. I had no idea what Holmes was doing, but I'd been sitting too long, and my legs were stiff. I unlocked the door and got out. I tied my shoe on the fire hydrant, jingled change in my pocket, crossed the street, and replayed Harry Heilmann's home-run call: "Trouble!—Trouble!!—Trouble!!!"— and shivered with a gust of cold wind.

A loud *thwok!*—like the crack of a good line drive between the outfielders—resounded from somewhere along the left side of the house. Startled, I looked up to see a side door swinging open and a thin, light-skinned, bare-chested, barefoot guy sprinting toward the front of the house, toward me. He was running all out, picking them up and laying them down, flailing his arms, one of which had a definite firearm protruding from the hand. He cut across the lawn, heading for me or the street and field behind me, I could not tell which. Seemingly off-kilter because of the weight of his weapon, he looked in each direction, like a late commuter frantically trying to catch an oncoming bus. Except there was no bus within a mile. Just concrete and weeds.

It took no genius to presume that this was Roscoe Miller, and, in these few, frantic seconds, I held my ground as he sprinted at me. Suddenly James Holmes appeared on the carport side of the house. Holmes also had a good dash going, and his gun was out and waving like a phallus.

Holmes yelled—or somebody yelled—something unintelligible, but Roscoe Miller kept advancing, his arms swinging with that handgun, a weapon so big it looked like a fake, a kid's squirt gun or something. I froze, not knowing what to do or who to pay attention to, and in an instant I realized that Miller was again coming straight for me. His face was twisted in a grimace of concentration or malice or both. There was no time to think or wonder if he just hated my looks or saw me as a human shield or had decided that I had keys to a drivable car.

Suddenly he stumbled or stepped on something so jagged or sharp that he veered crazily, hopping wildly and painfully. He had everything he could do to keep his balance, and I half expected his wild lurch to cause him to lose hold of the gun. Instead, he pulled up, still grimacing, no more than ten yards away from me, and raised the gat in my direction. It all happened, as I said, in split seconds, and I stood there like a batsman in the lethal path of a hissing fastball, like Mickey Cochrane staring at the fearful chin music of Bump Hadley.

I saw only the barrel of that now-steady gun, a round black hole that looked like famine, pestilence, war, and death. And I braced, I know I did, expecting like an idiot to field whatever came at me. Then I heard pops—sharp reports like tripped mousetraps. Not explosions, mind you, not the charge I would have expected from that barrel, but pistol shots, one, two, then a burst of three and four—I couldn't tell how many—and suddenly my right biceps burned as if the flesh had been sliced to the bone with a white-hot cleaver, and I spun and clawed at my arm and its acid pain.

I was then concussed by a deafening crack, and I saw Miller's cheek explode in a spray of pink, like a detonated tomato. The blow spun him, lifted him slightly, then threw him to his knees where he twisted and writhed as if some unseen force were pulling his legs in opposite directions. More pops, and suddenly I lurched forward, falling, and I tried to break my descent with my right arm. No use. My right wing was paralyzed with pain and useless, and I tumbled in a clumsy heap. The pavement came up to my face like a slap, and I kissed the grimy ground. I tasted blood and oil, and I heard Roscoe Miller choke and convulse, then cry—I swear, he cried.

I lifted my head to look but saw only James Holmes's black form moving above me, his eyes wild, the damn gun still out, and then I started spinning, spinning, and falling again, swallowing my own blood, tasting salt and mucus, seeing blackness in heavy, smothering blankets that were forced over my head, so hot and damp, and hearing Harry Heilmann say again and again, "Trouble!—Trouble!!—Trouble!!!"

Chapter
18

Some tough guy I am. I passed out cold, either out of shock or stupidity, certainly not due to massive injury. I had been shot in the arm, one of those flesh wounds that missed the bone but tore up the muscle and tendon. It was an injury right out of the movies, the kind the good guys get and flick off like a gnat bite, then continue to shoot it out with thugs or Apaches. An hour later they sport a bandage, but no pain, no trauma, no need for rehabilitation. Mine, on the other hand, bled like hell, on the sidewalk, then all over the leather of James Holmes's front seat.

He had pulled me like a bat bag into the car and sped off to St. John Hospital. I rolled and lurched with his driving, and bumped in and out of consciousness. It was a loopy, bad carnival ride run by a prune-toothed sadist. I lay there, my pants wet from the release one undergoes when he's shot, stinking and breathing with Wynton Mercer-like rasps.

"Hang on, Uncle Duffy," Holmes said.

He put his big Harlem Globetrotter hand on my sleeve and gave me a clutch. I've always felt myself to be a liberal man in matters of race, of hue, of religion and hair style, and never more so than at that moment when a black man was my beloved angel of mercy.

"What in hell happened, James?" I asked.

"Roscoe's potted," he said, not taking his eyes off the road.

"Potted!? What's potted?" I groaned. "Cripes . . ."

"Dead."

"Dammit. Why'd you—?"

"Me? I din't cap him! Hell, whoever it was came up *behind* you."

I managed a glare. My arm was killing me, and I was light-headed and stupid, but I thought I still knew horseshit when I heard it.

"Roscoe had you in the hairs," he went on. "That's when he caught it. From a *car*, Uncle Duffy. Drive-by. Like to blew his face off."

"I saw that," I said.

"Bet you did."

Suddenly my neck was rubber. My head lolled back.

"Squeeze it, pal. C'mon, Uncle," Holmes said.

He gunned the motor and blew through a light as crimson as the seepage from my arm. The jolt shot some sense back into me.

"I saw Roscoe and his gun," I said, "and I saw you coming with your gun. Who started shooting?"

"Cat from a car," he said. "Silver TC. Town Car. This year's model. Came up right behind you. *Boom, boom, boom.* Then took off."

"Who shot me?"

"Don' know. Maybe Roscoe. He got off a round. Maybe the other guy. I hit the grass when the shootin' started."

"Miller's dead? You sure?"

"Blown away."

With that, he swung into an emergency-room driveway, and within minutes I was being jostled and lifted, and my perfectly good sport coat, now with a bloody hole in it, was ripped off my back. I do not know if St. John is a good hospital or not, but I do know that they treated me like a wounded pontiff. In no time I was daubed, dressed, stitched, swathed, and sitting uncomfortably with my right arm in a sling. I had lost some blood, but my own left hand had stanched the flow. And James Holmes's fast car had made for quick repair work. The bullet went clear through the flesh, leaving a clean swath that a young female doctor told me would hurt like crazy as soon as the painkiller wore off, but would cause no permanent damage.

Other than that, there was nothing more to be done. My heart was strong, the wound patched, and there was no reason to stay here. Except that I had no sport coat and no trousers. One was cut up, the other soiled. After I was grilled for necessary payment information, I sat sedated in a recovery lounge beneath a hospital drape while Holmes called Petey to tell her to bring me a new wardrobe.

"She's comin'," he said. "Sit tight." And he stepped out again.

I looked for something to read and found nothing. Suddenly I started to shake, involuntarily, I presumed, and I wondered if my whole damn system was shutting down. Which would have been embarrassing. Getting shot is not recommended at my stage of the game, but it should not be reason to forfeit. I slapped myself—in the face, like Pete Rose used to do with his Aqua Velva.

And then I sat back and napped, the downers kicking in, for I don't know how long. I was jostled awake by a hand on my good shoulder, and I opened my eyes hoping to see the dappled countenance of Petey. Instead, I saw the stubbled mug of a cop.

"Duffy House?" he said. "Take the phone, please. Lieutenant Mercer, Detroit Police Department."

He handed me a portable job, a nice piece of equipment for an outfit that couldn't find paint for its headquarters.

"House!" Mercer barked. "Where's your head? You locate that felon and you don't call me? Now you're shot. How bad?'

"Bad enough. But I don't have to stay here."

"You could be dead," he groused.

"Teach me a lesson, right?" I said.

"Don't jack me around," he said. "You went along with that Holmes thug, right?"

"Yeah."

"Where's he now?"

"I don't know. And that's the truth. He got me here in time to get fixed, and now I don't see him."

Mercer cursed at that.

"Check outta there and go with my man back to the scene," he said.

I could hear him labor. When he was worked up, which was now, his system went into overdrive.

"Meet me there," he added.

I handed the gizmo back to the copper and told him I wasn't going anywhere without a fresh pair of pants. He bought that, but said something about the lieutenant having little patience.

Fifteen minutes later Petey showed up.

"Uncle Duffy, hey, I'm here," she said, her lovely face taut.

She rushed over and was about to give me a hug but held back.

"You all right? James said you were shot. You look awful. Sit down. What happened?"

"Slow down. I'm not going anywhere," I said. "My arm's got a hole in it, but I'll survive. Where's Holmes?"

"Haven't seen him. Just talked to him on the phone."

"That snake," I said.

She gave me my new clothes and helped me find a changing room, and I soon realized how difficult it is to put on your pants with one hand. My wounded arm felt like it was out to sea until I tried to lift it. Then pain shot through it. I was kind of groggy on top of that. I emerged with my shirt loose and my good hand holding up my pants, because my belt was unbuckled.

"I need some help, Pete," I said.

Like a good mother, she finished dressing me. The cop stood by looking anxious.

"Holmes come back yet?"

"No. Should I have him paged?" Petey said.

"Forget it. He makes himself scarce when he wants to. And right now, he wants to."

"Let's go home," Petey said.

"Can't. That's one of Mercer's detectives, and he's going to escort us back to the scene."

"Tell him to get lost," Petey said. "You're not under arrest."

"I will be if I do that," I said.

She exhaled and helped me out of the hospital and into the front seat of the unmarked squad. She followed us back to Kercheval and Drexel. I expected quite a scene, one of those barricaded jobs with yellow DO NOT CROSS police-line tape strung from pillar to post to keep back the hordes, with a couple dozen detectives and evidence men pacing the area. What I got was two cars, a black and white and a beige dick's sedan, parked in about the same place Holmes had parked me. Only a handful of neighbors stood around. Roscoe Miller had been zipped up and removed a half hour ago. A sickeningly thick puddle of his blood lay congealing on the sidewalk. Nearby was a much smaller, thinner blob, which I immediately recognized as my own. It made me gag.

A detective in a navy-blue slicker eyed my sling and waved me over just as a third car pulled up. Its front passenger seat was all beef in the person of Wynton Mercer. He rolled down the window.

"Get up to the house, House," he said.

With that, his car pulled around and into the driveway, where it drove around the vans and into the backyard. That's where all the action was. A half-dozen cars were parked helter-skelter up there. Petey and I trudged up the walk, our detective shadow right behind us.

We went in a rear door that led into a back kitchen area. The house had once been a grand *Upstairs, Downstairs* kind of place. Now it was a maze of rooms and phony partitions. Little black heads peered at us from behind doors and stairways as we came in. The place smelled of bacon. There were cops everywhere, and a rather bewildered old black woman with a silver wig stood in the main hallway scowling at all of us.

"Who's in charge here?" she shouted, and when nobody answered, she repeated herself every ten seconds or so.

"Whatta joint!" Petey whispered.

"Back here," our detective motioned, and we followed him to a side room that had once been a parlor, one with a pair of floor-to-ceiling alcove windows and oak woodwork. A rococo plaster-of-paris rosette, no doubt once centered by a chandelier, dominated the ceiling. A blipping circular fluorescent light now hung in its place. The room had been turned into a single-occupancy dive. Besides the bed, there was a microwave and a hot plate, cans of food, a makeshift closet with a sagging clothes pole, and a TV. And everything was a jumble, for the detectives had tossed the place with no mercy. They were still at it.

"Roscoe's dump," came a voice from an overstuffed chair in the corner. It was Mercer, having found a tarmac and landed.

I stumbled over to him. Petey hung by the door.

"Arm? Or shoulder?" he said.

"Arm," I said. "And thanks for asking, Lieutenant."

"I warned ya, and I don't wanna go into it now," he said. "Look at these."

He handed me photocopies of what looked to be floor plans. They were. Of Tiger Stadium, the different tiers, the clubhouses and press box, the suites, the whole layout. I'd seen them before; they looked like they might be copies from the Olson Survey. Only these had been marked up with arrows and circles. No words or instructions, no handwriting or telltale remarks, but somebody had obviously pored over these things.

"Kind of thing a fire setter could use, don't ya think?" Mercer said. "Found 'em in the stack."

"Find a gas can or some scorched sneakers?" I said.

"He wasn't that dumb," Mercer said, "but I lay you money he's our man."

"Score!" somebody said.

It was a detective in the corner. He'd been rummaging through Roscoe's toiletries, squeezing the toothpaste and testing for phony cans of shaving cream. In his hand was an economy-size box of sanitary pads. Below two of the real McCoys was cash, an inch-thick wad of fifties and hundreds, and below that was a bag full of white powder.

"He's our man," Mercer repeated.

There were smiles and compliments all around, and I stood there like a second-stringer. Mercer got back to me.

"Go walk my man through it outside," he said. "And come back and see me."

I retreated outside with Petey, and over the next twenty minutes I reenacted the gunplay as Mercer's operatives took notes and made drawings. They had already taken statements from a few others, including a woman inside the house who said she had seen it all. She had seen me and a fellow dressed in black who also had a gun. The cops now knew who that was.

I was about to go back inside the house when I saw Mercer's car coming down the drive; it stopped and he motioned me inside. Petey was not invited and she went back inside the house. For the next half hour I underwent Mercer's version of water torture. He grilled me without mercy, going over every detail, then going over it again. His driver took notes throughout.

"Miller got hit three times. Two in the front. One in the back. Any of them could've been fatal," Mercer finally said. "Means maybe your buddy Holmes blew him away."

"He saw Miller was shooting at me," I said.

"*You* got shot from behind. I checked with the medic on that."

"So I was just in the way?"

"Maybe."

"Either way, I'm nailed."

"I'll buy that. I'll buy it even better if Holmes says it to me. Problem is, we got a witness can I.D. that thug, and we got a bunch of shell casings near where you said his position was. Holmes's got a lot of questions to answer."

"He'll be able to give you the same story I did," I said.

"Then why is he long gone?"

"I don't know."

"I do. He came here to whack Roscoe. Roscoe saw him comin'."

"What about the Town Car?" I said.

"Yeah, the Town Car, right. We got others saw the silver Town Car. Could've been a Holmes accomplice. But we didn't find any shell casings near where the car had to be."

And then he went over it all again. I finally told him I had had enough, that I was feeling lousy, my arm was coming off, and I saw no point in drubbing the hell out of the obvious. The detective was short with me.

"Then you git. But we'll see you again," Mercer said. "You played real stupid comin' here. Ever been shot before? That arm's gonna eat you up tonight."

He wiped his wet face and brow with a green hand towel.

"Think about it, House," he went on. "You got scammed. Your pal Holmes was workin' you. Stays real close while you go and find Roscoe. You dug him up. You're good at that." He took an intake of breath. "Roscoe could add big to the shit we already got on Al Shaw's shoes, 'cuz Al's got a history with him. Shaw had one job for Holmes: Take Roscoe out. Now Roscoe's in a bag and James Holmes goes AWOL. He knows he's a murder suspect. You dig?"

"So who's in the Town Car, Wynton?"

"Ain't got that yet," he said.

He drank from a giant trainer's bottle. He was full of supplies.

"But we will," he said. He belched and gave me the back of his hand. I awkwardly pulled myself out of the car, and he drove off.

Petey was in the kitchen, leaning against the sink. A young black woman with her hair pulled tightly back, wearing jeans and a Pistons sweatshirt, sat at a Formica-topped table. She was leaning on her elbows and seriously smoking a long brown cigarette. She looked war-torn, as if the horde of cops rummaging through the bedroom were an occupying army. A boy of ten or so stood in the corner. He was lean and caramel-skinned, his hair razored with diagonal designs on the side, a dead ringer for the barefoot guy who had come at me on the sidewalk a couple of hours earlier. He was staring at Petey.

Petey gave me the eye.

"Tenille," she said.

The boy checked me out like a scared alley dog.

"And this is Sheneather," Petey said. "Sheneather Butler. She was with Roscoe."

She didn't look at me.

"They gonna rob the money?" she said through the smoke.

"That's her room. Shared it with Miller," Petey said.

"Where'd Roscoe get the cash?" I asked.

She shrugged.

"Your room, your possessions," I said. "They show you a search warrant? No. There was no crime committed in there. They have no reason to be there."

Sheneather perked up at that.

"Drugs with it," said Petey. "Cops could call it drug proceeds and keep it."

"Roscoe ain't no dope dealer," said Tenille. He punched the words across the room.

"How much you know about your daddy?" I asked.

"Shut up, T.Y.!" the woman said. Then she was on me. "What'd you say? They can't be in there?"

"Not legally. And they know it. They're hoping you don't."

"You a lawyer?" she said, suddenly on me with real glue.

"No, but I know that much law," I said.

"You tell them . . . they'd listen to you," she said.

"Will you talk to us if I do?"

"Anything you want."

"Butler. She-what?"

"Sheneather."

I went back into the room where Mercer's detectives and a pair of evidence technicians were having a picnic.

"I presume you have a warrant, gentlemen," I announced.

They stopped in mid-ransack and looked at me as if I'd just fired a pistol.

"This is Miss Sheneather Butler. She rents this room," I said. "She wants to see a search warrant. No crime was committed here, as far as we know. You have no right to be here."

"Hey, jump back a minute," the detective who had found the cash stash said.

"No, you jump back, Officer," I said. "I don't have to tell you the law. You don't search a premises unless it's a crime scene or you have a warrant. You leave everything you found right as it is. Especially the cash."

"We can arrest her for possession," one said.

"Do it," I said, "and it'll bounce out of court faster than you can say 'illegal search and seizure.' "

I had them and they knew it. Sheneather and Tenille looked at me as if I were Abraham Lincoln. The cops lifted their hands, looked at each other, and muttered things not suitable for a family audience.

"Tell it to the attorney, fellas," I said. "Leave everything where you found it. Including the box."

"We're back here in your face in a few minutes, doll," the lead detective said. "You don't touch nothing."

It was a hollow threat. What Sheneather Butler did between now and when they got back was her business. Then she smiled, one of those shit-eating smiles that is cause for justifiable homicide. I wanted to smack her myself. I hated the business of that bagful of white powder as much as anyone, but it and the cash were my lever with the only person who could tell me something about the late Roscoe Miller. I wanted that, and this was the only way to get it.

The cops retreated, one of them dialing Wynton Mercer as he went.

"We're in your face too—old man," the lead dick said to me.

A few moments later the four of us were alone. The room looked like a rummage-sale hell. The cash lay on the bed where the detectives had dumped and inventoried it.

"Unbelievable, Unk," Petey said.

Sheneather went for the loot. I stepped in front of her, unwittingly lifting my right arm and grunting with the pain. It was starting to throb.

"Payback time," I said. "What you do with that dope is your business, but first you tell me what you know."

"I don' know shit," she said.

"Halloween night," Pete said. "Where was he?"

"Start earlier," I cut in. "Where'd he get those maps of the ballpark? What'd he tell you?"

"He don' tell me. He's lookin' at 'em. I say, 'What you want with Tiger Stadium?' He say he want inside. 'Fool,' I tell him, 'they got guards.' He say he can buy and sell guards."

"Halloween night. Where was he?"

"He go out maybe noon," she said. "Don' come back till maybe next day."

She was suddenly very smart. She wanted that cash.

"When'd he get the money? I didn't say where, I said when."

"Next day."

"How do you know that?"

She cracked a little grin on that. She had good features, but she was drug thin, and aging too quickly.

"You wan' me to tell you? You wanna hear?"

"I want it all," I said. "I did you a favor, and I want something back."

Petey gazed at me like Della Street used to moon at Mason.

"Roscoe do lines and Roscoe do head. He need money for lines and he need me for head. So I *know* when he got money or when he don't. And that day, he had hisself money."

"How much?" I pressed.

"Enough to play 'Feed the Elephant' and 'Walk da Bed,' " she said. "When we play, he's talkin' alla time and he say ten large. Cash money. Got it day after Halloween. I *know* that. And he got that much in junk too."

She cocked her head like a peahen when she said it.

"That's my man. Gonna miss 'im," she said.

I considered her. While she talked, Tenille was working the room. He picked through the piles, pulling up and sifting.

"You telling me the truth, or what you think I wanna hear?"

"Truth."

"How about his clothing? Did he smell like fire . . . gasoline?"

"Not Roscoe. He had all kind of clothes. Went out in black. Came back in black, but different black. He's cool about that."

"He axed me did I see the fire," Tenille suddenly said.

"What'd he say, exactly?" Petey said to him.

"He say he watched it burn down," Tenille said. The boy seemed sincere and guileless.

Sheneather lit another brown cigarette and swatted at her own smoke.

"Why'd he run?" I said.

"He saw the man! Comin' in back with that gun," she said. "Man's a killer for Al Shaw! Roscoe knew the man!"

"He said that?"

She exhaled impatiently.

"Look. Day Roscoe get outta Jackson he goes after Shaw. I was there. He say Shaw owe him. All Roscoe want is to go after that man. He say he saved Shaw's life and he want his due. Man with all his millions and he tells Roscoe 'Fuck off!' He hired that thug. He say he gonna kill Roscoe if he finds him. Get him outta the way. That man you brought here—how'd you bring him here?"

She fixed me with a dagger on that.

"So he knew James Holmes," I said. "He saw him coming and ran."

"You lucky you alive," she said. "I saw it."

She was probably right.

I looked at my watch.

"Police comin' back," Tenille shouted.

Sheneather went for the cash and the coke.

"Where'd it go, T.Y.?"

"What?"

"My powder!"

"Ain't there. Ain't no bag was there!" the boy yelped.

She frantically searched the cash, the box, and anything else close by. The look on her face was highway robbery.

"God-*damn!* They ripped me!" she spat.

She gathered up the cash and disappeared into the kitchen.

Tenille turned to us and smiled at Petey. It was the kind of smile a kid offers you after you buy him ice cream, and it struck me: Did he know his father lay in a morgue? Did he understand?

"You look like my teacher," he said to Petey. "That red hair— I love red hair."

Petey loved that remark. She looked like she wanted to adopt the kid.

"You want Roscoe's pants?" he said. "Got his wallet in it. She already take the money out."

"Oh my, yes!" said Petey, and she grabbed the slacks and rifled the pockets. The wallet was long and thin, and she slapped it against her palm. Outside, the detectives remained in their cars. Tenille stood next to Petey like an Eagle Scout.

Sheneather Butler reappeared.

"How we get Roscoe back? To bury him. How we do that?" she said.

"They'll autopsy him. Release him in a few days," I said. "You have a problem, you call me."

We left the house through the back door. I was exhausted, and

Petey gave me her shoulder. Mine was killing me. The cops glared at us, but I knew they would. It was cold, looking like it might even snow. I needed a shower and a bed. When we got to the sidewalk we heard footsteps behind us. It was Tenille.

"You comin' back?" he said to Petey.

"I'll come and see you," Petey said.

He nodded big at that, then caught sight of the blood on the sidewalk. He leaned down over it, and I half thought he was going to put his finger in the puddle.

"Blood," he said.

"I'm sorry about your daddy," Petey said.

"He wadn't my daddy," Tenille said. "My aunt say he gone too long to be my daddy. He was just Roscoe."

With that, he looked at Petey and, I swear, he blew her a kiss. Then he scooted back up to the house.

The wallet lay on my lap as we drove away. I fell asleep as I was about to go through it, and stayed in that state all the way home.

Three hours later I picked myself off the bed in my room. My mouth felt like soldiers had bivouacked in it. The inside of my lip was cut, and my arm ached.

Petey was sitting on the sofa watching TV.

On the coffee table in front of her was Roscoe Miller's wallet, the contents displayed like a bad collage.

"Score," Petey said. She'd heard that someplace.

I groggily went over.

"Two keys and some phone numbers," she said. "One is to a lock system called Best. I did some research. It's a commercial security lock. They use them in ballparks. Tiger Stadium for one."

I suddenly became very lucid.

"And the numbers?" I asked.

"EX-CON, of course. And Al Shaw, home and car. Kit Gleason, office—that's the S.O.S. private line—and, get this, the number to the lust apartment. And also her home number. That's the same home number as Cooper Nance, I might add."

"So Roscoe was right in the middle of it," I said.

"He got around," Petey said. "Knew all the key players."

"And suddenly he had cash," I said. "Ten thousand in cash and that much in drugs, if we believe his floozy. According to Deacon McGuire, there was ten thousand on the street to torch the ballpark—"

"And maybe another ten on Kit's head," Petey added.

"Damn cheap, if that's the case. And it's outrageous. People are animals."

"I'll bet Roscoe Miller knew who was in that Town Car," Petey said.

And now he was cold, grist for the pathologist's hacksaw.

"Wish *we* did," I said. "And I wish we knew the real story on James Holmes." I searched for my medicines.

"You okay?" Petey asked.

"Two things bother me," I said. "The hole in my throwing arm. And not knowing what in hell is 'Feed the Elephant' and 'Walk the Bed.' "

Petey hooted.

And then she would not tell me.

Chapter 19

"The lieutenant wants a piece of you," Petey said, "and maybe not one you can spare. He called three times. I told him you were in a a drug-induced coma."

"I'll face the music," I said, going for the phone.

"He's sitting on the Roscoe story as far as the fire is concerned," she added. "The TV guys don't have it yet."

"Then he's waiting for the long ball. Wynton's a pro. He knows what a big one like this can do for him."

"Jimmy Casey called too," she said. "All upset and crazy. Said it was his fault, he got you into this, that stuff."

"It's true. He did," I said.

"Did you put him to work on Mickey Schubert?"

"I did."

"Well, he got something," she said. "Said Schubert drives a silver Lincoln Town Car."

I shook my thick head.

"Of course," I said.

I called the giant gendarme and, I swear, his phone did not ring before he picked up.

"You got in my face over there, House," he started. "I don't like it when my people get blown off."

"You had what you wanted—the maps, the cash, the dope," I said. "Your men were making mischief."

"*I* decide what's mischief. Shoulda had you busted for impeding an investigation. Jerk you down here and ice your old behind for a day."

His tone was nasty. He was sputtering worse than usual, and I was glad I was not close by.

"Then we fight," I said.

He sniffed at that.

"I mean it," I said. "Ask your boys where the cocaine is. That big bag they found with Roscoe Miller's cash. When they left, it left with them."

He held his gasp at that.

"No. Don't tell me that," he said.

"I didn't make it up," I said. "You got some serious questions to ask your people."

"Who knows this?"

"My niece and I. And the woman—Roscoe's roommate. 'Cept I don't think she's going to file a theft complaint."

"More damn shit," he murmured.

"The girl talked some," I said. "She said Roscoe went out the afternoon of Halloween and didn't come back till early the next morning. And he came back with all the cash."

"Makes sense," Mercer said. "We heard ten large on the street to set it."

"She also said Roscoe Miller knew James Holmes," I went on. "That's why he ran. Seems when Roscoe got out of prison, he went after Al Shaw to settle some prison scores—"

"Shake his ass down, that's what he did. I told you that."

"Whatever, but Shaw told him to get lost. Or worse, he threatened him. The girl said Roscoe knew that Holmes worked for Shaw and thought he came there to kill him."

"She's got that right. You can testify to what she said?"

"Every word. To me, not to your people, Lieutenant. They were too busy tearing the hell out of her room."

"Yeah, well, I'll find out about that," he said. "In the meantime, we got a red flag on our silver Town Car. We know the deceased— the Gleason woman, that is—owned one. Far as we know, it's been sitting in a parking garage downtown ever since we got done with it."

He paused and made a chugging noise.

"But our computer got another one that jumps out at you because it belongs to Mickey Schubert."

"Heard of him."

"Bet your ass. McAllister's thug. 'Course, there's a lotta silver TCs around. Couple hundred in Wayne County alone. But I like the coincidence."

"Your people do good work," I said.

"Oh, now they do, huh?"

"You know what I mean."

"I'm still not done with you, House."

"I know, Lieutenant."

There was a pregnant pause there. It was almost eight at night. I wondered if the guy had a life outside his office.

"I didn't notice where the press or TV knew about Roscoe Miller the arsonist," I finally said.

"And they won't until they have to or until we're good and goddamn ready," he said. "You got that? Tell your niece too."

"Deal," I said.

"By the way," he said, "a nine-millimeter slug got you. Probably a Beretta ninety-two. Your friend James Holmes has a license to carry. But I'm sure you knew that."

"I was shot from behind, Lieutenant."

"That's a popular gun. More popular than silver Town Cars."

The scene replayed in my mind. Had I turned around a simple second sooner, gotten a sign or a tip or just a lucky nudge, I could have caught a look at our man.

"Would've broke your arm if it hit the bone, House," Mercer interrupted.

"Doctors told me that, thank you."

"As it is, it's gonna ache real sore."

"You ever been shot, Lieutenant?"

"Been shot at," he said. "Back in my leaner days. I hear it's not comfortable. You can tell me about it. Keep a diary. Do that, and here's another recommendation. No, call it an ultimatum: Sit your ass tight. Don't get in the way anymore."

The rest of my night was consumed by the carpet of darkness that the drugs brought on. I slept fitfully, jolted every so often by the spike driven in my shoulder. It was the stuff nightmares are made of, but I had none. No ogres of plots past presented themselves, not even the lady in Los Angeles who had sliced my ear, and she's wont to show up in the swirl of my coffee. I simply laid me down to sleep, too ravaged to even loft a prayer of deliverance, should I die before I woke.

Petey awoke and went off like a marathoner at dawn. In jeans and sneakers, a windbreaker, and her hair pulled back in that ass-kicking single braid, she put the Volvo in overdrive. She had the two keys, she told me later, and she wanted to know exactly what locks they fit. Not calling ahead, she drove directly to Tiger Stadium. She never said as much, but going blind into the fray is something attractive women can get away with, and she knew it. My experience comes from ballparks, places where people are constantly trying to get into areas where they do not belong. Pretty girls work them like safe crackers on old Moslers. Male security guards are like rosin bags in their hands. The rest of us are always questioned, always denied.

Petey drove over to Trumbull and Kaline Drive, and in no time she was throwing leading questions at the lone security guard. He was a young white guy, obviously bored, Petey said, guarding an empty ballpark in the off-season, even one that had recently been penetrated by an arsonist. He invited her to park inside the lot, which was a good sign, then he motioned her inside the small guardhouse. The proximity must have been enough to make him light-headed, for soon he was disgorging the ins and outs of his post like a double agent.

She finally asked him about the keys. He had the key ring of a jailer, if jailers still had keys, and he went through it one by one for her. He was a man who loved his work. The Best keys, he said, were to various inside gates and doors that led to such areas as the clubhouses, the suites, the Campbell Box, and even one for the elevator to the press box. That one interested Petey, because it looked like one of the keys we'd discovered in Roscoe Miller's wallet.

Best keys were security-system keys, he said, not ordinary house slugs. The difference was in their inability to be duplicated.

"Only special machines at a few places can cut these," he said. "And then they don't do it for just anybody."

"You ever see punch marks on keys?" she asked. She would have shown him the genuine article except she feared he'd want it, or ask her where she got it, or simply do something to complicate matters. She doubted it from this pudding-head, but it was not worth the risk.

"Alla time," the guard said. "Shops guarantee their cuts. Put a punch prick on the head to make sure it's theirs."

"Once saw one with a little *M*," she said,

"MiKey's," he said. "On Gratiot. They do all our work."

She was much obliged, but had to turn down his offer for coffee. He even wanted to take her on one of his rounds, but she begged off. His last try was in giving her a Tiger schedule with his name and phone number on it. Petey took that with a wink, then took off. Once they have what they want from you, the sirens throw you to the rocks.

From there she cut across town to MiKey's, a lock shop that she knew was in the same building as the Gratiot Central Market, next door to the Busy Bee hardware store. MiKey's was busy, full of guys leaning on a counter, waiting for keys and lock parts of every description. Security was a rock-solid business in Detroit. She took a number and bided her time looking at dead-bolt lock displays. She was the only female in the place, something that never bothered her. She feared only that her business would take time, which these harried clerks did not seem to have.

She remedied that by letting the shop clear out some before she hogged a clerk. His shirt said his name was Mike, which made sense in this place, and his pocket protector said he was the kind of guy who had long ago forsaken fashion for efficiency. He was maybe thirty-five, with thin hair on top and a bushy mustache.

"Why do I think you may be trouble?" he said.

She liked that, and gave him a thumb up.

"Because I got a short question that may need a long answer," she said.

"No essays," he said.

She handed him the Tiger Stadium key.

"Do you recognize that?"

"Sure do," he said, without touching or examining it.

"Has an *M* punched in it," she said.

"I know."

"Where would somebody get a key like this?"

"Where'd you get it?"

"I mean, somebody besides me," she said.

He threw her a look reserved for shoplifters.

"It's important," she said.

"I deal with a couple guys in stadium operations," he said. "Who they give their keys to is their business."

"Ever copy one for somebody besides the Tigers?"

"Rarely, and only on their say-so," he said. "I'd lose the account if I did."

"Would you know if you cut an extra key, say, in the last month or so?"

"I'd know, because I'm the only one who does it."

"And?"

"This have to do with the fire?"

"Yes."

"I'd be dumb to tell you."

"I already have the key. You had nothing to do with that," Petey said.

"Those assholes," he said. "Pardon my pig Latin. But their system sucks."

"Maybe they wanted it that way."

"Yeah. So what'd you wanna know?"

"Who'd you cut these for in the last few weeks?"

"Maybe a half dozen for Stadium Operations. The usual. A couple for a TV station. Did a couple for Save Our Stadium— the woman who was killed, you know?"

"She ordered them personally?"

"Well, a call came in. And they were cleared," he said. "I don't know why, but they're on the list."

"When was that? You remember?"

"Sure. August. Last week of the month," he said. "Did a couple of others too. Two Segals and a Medeco."

Petey smiled.

"So, was I trouble?"

"I can handle it," he said. "Hope you can."

"Whataya mean?"

"Hey, we're locksmiths. We know things," he said. He tamped his mustache with a single finger. "That woman should never have been in the stadium. Worst key I ever cut."

"I understand," Petey said.

"Hope so," he said. "And I'm not gonna ask you where you got that key."

She smiled again, realizing she was two-for-two this morning.

"And you're not going to tell me," he said.

She smiled again.

While Petey legged out those leads, I fielded one in bed. It was the phone, and a familiar jive voice on the other end.

"What say, Uncle Duffy. How's that wing?"

"That you, James?"

"Can't say. I'm in-cog-nee-to."

"You're in trouble, that's what," I said. "Then again, thanks for getting me to the emergency ward."

"I gotcha," he said. "I gotcha."

"Why'd you shoot him, James?"

"He was gonna stitch you, man. Who you been talkin' to?"

He was into his innocent yelp.

"Roscoe's lady said they saw you comin'. Said you were there to whack Roscoe and ask questions later."

"The bitch is wrong, Uncle."

"So fill me in, James. It's important now. Did you go in to hit Roscoe? Used to get to him?"

"Hell no! This is me talkin' now, not some coked-up sister," Holmes said. "I didn't go in to kill nobody. But the man's been to Jackson so I don't go in without a full clip."

"He got one in the back. That's you. Three or four in the front. From the Town Car."

"You got that right."

"What'd you see? Who was in the car?"

"I saw the gun and I ate weed, Jack," he said. "All happened like that and the car was gone, you know? You was down before you could check your fly."

He was right. Gunplay is nothing if not lightning quick.

"Car fishtailed out. Windows up. Gone. And all I see is Roscoe's head blown half off and you holdin' your arm."

"It's me now, James. You can come clean."

"I'm clean, Uncle Duffy! That don't mean I'm gonna get out of that fat man at Beaubien kickin' my ass."

"Lieutenant Mercer. He wants to."

"Mean man. Mean."

"Let's say I believe you, James. Roscoe's dead. So what now?"

"Albert's still hot. They think he hired me to cap Roscoe. And he ain't exactly steppin' up to speak for me, is he? Check that out. Heat's on me, fine with him. Muthafuckah! So I stay lost 'cuz I can't do shit from a cell, and Albert ain't gonna bail me. Meantime, I got two things you can check out. How's Petey? Boy, she be a peach, an' I love to shake her tree."

"Come on, James."

"Yeah, well, one thing is the doctor owns a nine-millimeter Beretta ninety-two. Dr. Nance. Check it out. That be a hell of a pistol for your law-abidin' citizen of Grosse Pointe."

"You certain?"

"Hey, Uncle Duffy, don't doubt a private investigator," he said. "I can look in your pocket and count your change. Man like the doctor puts it all on record. James Holmes, private eye, can get to the record."

"All right. That makes him a possible shooter. What else?"

"Damn right it makes him a shooter. Second thing, now check this out: My man Larry at the Millender says the doctor took out elevator time for this afternoon. You gotta do that if you wanna move out. Two to three o'clock. He's cleanin' out the place. You dig?"

"I dig."

"Good. They got you doped up?"

"Yeah. But I can function."

"I feel for ya, man. Been shot three times. Twenty-two in the foot, pellet in the hand, got a thirty-eight in the ass. Hurts, don't it?"

"It hurts," I said. "Worse now than when it happened."

"I heard that."

"Where are ya, James? Where can I get to you?"

"Low. Low, low. That's where. I get to you, Uncle Duffy. Lean on that face doctor for me. He's dirty."

Police and evidence technicians always talk about a crime scene being "contaminated." That is to say, a crime scene that has been invaded by paramedics, police, bystanders, relatives, detectives, or anybody else without evidence expertise can unwittingly alter or destroy important aspects and crucial clues. I learned that soon after getting into this queasy business, and it jumped out at me like a cut fastball when James Holmes tipped me on Nance's afternoon clean-out of Kit Gleason's Millender Center apartment. Once a scene is contaminated, detectives rue, it can never again be made whole. Anything lost is lost for good. The apartment was not a crime scene, but pretty close. Wynton Mercer's men had taken enough out of there to serve Al Shaw his lunch, and I now wondered how much Dr. Cooper Nance was going to remove.

I had to make a stab at finding out, at confronting the physician—whom I'd seen but once and whom Petey and James Holmes were rinsing with guilt. He had been seen in the Millender Center. He had access, no doubt, to his wife's key ring, which meant he could drive her silver Town Car. He was said to own a nine-millimeter Beretta. In all it qualified him to be the gentle person responsible for blowing Roscoe Miller's head asunder and ripping the tunnel in my arm. Which hurt more now than ever.

I dialed Petey's beeper, then I called Georgia Stallings at S.O.S. I got her recording, which said the office would open at noon. Which was fine. In the meantime I could get down to the Penobscot Building on my own. I wanted to find out if a certain Town Car had been taken for a ride yesterday or recently.

Petey returned my call from a phone booth near the stadium. I told her of my plans and that I'd dial her from S.O.S.

"We're peeling his skin back," Petey said of Cooper Nance.

I wasn't sure about that, and I'm not fond of dermatological metaphors, so I signed off.

After going through the ritual of showering and dressing myself with my shoulder in a sling, an exercise comparable to a turtle doing sit-ups, I was dropped off in front of the Penobscot Building by a young cab driver who pulled the entire trip with stereo headphones on. That allowed me to read the *Free Press*. The shooting of Roscoe Miller was reported in a page-eighteen column of mayhem which included: an account of a guy who was run down and killed by a man he'd just slashed in the throat during a fight precipitated by a traffic squabble; a murder in a bar; two people found shot to death in parked automobiles; two found dead in alleys; and another killed in his own grocery store. Roscoe's demise did not stand out. I was not mentioned.

I went inside the Penobscot Building and took the elevator down to the garage. It looked like every other subterranean parking lot except that it was a little more aged. The lighting was fluorescent but spotty, the walls seeped efflorescence. It smelled moldy and echoed every sound. Before I found the attendants' kiosk, I snooped around on my own. I made no attempt to be covert or secretive. I walked up and down the aisles, in and out between the parked automobiles. If cameras were watching, they easily captured my movements. My aim was simple: to determine if anyone could enter and leave unbothered. It appeared so.

Finally, I spotted a silver Lincoln Town Car. It gave me pause, parked there like a silent conspirator, dusty—it was definitely dusty—its smoky side windows giving it the look of a hearse. I could not be certain if it was Kit Gleason's, for I had never bothered to research the license number. Yet I figured it was; I almost willed it so.

I leaned over and cupped a hand around my eyes to look inside. Its interior was unremarkable as luxury cars go. The front seat was bare. I looked in back and saw an umbrella. On the floor, however, and I had to cock my head to see, was what looked like food wrappers. A potato chip bag, a candy wrapper, an empty cup of soda. It was the kind of refuse you'd find in your kid's bedroom and remind him of when he didn't eat supper. I gaped at it for a while, those familiar leavings of convenience stores and the American packaging industry, and I wondered if they came from Kit herself or the pack of cops who had vacuumed it.

But that was all, and after setting my imagination in motion with all the episodes this automobile could have been a part of, I stepped back and saw it only as the inert, motionless hunk of metal that it was. Without Kit Gleason behind the wheel, it had nowhere to go. Or so it seemed.

I retreated from the Lincoln and found the garage attendants' office. The two young guys sitting there looked like middle relievers in the late innings: that is, apart from a radio and a pintsize TV playing simultaneously, not many muscles were flexing. I asked about Kit's silver Town Car, and they did not light up at the mention of it. One suggested only that it existed, which was comforting, and told me where he thought I could find it. He was close. Neither individual had a sliver of an idea whether or not it had been driven in the last day or so. They were about as helpful as last year's scorecard, and in so being, I realized as I considered their supine forms, they were very helpful.

With that, I made my way back to the lobby and took an elevator up to S.O.S. Before I rang, I tried Roscoe Miller's second key in the door lock. It did not work. A moment later Georgia Stallings appeared. She was considerably warmer than the building's car jockeys.

"Duffy, my God!" she exclaimed. "I can't believe you're walking around. You were wounded, for goodness sake!"

"Goodness never showed," I said.

She put her arm around me and guided me into the office like a good trainer.

"Tell me what happened," she insisted, after all but forcing me into a chair. "The police swarmed all over EX-CON's files. Drove me nuts, and those girls were so inept. They were looking for anything on an inmate who knew Al Shaw at Jackson."

"Named Roscoe Miller. A thief, cat burglar, arsonist, maybe even a murderer. At least he was. What missed me killed him."

I went on to fill her in, from the initial tip of Roscoe Miller to the shoot-out and the silver Lincoln Town Car. She lit a cigarette and listened, shaking her head like an amazed aunt, mouthing an occasional "That's *unbelievable!*" The office phones were quiet now, the hubbub subsided. Still, Georgia was dressed for business in a navy-blue skirt and blazer. Her makeup was in place, her short gray hair freshly brushed.

"I can't imagine that you even went out looking for that loser," she added. "This is Detroit, Duffy. These people have nothing to lose."

"I found that out," I said. "I thought my partner was going to do the heavy work for me."

"Some partner. You said the police think Shaw wanted him— what's his name?—to kill Miller?"

"That's what they think. And I'm not so sure they aren't right."

"Oh, Al," she said, exhaling an impatient gust of smoke. "He's getting in deeper and deeper."

She recovered and asked me if I wanted some coffee, and I nodded, then followed her into Kit's office, where the machine was still set up. The office itself, however, was being dismantled. There were boxes on the floor, the desk was clean, the curios gone, and the photos had been taken down.

"Tell me," I said, "how often did Shaw come around here?"

"Oh, he came around," Georgia said. "I think he wanted Kit and me to run EX-CON. He once told me he thought S.O.S. had a dim future and that we should both work for him."

"Did he have a key?"

"A key? To this office?"

"Yeah."

"I don't know. Kit could have given him one, that's for sure. But I don't know why he'd want one."

Our words seemed muffled in the room's low light. I looked at the walls and the tiny pockmarks where nails had been. They had been daubed with white.

"Toothpaste," Georgia said. "It's an old trick for picture-nail holes. Paint right over it."

She thought of everything. I absently lifted a flap of one of the boxes and spotted one of the many photos of Kit inside. This one was with Kirk Gibson.

"Ever find that shot of Kit and Shaw? The one where he's wearing the old uniform with the tiger's head on it?" I asked.

"It's here somewhere," she said. "Why?"

"I'd like to have it," I said. "I saw a duplicate of it in Kit's apartment, you know. It jumped out at me. It was Kit at her best. She must have thought so too if she made a copy."

"All this belongs to Dr. Nance," she said.

"But with Shaw in the photo, perhaps he'd just as soon pass on it."

"You'd have to ask him."

"You're packing up. Is he coming in?"

"I'll have this delivered," she said. "He has too much on his mind right now to bother with it."

The coffee was good, but straight and black. No flavorings or creams à la Kit.

"My niece tells me I should wonder about the doctor," I said. " 'When wives are killed,' she said, 'find out where the old man was.' "

"She was raised on television," Georgia said. "She saw fifteen thousand murders before she was twelve."

"I remember looking around these walls when I first visited," I said, "and I saw no evidence of Dr. Nance."

"This was Kit's world," she said. "He didn't share it with her."

"Did he resent it? And Al Shaw, for that matter?"

"Maybe," Georgia Stallings said, "but wouldn't we all?"

The phone rang and Georgia went into the other office to answer it. It was a few minutes after high noon, and I still had not contacted Petey. I called her beeper once again and gave her the S.O.S. number. If she and I were to rendezvous at the Millender Center—and I surely wanted to—then we had to make contact soon.

I finished my coffee and Georgia returned.

"You have a lot of guts," she said.

"No I don't."

"If anybody ever shot at me, and then drove away, I'd be scared out of my mind."

"I'm not exactly smug. I would like to know who was driving that Town Car."

"Like Kit's, you're thinking," she said.

"Yes," I said. "And also like one belonging to a fellow who I've learned is a right-hand man to Sport McAllister."

"Mickey Schubert," Georgia said.

"That's him."

"Scum. Hustler. Now a murderer," she said.

"The kind of a guy who would hire an ex-con to torch his boss's ballpark, then pick him off before he talks?"

"Now you have an insight into ownership," Georgia said.

The phone rang, and she retreated once again.

"For you," she called from the outer office.

I picked up.

"Unk," Petey said, "my beeper's overheated from your calls."

"At least it works," I said, and told her what James Holmes had said about Dr. Nance and moving day.

"I think we should meet him in the lobby," I added, "so let's have lunch and get over there a few minutes before two."

"What's to say James doesn't show up too?" she said.

"Nothing. And that's what I'm afraid of," I said.

We synchronized watches, and agreed to meet for a hot dog at Gus's Coney Island, just down the street from where I was.

I lingered a little before I left S.O.S. The *Free Press* had run another article on the stadium's fire damage and what the engineers were now saying. Georgia fumed about Yeager's blind insistence on playing in Pontiac next year.

Before I left, I swallowed another dose of pills.

"Those don't interact negatively with caffeine, do they?" Georgia asked.

"Just my luck," I said.

"Just wondering—I'm an old nurse," she said.

"Old nurses never die . . ." I said.

"They just lose their patience," she finished.

I laughed, and she told me to be careful, and, like a good nurse, told me to take aspirin and call her in the morning.

Chapter
20

I WALKED OUT OF THE PENOBSCOT BUILDING AND ONTO THE SIDE-walks of Fort Street. The sky was the color of the sidewalks and it was cold. November in lower Michigan is occasionally crisp and invigorating, but most of time it makes your teeth clatter under a too-thin jacket, your illusion that winter is not here yet. Today was one of those. I grew up in weather like this—drab, biting days with air you could taste, offering no excuse to gambol or shirk business. It is no wonder to me that men and women in this city made wheels and chassis and motors all those years. The climate told you to stay inside and get something done. Three shifts' worth.

I walked over to Cadillac Square and turned on Randolph. The pills were kicking in and my shoulder was flattening out, and I walked with my head down and my mind elsewhere. *Elsewhere* was on the second key in Roscoe's wallet. It did not fit the door to S.O.S. So where were its friendly tumblers? And why was it a ring mate to the Tiger Stadium key? I wracked my drug-addled brain trying to figure it, to get into the mind of the person who had supplied Miller the ring, to think like a killer.

And then, just a few yards from Gus's Coney Island, with the smell of grilled onions romancing my nostrils like jungle flowers, it came to me. I was certain of it. Petey had found a meter and was standing out front, rubbing her hands together. She was all but salivating for a Polish with all the roses.

"Come on," I said. "No time for grease or gas."

"Wha—? Wha—?" Petey said.

I took her elbow and pushed her past the dog stand and toward the Millender Center. I explained my morning and my hunch.

"Consider," I said, "if you wanted to kill your wife and get away with it, you'd choose the two places where you knew she spent a lot of time and where you, or anybody else, did not. The apartment or the ballpark. That gave Roscoe a choice. If that second key doesn't fit the apartment, then I don't know Mickey Cochrane from Lou Berberet."

"Lou Berberet?" Petey said. "You drop names, Unk, like most people drop dimes."

"A lifetime of rosters, Petey. All inconsequential collections of data. If I'd channeled all that memory to something important, I'd be Lech Walesa."

"Stop punishing yourself," she said.

"My arm's killing me," I said. "And I'm worried about something else. Namely, James Holmes."

"I know what you mean, but tell me anyway."

"Holmes gave me that tip about moving day. He wants Nance's head. And he's a guy who carries a gun that shoots fifteen bullets in three seconds. For openers."

"Don't worry," she said, "he likes me."

I growled at that.

"For all of his thick cream and strawberries, Pete, he's a hired gun. A Hessian."

"God, I love your vocabulary," Petey said. "Will it to me, huh?"

"I'm in no mood, Pete."

"So what's your hurry?"

"We get over there long before Nance does. Try the key. Maybe even trespass. Catch him unawares, see if he slips up. Plus, I want to take a look at a picture on a wall."

"You've lost me again."

"Remember when I mentioned a photo of Al Shaw and Kit where Shaw was wearing an oldtime uniform? The one with a tiger's head instead of a *D* on it? It struck me when I saw it, because I'd never seen that uniform before. It goes way back to the Fat Fothergill days. I first saw it on Kit's wall in her office. It was affectionately signed by Shaw—"

" 'Token love.' I remember." Petey said.

"That's it. And then it was in the apartment. I figured it was a duplicate. Now I'm not so sure. It could easily have been moved, something to add to the frame-up of Al Shaw."

"Didn't the police take it?"

"I don't think so. Then again, I can't be sure."

"And you want to see if it's still there?"

"And if it is, whose fingerprints are on it," I said.

"If they're his, we got him."

"Not necessarily. There's no law against rehanging a photograph," I said. "But if Nance moved it, and he knows that *we* know he moved it, he might blink. It's a stab, but if this key fits and that pic is there, it's a good stab."

"I like it," Petey said. "We get in his face. Find the telltale scars."

"If we're lucky. He's damn good, you know."

"Maybe too good," Petey said, "like a pitcher who's trying to be too fine."

I liked the analogy, and had I a few more blocks to walk, I would have dwelt on Jim Bunning, who was never fine and who busted any hitter who staked a claim to the plate, or John Hiller, that Detroit lefty who had a rotten personality until a heart attack rearranged his ego and somehow transformed him into the Tigers' best relief pitcher ever. But by then we were on Brush Street and the thirty-three floors of the Millender Center loomed over us.

Just as we opened the door to the now familiar lobby, I saw something. At least I thought I did. In a flash of speed and motion, it pulled in the parking area adjacent to the security desk: a silver Lincoln Town Car. I was certain of it, of the metallic shine, the scrape of rubber, the heavy hiss of the engine, all in a swipe before it disappeared into the parking garage.

Or maybe not. Maybe I was not certain. Maybe it was a silver hallucination brought on by the drugs, déjà vu all over again, a vision of Sparky Anderson's silver pate or the 1968 line drive by Jim Northrup, "the Silver Fox."

"Over there," I said, nodding toward the area.

"Whataya got?" Petey said.

"The silver car. You see it?"

"No. Are you sure?"

"Yes. And no."

She shook her head.

"You okay, Unk?"

"I've been better," I said.

I went for the desk. Our friend Larry was there, and he was glowering like a bouncer. I knew he recognized me, but he acted as if I had come to collect child support.

"It's Larry, if I remember correctly," I said.

Nothing.

"Tell me, you got anybody who belongs to a silver Lincoln Town Car?" I said.

Still nothing.

"Give me one of those rental brochures," I said. I knew his hustle and was prepared for it. I put a fifty inside and handed it back to him.

Larry gve me his almost imperceptible nod.

"Tigers got three units on twenty-seven," he said. "Lotta people on their list. One dude with a mustache could be your man. 'Bout forty. Golf shirts. Likes blondes, vodka, and a bucket of chicken wings."

It was a thumbnail sketch of Mickey Schubert.

"Here now?"

"Don't know."

"You called my man Holmes. The elevator still reserved?"

"Uh-huh. But you're too early."

"That bother you?"

"Everything bothers me."

"There's more where that came from."

"Better be."

"We're going up."

"Suit yourself."

"Appreciate a buzz if someone shows up."

"Gets expensive."

"Keep a tab."

He buzzed us over to the elevators.

"What a creep," Petey said. "You sure you gave him enough?"

"Impossible. No way he'll stay bought. That's the trouble today—nobody stays bought."

The elevator arrived. It was empty and we rode up without stopping.

"That's McAllister's man he was talking about, right?" she said.

"That's him."

"You sure we're not walking into something instead of the other way around?"

"You got your weapon?"

"No."

I couldn't believe it.

"A one-armed sportswriter and a defenseless lady," I said. "What a team!"

"Wish James were here."

"Who said he isn't?"

She chewed on that as we rode up to the eleventh floor.

"Not only that," I said, "but we don't even know if we can get inside. If not, we stand at the end of the hallway like mopes."

The hallway was tastefully lit, carpeted, and deserted. All hallways are created equal. We padded to the door of the apartment. I gave her the mystery key.

"Ready or not," Petey said.

She inserted the key as if she owned the place. It turned over with no protest.

"One for the good guys," Petey said.

We went inside. The apartment was airless and in disarray, but that was the least of my interests. I walked past the kitchen and the small dining area, knowing exactly what I was looking for. On the long wall of the living room Kit Gleason's photographic collage remained, and there was the photo: Kit Gleason and Al Shaw in much happier days, framed at close range but vertical enough to see that ragged tiger's head on Shaw's 1920s-vintage uniform. I studied the animal's white eyes and oversized teeth, an almost comical fierceness, and it was obvious why the logo design had not survived. I reread the inscription in Shaw's exaggerated cursive. *Token love.*

"Two for two," I said. "Nobody's touched it."

"Now what?" Petey asked.

"We sit tight."

"Or we quit while we're hot," she said. "Take the photo, get out of here. Don't wait around for Cooper Nance or Mickey Schubert or James Holmes or any other comedian."

I snapped off a look at my niece, the same person who crossed before looking both ways, who did not wear seat belts, who dated felons. *Askance,* I think, is the proper term.

"I didn't mean it," she said.

"No, let's think this over," I said. "We're trespassing. The guy downstairs will sell us out to the first offer. Especially if it's Mickey Schubert, who probably wouldn't miss this time. Then again, if Nance shows up, he can have us arrested. Wynton Mercer will gladly comply."

"So why are we staying?"

"Like Sparky used to say, 'I can't believe they're paying us for this—something we did for nothing as kids.' "

"He was talking about baseball, and we're doing something that got you a bullet in the arm."

"Another thing Sparky said, 'Bullets are serious.' "

"God, Unk, you shouldn't take drugs," Petey said.

She went over to the door and locked the dead bolt. The same key fit both locks, but took more time.

"That gives us a little advance notice," she said.

"About as much as you get with a suicide squeeze," I said.

We looked for a suitable blind. We had a cushion of over three quarters of an hour. We dismissed the kitchen, because it would give us no cover. The bedroom was farthest from the entrance and the likeliest choice, or the bathroom, or even the balcony. We felt like Alfred Hitchcock blocking a scene. We almost decided on the bedroom's walk-in closet, an enclosure near the bedroom door and big enough for the two of us. Then again, doesn't everybody hide in the closet?

We finally retreated to the mirrored bedroom. From its doorway we had a view of the photo wall in the living room. The bedroom was the mess that Mercer's detectives had left it. I sat on the unmade bed, a water bed I rediscovered with the first undulation, and felt queasy. Maybe we *should* loot the wall and run. Petey got up and snooped in the closet. I could smell Kit Gleason's fragrances and creams. Those smells more than anything made me feel like an intruder. That and the mirrors; everywhere I turned I saw myself. I looked like an emeritus sportswriter with his arm in a sling sitting on a water bed.

Suddenly the front door lock sounded, that telltale sound of a key slipping against tumblers, and Petey and I froze. The handle turned—we could hear it clearly—but the door held because of the dead bolt. Then it too was engaged. I stood up and went over to the bedroom door. Petey stepped quickly to my side. Hiding now was almost useless, but neither of us made a move into the brief hallway where we might get a look at the entrant. The dead bolt snapped back and the door opened. We strained to hear any sound, but there was nothing. Whoever was coming in had cat's feet.

I waited, holding my breath and most anything else that could be held, feeling the clutch of Petey's fingers on my arm and my own heartbeat in my throat. The suspense was scalding and ridiculous, and suddenly I caught a glimpse of clothing. It was dark, black or navy, a blazer and a familiar one, a recent one. Then, like tumblers hugging a key, it all fell into place, this whole Detroit odyssey. In a single, golden moment I experienced an almost dreamlike flood of insight, a sleuth's epiphany, one of those orgasmic sequences when the ball looks as big as a cantaloupe and you are Ty Cobb.

Standing at the wall of memories, about to remove the Kit-Shaw photograph that she had placed there herself, was Georgia Stallings.

"Her!" Petey breathed. "My God, Unk, it's her!"

Her. I mouthed the word but nothing came out. I was speechless, my gut churned. I would like to say that I was as cool as Sherlock Holmes, Hercule Poirot, or Bob Scheffing when the realization hit me, but I was nothing of the sort. Seeing her there, Georgia Stallings, Kit Gleason's adjutant and the rock of S.O.S., almost took the wind out of me.

Yet this was no time for deep breathing, and I rushed into the living room.

"Don't touch it!" I said.

Stallings spun around. She was truly startled, a condition rare for her, I was certain, and her face twitched and her lips quivered in a kind of smoker's panic.

I advanced on her and with my good arm grabbed her elbow and yanked. I played a little ball in my days, so there's some pull in my wings, enough, at least to throw her off balance. She soon realized what I was doing and struggled to get back to the photo. That's where Petey leaped in and threw her body between Georgia and the wall much like a beefy coach does to a player who is going at it with an umpire.

"You *won't* touch it," I repeated. "You put it there in the first place. Your prints are all over it."

Stallings fell back a few feet, where she stood and glared at the two of us, conjuring furiously, no doubt. She was a tough nut, but not so tough that she was not biting the dickens out of her inner lower lip. I knew we had her.

"I'm only here to help Dr. Nance," she blurted.

"You've helped enough," I said. "Don't move or I'll have Petey tie you up like a common thief."

Stallings considered that, checked her flanks, and I suddenly worried about the balcony. The last thing I needed was for her to fly over the railing and land all over Brush Street.

"Lock the balcony door, Pete," I said. "Draw the drapes. Call Lieutenant Mercer. We just scored some runs."

Petey did what I asked, but not before she looked at me as if I'd announced a cure for the hanging curve. Stallings sat on the arm of the sofa and searched in vain for a cigarette. In her haste she had not brought them along.

"I took you for a true Tiger fan," I said. "Al Shaw was your hero. And yet you tried to put him back in a cell."

She sneered at me.

"Don't be silly," she said.

She was digging in, obviously regaining her nerve. I wasn't Sam Spade and she wasn't Brigid O'Shaughnessy, and she figured there was no reason for her to come clean.

"Come on, Duffy House, baseball scribe and super dick," Stallings said. "Give me your best stuff. Impress your red-headed Watson here."

I wasn't sure if I had any stuff at all, but what the hell. She was waiting for it, and I decided to grip the seams and throw some chin music.

"You knew we'd be here," I said, "because you listened in when Petey called me at your office. You always listened in, didn't you, Georgia? You are the perfect personal secretary, aren't you Georgia? Every detail, every contingency."

She sat there unmoved, unbending, her arms crossed and her jaw set like a Third Reich librarian.

"You had a key to this apartment because you have all the keys," I went on. "You ordered them cut. Even the ballpark key that Kit got from Jimmy Casey. You had them duplicated. You knew Kit Gleason's every move because you scheduled most of them. You knew when she was with her husband. You knew when she was with Al Shaw. You drove Kit's car. You brought it over to the stadium the night of the fire like you often did when Kit said she was going there later on. The security guard knew you on sight. And you knew what Al Shaw was doing, because you had your fingers in EX-CON. You ran the office, even answered their phones.

"And you knew what Dr. Nance was doing, because you used to work for him. You go way back with him, don't you, Georgia? Not just ten years like you told me, but at least twenty-five years. Remember, Pete?"

"That's right. That's right. The woman in Livonia—" Petey said.

It had little effect on Stallings. She sat there like Lot's wife, like Ralph Houk minus the chaw.

Then the phone rang. I took it in the kitchen.

"Po-lice comin' up," Larry said. "Big cat."

Chapter
21

I SUSPENDED MY NARRATIVE, SOMETHING THAT GAVE ME TIME TO reconsider the details. Mercer took some time, but finally there was a knock on the door. Accompanied by one of the detectives I'd seen at the Roscoe Miller flat, the mammoth lawman trudged into the apartment. His liquid eyes looked at me, then at Petey and Georgia Stallings, and leaked plenty of skepticism and even more impatience. He rocked backward onto the sofa.

"What do we have here? Tell the authorities all about it, why don't we?" he said. It was as much of a salutation as he was going to offer.

I backfilled and embellished. Stallings had put a crust on, and showed no reaction to anything I said. Petey handed the two keys to Mercer, and I could tell he was wondering where we got them and how long we'd had them.

"So she set up the apartment around the night of the fire to reek of Al Shaw," I said. "The glass with his fingerprints was easy. Shaw came around the S.O.S. office often enough for her to appropriate that. Same thing for the bottle of cologne. Even the pubic hair she gets from the bathroom down the hall at S.O.S."

Mercer lifted an eyebrow at that. Finding pubic hairs in strange places has not been the right thing to do for a few years now.

"But the photograph is overkill," I went on. "The one overdone detail. That photo was on Kit's wall in her office. First thing that took my eye when I met the lady. The tiger's head on the uniform. Real unusual to see something besides that Gothic *D*. Stood right out. At least it did to me. So when I didn't see it later on, I asked. And Georgia said, 'Oh, it's around here somewhere.' I dropped it. Then I asked again. And then we made a move to come back here and she *knew* she had to come and get it before I saw it. I'll bet her fingerprints are on it."

Mercer breathed through his nose and looked aggravated.

"Better have more, House," he said.

I did, but this was the hard part, the cadenza, the creative portion of the narrative where finesse might have to cover up the lack of content.

"We got the keys, Lieutenant, from Roscoe Miller's girlfriend," I continued. "She had his wallet, and there they were. A key to the ballpark and a key to this apartment. The two were put together by only one person. Gave Roscoe two options. And how'd she get to Roscoe? EX-CON. It's a natural. She could take her pick of the convicts there, because she ran their computers. She could print out any felony she wanted. But because she knows everything, she somehow knew about Roscoe Miller. She knew about him and Al Shaw in prison and she probably knew that Roscoe tried to shake him down. And she made her move. With Roscoe Miller, all that took was cash."

Mercer nodded at that.

"You got the keys off of Miller? This one works the ballpark?—"

"The upper suites by the press box. Kit Gleason's favorite night-time perch," I said.

"—and this one fits here."

"And I got a key maker who said he cut them for S.O.S.," Petey said.

Mercer looked at her and then at Georgia Stallings.

The phone rang again. I looked at my watch. It was time for our official visitor. I answered and Larry confirmed it. Dr. Cooper Nance was here.

"Another player's coming up," I said. "The widower."

My eyes were on Georgia Stallings when I said it, and though she was as icy as a late reliever, I was certain I saw the flinch, a slight, involuntary contraction of her body and, perhaps, her soul. I knew then that I had her.

"The plastic surgeon," Mercer said. "He's welcome. Why don't we ring up Al Shaw. Get him over here. And that thug Holmes. We can have a panel discussion."

Petey smiled at that, though Mercer was not aiming for a laugh.

"You done yet?" Mercer said to me.

"No," I said, "but I'll wait for Dr. Nance."

The wait wasn't long. With his own key, the third one to enter the lock that day, Nance came in and just about jumped out of his lovely skin at the sight of us.

"What's going on here?" he asked.

His eyes shot around the room, his head swiveling on his neck like a periscope run amok.

"You!" he said to Petey.

"Georgia!" he said to Stallings.

"Remember me, Doctor? Lieutenant Wynton Mercer, DPD. We've been waiting for you."

"What the—! This is improper!" he sputtered. "I'm going to call my attorney." His tan flesh was flushed.

"Can it for a minute," Mercer said. "We've got a drama here. It involves your late wife."

He clammed up at that, and put his hands on his hips. He was dressed casual today, a pair of chinos, a leather jacket over a plaid shirt. But there was nothing casual about him as he stood there, as we all did, the five of us fanned out around the considerable constable like the fingers of a fielder's glove. Mercer brought Nance up-to-date, doing so in his inimitable gasping style, but without omitting a fact. The detective's brain was a sweeper.

I kept my eye on Georgia. She had gone frosty again, a pose, I noted, that contrasted sadly with the smiling countenances of Kit Gleason in the photographs behind her.

"You take it from here, House," Mercer said. "We got Roscoe with the keys he got from the lady here—"

"And Kit and Al Shaw are on for dinner," I resumed. "Miss Stallings knows this, because she keeps the schedule. Roscoe leaves his place that afternoon, and nobody sees him after that. Shaw and Kit go to Roma's restaurant, and then they go to the ballpark. Georgia knows this too, because it's her job to shuttle Kit's car over to the stadium parking lot. She's done that so many times the security guards know her. She brings the car over at six o'clock or so, and leaves in a taxi. Security told your detectives that.

"But this time she brought a passenger. Roscoe was hiding in the backseat, something the guards did not pick up on because of the smoked windows. He stayed there and saw Kit and Shaw arrive and go into the stadium together. And they argued. Shaw admits to that, and a while later, he left. You have that on record, because he told you he got paged by his wife. He thought there was an emergency at home, so he left. Or maybe it was a good excuse to get the hell out of there. At any rate, it was enough to get him to leave.

"Except, and this is a big *except,* when he got home, there was no emergency. His wife wasn't even there, Al said. Only one reason for that. He was paged by Georgia Stallings, the one person who would not only know his pager number, but who would know his home phone number and might even know that when Al saw it on his beeper, he would move. That took him out of Tiger Stadium and harm's way. Never forget, Miss Stallings is a fan. And the idea of losing the franchise was too much even for her.

"But with Shaw gone, Kit remained, and Roscoe Miller moved in."

Mercer shifted his bulk on that.

"And if you say he started the fire to cover up the homicide, I got problems with that," he said.

"So I won't say it," I went on. "He torched the place because he had a contract to do that too. Roscoe was an arsonist, my prison informant told me that. And an opportunist. He's already going in on one job, so he moonlights another. There was ten thousand out on the street to torch the place, and don't think Roscoe didn't know it. Besides, the last thing Miss Stallings wanted out of this was a fire in Tiger Stadium. It would be a sacrilege to her."

Mercer turned to Georgia, who stood like a pillar.

"You want to jump in here anytime, you go right, ahead," he said. There was no humor to it.

She looked over at Cooper Nance, but said nothing. Her expression was still a mask, but one tinged with disdain.

"That's my gut feeling, Lieutenant," I cut in. "On the fire. And we may never know one way or the other about who put up the money. But I don't think this woman commissioned it."

"I'll buy that, House," Mercer said. "So who took out Roscoe?

And hit you in the process, my friend? Who shoots a nine-millimeter Beretta?"

"Ask the Doctor," I said.

Nance wheeled around toward me.

"I don't have that gun anymore," he said quickly. It was a knee-jerk reaction, and he wanted it back as soon as the words were out.

"Your nine-millimeter Beretta," I said. "What happened to it?"

"A Beretta? You don't say," said Mercer.

"I got that for Kit's own protection as soon as she started coming downtown," Nance offered. "She had it in the office."

Bingo, I thought to myself, because that was news to me.

"Kit could handle a weapon like that?" Petey said, her voice cutting through the male repartee.

"No." Nance responded softly. And with it his expression dropped. "Georgia could. She took up shooting so she could handle weapons."

At that we all turned to her. She was trembling now, there was no doubt about it. Her earlier look of defiance had cracked some, at least it had to me. I was ecstatic—she was a shooter, who would have imagined it!—and yet I suddenly worried about the balcony once again. And my arm hurt. I was standing only a few feet away from the person who had stitched me from behind.

"The silver Lincoln Town Car is parked in Penobscot garage," I said. "Available to Miss Stallings anytime. Including the day James Holmes and I visited Roscoe Miller on Drexel Street. With Miss Stallings tailing us."

Cooper Nance suddenly punched his fist into his palm, startling us all.

"What the hell? Is this all on the level?" he said, his voice incredulous and nearly cracking. "Why, Georgia? If this is true, why? Why would you do it?"

"She hated Kit, that's why," I said. I was ready for this, and I wanted the floor. "Raw, skinless hatred. She hated Kit because she was her boss, and Kit got all the credit for her brains and her organization. She despised Kit because Georgia had forgotten more about the Tigers and Tiger Stadium than Kit would ever know, yet Kit got raves for S.O.S. The Olson Survey was Georgia's idea, and Kit's name went on the cover. She hated your wife because she was beautiful and rich and never had a bad thing happen to her in her whole life—"

"That's not true," Nance said. "Georgia, I've known you for twenty-five years. . . ."

He let it hang there. I hesitated to continue, but he offered no more. And she stood mute.

"It is true," I finally said, "and I should have laid into this a long time ago—Georgia hated your wife, Dr. Nance, because she had *you*. That's right, Georgia was someone you'd worked with for years, and when you work with a person so closely for that long a time—longer than most people are married—you know their every itch and tic. People tend to fall in love like that, and they stay that way."

That locked the doctor's stare on his former nurse.

"Is that true, Georgia?" he said. He seemed more naïve than a man of his age and his status could possibly be.

She returned his look, and without a trace of naïveté.

"You never saw it, did you, Cooper?" she said.

Her words hung in the air, and none of us dared interrupt.

"You're so blind," she went on. "You looked at me for all those years and all you saw was your nurse. I was nothing more than an L.P.N. to you. I could have protected you from people like Kit. I *tried* to protect you—"

"Don't, Georgia," Nance said. "Don't do this. Kit and I both loved you. You knew that."

She snorted.

"*Love* me? *Love* me?" she said. "Love me so much you closed me off. Shut down your practice and farmed me out to work for that woman—"

"You didn't have to," Nance said. "I said it was up to you. But it was the Tigers, and baseball—it was perfect for you."

"Oh, Cooper," Stallings said, and now I had the feeling this was between just the two of them, "how could I *not* do it. I always did what you wanted. All those years I did what you wanted. Even if it meant enduring that woman in the other room sipping hazelnut cappuccino and beating up on the Tigers."

That's it, I said to myself, *now she's getting into it.*

"Oh, yeah," Georgia went on. "She thought she had them. Yeager, McAllister. 'The two stooges,' she used to call them. As if they were going to invite Kit Gleason in to define the future of the franchise. Get down on their knees and plead for her wisdom. She really believed that. And, of course, she *never* told anybody how she used to come to me for three-by-five cheat cards whenever she had to speak somewhere or say two words at a benefit."

"But that's not what really got you, was it, Georgia?" I asked. "That's not what turned the worm."

She glared at me, and I hoped for a little hand wringing or clenched teeth.

"You saw her go after Al Shaw," I continued. "That's what drove you over the edge. That you couldn't stand."

"He was a plaything to her," Georgia said. "She was so damn cruel. Using him like she used me and you, Cooper, and everybody else. And she loved it. She loved getting just what she wanted. And she was getting away with it. That big, stupid, wonderful outfielder. She was killing him."

"And you couldn't let that happen, so you killed her," I said. "Not only was she cuckolding Dr. Nance, the love of your life, but she was toying with the real guts of the franchise. You pitied Shaw and you resented him for it."

I stopped. I had talked too much. She stood there like an accused witch of Salem. She was a spurned lover, a second banana, a desperate fan. And for a moment my heart went out to her. I even felt a kinship with her. The passions of middle age are not much respected nowadays, and Georgia Stallings's passions ran deeper and more acute than any of us in that room really knew.

"I did not burn down Tiger Stadium," she said softly. "That little weasel did that. It made me sick."

"I would assume you still have the Beretta?" Mercer asked.

She did not answer.

"We better go downtown," the lieutenant said.

He maneuvered himself in an attempt to stand.

I looked over at Cooper Nance. He had turned toward the balcony, looking blankly into the closed drapes. Petey and I stared at him, and for the first time in this whole thing felt true pity for him. Behind his silvery head was the wall of photographs, the celebrity gallery of Kit Gleason's fanciful world, and all of the photos were lit by her lovely, omnipresent, manipulative smile. It was the fuse in all of this, the fire, the ice, the awful toll.

My musings were interrupted by the monotone phrasing of Mercer's detective as he recited Georgia her rights.

Box  Score

I AM NOT CERTAIN OF WHAT HAPPENED IN THE ENSUING HOURS. I was chauffeured back to the Dearborn Inn. I took some more drugs. I slept some. No, maybe I slept a lot. I dreamed lurid dreams of one-armed outfielders and midget pinch hitters. In the room on the other side of my wall, Petey made a triumphant call to Marjorie and Grand Chambliss, and she basked in their kudos and congratulations. She also surfed the local channels of her television as the news stations reported the arrest of Georgia Stallings.

It was all rapturous for her, and rightfully so, I guess, for she had swooped and gathered in her quarry. I did not join her. I unplugged my phone, covered the message light, and drew the draperies. I crawled under my blanket. I found no elation, no gratification. Call it sadness, or the morning-after dew that settles on a battlefield. Lives taken. Lives ruined. Two decent, bright, remarkable women, destroyed. Hatred and treachery. A primeval city bleeding anew.

It was a full twenty-four hours later that I surfaced. I flexed my arm and felt the pain, and I threw the analgesics away. The bite of healing was good for me. Petey was anticipating my resurrection, and she greeted me with a list of phone messages and a stack of newspapers.

"It's the talk of the town," she said. "And Red Carney's coming in."

"Come again," I said.

"Red called from Palm Springs and said he was so impressed and so bored in the desert that he's flying in and meeting us at Carl's Chop House. Plus, he wants to see how bad the stadium is."

"When?"

"Tonight at seven."

"I'm game," I said.

"And Jimmy Casey. He wants to come."

"No. Give Jimmy a rest. I got a better fourth."

"Who?"

"Holmes."

"James?"

"That's the one," I said. "The guy who got us up in the apartment before Georgia got there. The guy who got us to Roscoe Miller. The guy, I've decided, who may have jeopardized and saved my life all in one reckless afternoon. I think I owe him a steak."

"Great choice, Unk," she said, and went off to the telephone.

I felt like a dose of Red Carney, the goggle-eyed Cubs' play-by-play announcer and an old friend who can tell you that it was the Tigers' Bob Cain pitching and Bob Swift catching when Eddie Gaedel took his midget strike zone up to the plate in 1951. And that he walked on four pitches, and Jim Delsing, later a Tiger, ran for him. Red would want a recap, a tenth-inning rundown of the guns, hits, and liars.

He met us at Carl's Chop House on Grand River. Even though he ran in the National League circuit, Red was no stranger to Carl's, a red-meat and hard-liquor place. It was near the ballpark and just down from the UAW offices, a place that still attracted the owners of black Lincolns and white Cadillacs even though it was now surrounded by uninhabited buildings. The valets were jockeying them as we drove up, and it was a pleasure to give them my scarlet Volvo and admonish them to treat it like a newborn.

"Mister," said one, "nobody's gonna go for this thing."

I took it as a compliment.

We did not have to search for Red; we heard him. He was sitting in the middle of the long, dark-oak bar and bellowing forth with old Van Patrick stories. Dressed in a red polka-dot shirt open at his tanned collar and a pair of Sansabelt slacks that did all they could do to contain his massive midriff, Red was full of helium and taking on Jack Daniels. He cut them short only because he doesn't miss anything, and anything was Petey. She was dressed slinky and Red could glimpse slinky from a bleacher seat.

"Take me, boys!" he announced. "Take me to this vision of loveliness!"

"Hey, big hitter," Petey cracked, "is that a bat in your hand or are you just happy to see me?"

And the two of them did some shameless smothering.

"Did you bring your grip, my darling?" Red said. "Our flight for the Virgin Islands leaves in a few minutes."

"We'd make that place a misnomer," Petey said, and gave him a shot in the ribs.

I stood back, because Red was a back slapper and I did not need my shoulder slapped out onto Grand River Avenue.

"And you, old friend," he said. "I was worried about you."

"No need," I said. "I bite a bullet with the best of them."

"He's lying," Petey said.

"Just glad it didn't hit you in a vital organ," Red said, putting his paw on my good arm. "Then again," he added, and I knew it was coming, "how vital is your organ?"

They got a good laugh at that, and what the hell. Then we peeled off to one of the two dining rooms full of round tables and populated mostly by men—men talking business, men talking sports, men drinking liquor and lacerating red meat. You expected Jimmy Hoffa to walk in anytime. When Petey ordered a glass of white zinfandel, you got the impression they would have to send out for a bottle.

We were sitting and small-talking for a quarter of an hour when Holmes arrived. He was worth the wait. Dressed in a black double-breasted suit and a starched black shirt, his head shaven as smooth as a balloon, he looked like a point guard for the Pistons. Except for his tie, which, when he undid his suit-coat buttons, flaunted the hand-painted likeness of none other than Satchel Paige.

"Leroy," Red said.

"Magnificent," Petey said.

Holmes beamed, and I half expected a ruby to shine from his front tooth.

"My lady friend makes these and she's lookin' for backers," he said.

"Who do I make the check out to?" Red said, and I think he meant it.

Over drinks and appetizers, we explained to Red what James Holmes had done for us, and James enjoyed the attention.

"Now it can be told," Holmes said while devouring a double order of giant shrimp coated with cocktail sauce. "The investigator was worryin'. I just was never sure Albert Shaw, my main account, weren't in severe trouble on this. Never sure. Never sure."

"Neither was Al," Petey said. "He was in over his head with Kit Gleason."

"And he still isn't out of the inning," I said. "Unless Georgia confesses—and Roscoe isn't around to testify against her—her defense will be that Shaw did it. That Kit was dead when Roscoe got there. Deny, deny, deny."

"But she wanted Kit dead, Uncle Duffy," Petey said. "That's what she admitted to in the apartment."

"You heard it. I heard it." I said. "But that doesn't mean a judge and jury will ever hear it."

"Could be a hell of a trial," Holmes said.

We paused occasionally to fill Red in on the dramatis personae.

"And Cooper Nance may be her biggest ally," I added.

"That cad," Petey said.

"Maybe so, Petey, but he can testify that he knew about Kit and Shaw," I went on. "He could say Kit was too much for him from the start. Sixty-year-old guys tend to get by on former glory . . ."

"That's no joke," Red said.

". . . and as much of a wolf as he thought he was, he was as powerless as a utility infielder. He accepted it. Al Shaw did for his wife what he couldn't do. It might have been irritating, but it wasn't a motive for murder."

I had their attention.

"Keep going, Unk," Petey said.

"Except to Georgia," I said. "It burned her. Just seared her in the gut. And yet she was too much of a fan to take Shaw out of the lineup. She knew he'd get the best criminal defense and he'd never be convicted of murder on circumstantial evidence. He'd be chastised and humiliated and it would cost him a fortune, but he'd beat the rap and be batting cleanup on Opening Day."

"A baseball woman," Red said.

"Lady had me goin'," Holmes said. "How'd she get that cologne, and that you-know-what that comes from you-know-where?"

"You mean the pubic hair, James?" Petey said.

"What the hell—?" Red blustered.

"Good secretaries always tidy up," Petey said. "A simple walk down the hall to the men's room after Shaw visited. You men are always leaving things behind."

We let that sit for a while.

"Who burned down the ballyard?" Red finally asked.

"We may never know unless Roscoe Miller taps back at the séance table," I said.

"Georgia knew that too," Petey added. "Roscoe was the only guy who could finger her, so she had to whack him."

"You got that, Jack," Holmes cracked. "I laid one in him, but she got him first."

"You sure?" I said. "I say Georgia's ditched the gun and won't confess to even being on Drexel Street."

"Too late on that, Uncle Duffy," he said. "I got it covered. Found me a can picker got his shopping cart smashed up by Georgia in the silver Town Car when she scooted. Found the car too—"

"In the Penobscot garage?"

"That be the one," he went on. "Got nasty chrome marks from my man's cart."

"Lieutenant Mercer may pinch you anyway," I said.

"That nasty fat man already got back to the Town Car," Holmes said. "I seen to that. He picked it up for evidence 'fore the lady could put it in the river."

"So you're a free man, James?" I said.

"Din't say that," he said. "Police come after me, I'm gonna need you, Uncle Duffy. You remember Roscoe with that cannon, right? Tell me now."

"Vividly," I said.

Holmes smiled.

"Then you can tell 'em I was savin' your neck when I popped him."

We toasted James on that, and then leaned back while steaks and chops and lobsters were put in front of us. We deserved excess, and the Chop House obliged. I ate with my left hand.

"To answer your question, Red," I said, "I'm convinced Roscoe Miller torched the place. Utterly. For whom? Who knows. The job's got Mickey Schubert's name all over it. Maybe for his boss. Maybe he reached out on somebody else's behalf. And without even meeting up with Roscoe. That's the kind of thing he does real well."

Petey suspended a morsel of lobster tail in midair.

"I don't think Schubert would have had Kit murdered," she said. "That's too dumb even for him. Too risky."

"Love to visit that sucker," Holmes said.

"Just don't work for him," Petey said.

Holmes drew back at that. "Whataya take me for, sistah?" he yelped.

"You want me to answer that, James?" she said.

He grinned. He was working the daylights out of a New York strip and his napkin looked like a paint rag. The man could eat.

"I'll always wonder about Schubert," I added. "I think he was in this thing more than we know."

"We saw a lot of silver Lincoln Town Cars in the rearview mirror," Petey said.

"Bad tint," Holmes said. "Black. You gotta run with black."

We sliced and ate and never once mentioned cholesterol or the amount of grain it takes to feed beef cattle.

"Tell me what did it, Unk," Petey finally said. "How did it all come together for you."

She nodded at me.

"He was masterful in the apartment when we finally had Stallings," she said.

"Thank you," I said. "I must admit, sometimes I amaze even myself. But it started with the keys. The ballpark, and then the apartment. Why have a person murdered in one of those two places if you weren't trying to make a statement? I mean, in this day and age you can have somebody murdered as they take the groceries from the car. It can be done anywhere. Georgia was inside Kit's life. But *anywhere* wasn't good enough for this perpetrator. Which is why I thought the doctor did it, because he so hated what Kit did in those two places. Why, he'd even have the ballpark burned to add insult to injury.

"But that photo bothered me. I didn't know why, and I decided it was because Georgia brushed me off when I asked her about it. 'It's around here someplace,' she said. Not her. She knew where everything was. Every detail. That's why she gave Roscoe the keys. She attended to every detail. Then she missed a detail. That was with Kit's car. When I found it in the garage, I looked inside and saw junk-food wrappers on the floor of the backseat. Just in the backseat. That wasn't like Kit. In fact, it was so unlike Kit that Georgia didn't even notice it when she drove the car. When I saw that stuff, I finally figured out how Roscoe got inside Tiger Stadium: Georgia drove him there. Then he sat in the backseat and waited, and ate junk food."

"Brilliant, Duffy," said Red. "You figuring that out. Like a manager stealing signs. 'Member Charlie Dressen? Used to manage here in Detroit, Charlie did. Greatest sign stealer I ever saw. He was managing the All-Stars one year, and when he got together with the players to set signs, he said, 'Hell, I'll just give you the signs you use on your own team.' "

"Nah, I wasn't that sharp—I was lucky, Red," I said. "The lady was brilliant. But she was too brilliant. She overmanaged."

"Sparky used to say it was the little things that win in the long run," Petey said.

"And Georgia loved Sparky," I said.

"Hell, *I* love Sparky," Holmes said, "but that doesn't mean I wax my boss."

"You're self-employed, James," Petey said.

Holmes liked that, and bucked his head in laughter. He did it with such gusto that his tie, specifically the long lead leg of Satchel Paige, landed in his creamed spinach.

Some time later, after plastic from the commissioner's office covered the check, we moved our sated torsos away from the table and headed for the door. Red had wanted to see the damage to the stadium, and I figured Petey could talk our way in.

Before we got to the exit, however, we came upon a commotion of patrons in front of the large-screen television at the end of the bar. There were cheers and raised steins, and we wondered why.

"So long, Little Joe," yelled a patron.

He was talking to the figure of Joe Yeager, who was standing next to Sport McAllister and a bunch of other googaws.

"He's sold the club," said a bartender to Red.

"Holy cow!" Red bellowed.

We stood and listened to the chatter, to Yeager and his prepared statement filled with more platitudes than his pasta primavera had vegetables. He was selling the club with a heavy heart, blah, blah, blah.

"Who's the new owner, you dipshit?" bellowed Red. The patrons roared.

That information soon followed. The newest proprietor was to be another Michigan fast-food tycoon, this one in sushi bars. He had hundreds of them in malls all over the country.

"With all due respect to my predecessor, the Tigers are staying at Michigan and Trumbull," said the new owner, a swarthy fellow who, according to the sports jockeys, had once played minor-league ball and always had a hankering for the Tigers. He was wearing a Tigers cap with its venerable *D*. I thought of the tiger's head on Al Shaw's vintage uniform.

"We'll patch up that great old ballpark," he went on. "Owning the Tigers is a dream come true for me, and the Tigers belong in Tiger Stadium."

We raised our collective eyebrows at that, then drowned our skepticism in a round of drinks bought by the house.

"Don't know 'bout you," James Holmes said to me, "but fast-food dudes make me nervous."

"Sushi," Red said. "Stuff ain't even cooked."

I rubbed my belly at the thought of it, and felt queasy.